Alice Munro's

THE MOONS OF JUPITER

"Of all the writers at work in the field today, few can move us as deeply as Alice Munro. *The Moons of Jupiter,* her fourth collection, is a triumph of sentiment over sentimentality."

—*Newsweek*

"From [Munro's] naturalistic, classically composed short stories there rises a melodic line that catches at the heart with its freshness. In her seemingly effortless prose style, Munro has etched portraits of people living underground dramas of high intensity. Writing about ordinary life is hazardous; it may induce the boredom that is its subject. Munro defies the danger, and triumphs."

—*Time*

"Alice Munro's fine and intelligent stories are like Edward Hopper paintings, lit with a relentless clarity, and richly illuminating the perplexities of human connections, their possibilities and pain."

—*Washington Post Book World*

"Witty, subtle, passionate, [*The Moons of Jupiter* is] exceptionally knowledgeable about the content and movement—the entanglements and entailments—of individual human feeling. And the knowledge it offers can't be looked up elsewhere. A gifted evoker of place . . . is also an uncommonly powerful summoner of passionate physical encounter."

—*The New York Times Book Review*

"Munro is mindful of space, and her preoccupation with this, whether real or metaphorical, is echoed in her elegant prose where each word seems surrounded with a peculiar space of its own. Not the least of her gifts is a delicate, illuminating precision of language. Alice Munro often articulates the barely perceptible and her voice shows tremendous assurance. She creates and sustains moods with an almost magical exhilaration, giving us characters true and memorable. One finishes this book and immediately misses it: that's how good Alice Munro is."

—*Cleveland Plain Dealer*

"Lovers of the art of the short story will rejoice. . . . Munro has deftly lifted the blinders from our eyes for a peek at the not so mysterious forces that determine our relationships with the world. A writer of crystal clarity and stunning word craft, Ms. Munro is undoubtedly one of Canada's finest exports. *The Moons of Jupiter* is a stellar effort."

—*Kansas City Star*

"A major talent is at work here; beyond the frustration and bitterness of social movements, Munro operates in the larger company where each heart must thump by itself."

—*Los Angeles Times*

"Alice Munro . . . writes of her brave, vulnerable women in a clear-eyed unsentimental way. Although many of her stories are bleak and somber, her writing is so sharp and brilliant that it lights up the imagination and makes this work an absolute joy to read."

—*San Francisco Chronicle*

BOOKS BY ALICE MUNRO

Dear Life

Too Much Happiness

The View from Castle Rock

Away from Her

Carried Away

Runaway

Hateship, Friendship, Courtship, Loveship, Marriage

Vintage Munro

The Love of a Good Woman

Selected Stories

Open Secrets

Friend of My Youth

The Progress of Love

The Moons of Jupiter

The Beggar Maid

Something I've Been Meaning to Tell You

Lives of Girls and Women

Dance of the Happy Shades

THE
MOONS
OF
JUPITER

stories by

Alice Munro

Vintage International
Vintage Books
A Division of Random House, Inc.
New York

First Vintage International Edition, May 1991

The following stories have been published previously,
some of them in slightly different form: "Chaddeleys and
Flemings: 1. Connection," in *Chatelaine*, November
1979; "Chaddeleys and Flemings: 2. The Stone in the
Field," in *Saturday Night*, April 1979; "Dulse," in *The
New Yorker*, July 21, 1980; "The Turkey Season," in
The New Yorker, December 29, 1980; "Accident," in
Toronto Life, November 1977; "Prue," in *The New
Yorker*, March 30, 1981; "Labor Day Dinner," in *The
New Yorker*, September 28, 1981; "Mrs. Cross and Mrs.
Kidd," in *Tamarack Review*, winter 1982; "Visitors," in
the *Atlantic Monthly*, April 1982; "The Moons of
Jupiter," in *The New Yorker*, May 22, 1978.

Vintage is a registered trademark and Vintage
International and colophon are trademarks of Random
House, Inc.

Library of Congress Cataloging-in-Publication Data
Munro, Alice.
    The moons of Jupiter : stories / by Alice
Munro.—1st Vintage contemporaries ed.
        p.   cm.—(Vintage contemporaries)
    ISBN 0-679-73270-5
    I. Title.
[PR9199.3.M8M66   1991]
813'.54—dc20   90-50493
                                CIP

For Bob Weaver

Contents

The
Moons
of
Jupiter

Chaddeleys
and Flemings

I CONNECTION

Cousin Iris from Philadelphia. She was a nurse. Cousin Isabel
from Des Moines. She owned a florist shop. Cousin Flora from
Winnipeg, a teacher; Cousin Winifred from Edmonton, a lady
accountant. Maiden ladies, they were called. Old maids was too
thin a term, it would not cover them. Their bosoms were heavy and
intimidating — a single, armored bundle — and their stomachs and
behinds full and corseted as those of any married woman. In those
days it seemed to be the thing for women's bodies to swell and
ripen to a good size twenty, if they were getting anything out of life
at all; then, according to class and aspirations, they would either
sag and loosen, go wobbly as custard under pale print dresses and
damp aprons, or be girded into shapes whose firm curves and
proud slopes had nothing to do with sex, everything to do with
rights and power.

My mother and her cousins were the second sort of women.
They wore corsets that did up the side with dozens of hooks and
eyes, stockings that hissed and rasped when they crossed their
legs, silk jersey dresses for the afternoon (my mother's being a
cousin's hand-me-down), face powder (rachel), dry rouge, eau de

cologne, tortoise-shell, or imitation tortoise-shell, combs in their hair. They were not imaginable without such getups, unless bundled to the chin in quilted satin dressing-gowns. For my mother this style was hard to keep up; it required ingenuity, dedication, fierce effort. And who appreciated it? She did.

They all came to stay with us one summer. They came to our house because my mother was the only married one, with a house big enough to accommodate everybody, and because she was too poor to go to see them. We lived in Dalgleish in Huron County in Western Ontario. The population, 2,000, was announced on a sign at the town limits. "Now there's two thousand and four," cried Cousin Iris, heaving herself out of the driver's seat. She drove a 1939 Oldsmobile. She had driven to Winnipeg to collect Flora, and Winifred, who had come down from Edmonton by train. Then they all drove to Toronto and picked up Isabel.

"And the four of us are bound to be more trouble than the whole two thousand put together," said Isabel. "Where was it — Orangeville — we laughed so hard Iris had to stop the car? She was afraid she'd drive into the ditch!"

The steps creaked under their feet.

"Breathe that air! Oh, you can't beat the country air. Is that the pump where you get your drinking water? Wouldn't that be lovely right now? A drink of well water!"

My mother told me to get a glass, but they insisted on drinking out of the tin mug.

They told how Iris had gone into a field to answer nature's call and had looked up to find herself surrounded by a ring of interested cows.

"Cows baloney!" said Iris. "They were steers."

"Bulls for all you'd know," said Winifred, letting herself down into a wicker chair. She was the fattest.

"Bulls! I'd know!" said Iris. "I hope their furniture can stand the strain, Winifred. I tell you it was a drag on the rear end of my poor car. Bulls! What a shock, it's a wonder I got my pants up!"

They told about the wild-looking town in Northern Ontario where Iris wouldn't stop the car even to let them buy a Coke.

She took one look at the lumberjacks and cried, "We'd all be raped!"

"What is raped?" said my little sister.

"Oh-oh," said Iris. "It means you get your pocketbook stolen."

Pocketbook: an American word. My sister and I didn't know what that meant either but we were not equal to two questions in a row. And I knew that wasn't what rape meant anyway; it meant something dirty.

"Purse. Purse stolen," said my mother in a festive but cautioning tone. Talk in our house was genteel.

Now came the unpacking of presents. Tins of coffee, nuts and date pudding, oysters, olives, ready-made cigarettes for my father. They all smoked, too, except for Flora, the Winnipeg school-teacher. A sign of worldliness then; in Dalgleish, a sign of possible loose morals. They made it a respectable luxury.

Stockings, scarves emerged as well, a voile blouse for my mother, a pair of stiff white organdy pinafores for me and my sister (the latest thing, maybe, in Des Moines or Philadelphia but a mistake in Dalgleish, where people asked us why we hadn't taken our aprons off). And finally, a five-pound box of chocolates. Long after all the chocolates were eaten, and the cousins had gone, we kept the chocolate-box in the linen-drawer in the dining-room sideboard, waiting for some ceremonial use that never presented itself. It was still full of the empty chocolate cups of dark, fluted paper. In the wintertime I would sometimes go into the cold dining room and sniff at the cups, inhaling their smell of artifice and luxury; I would read again the descriptions on the map provided on the inside of the box-top: hazelnut, creamy nougat, Turkish delight, golden toffee, peppermint cream.

The cousins slept in the downstairs bedroom and on the pulled-out daybed in the front room. If the night was hot they thought nothing of dragging a mattress on to the verandah, or even into the yard. They drew lots for the hammock. Winifred was not allowed to draw. Far into the night you could hear them giggling, shushing each other, crying, "What was that?" We were beyond the streetlights of Dalgleish, and they were amazed at the darkness, the large number of stars.

Once they decided to sing a round.

Row, row, row your boat
Gently down the stream,
Merrily, merrily, merrily, merrily,
Life is but a dream.

They didn't think Dalgleish was real. They drove uptown and reported on the oddity of the shopkeepers; they imitated things they had overheard on the street. Every morning the coffee they had brought filled the house with its unfamiliar, American fragrance, and they sat around asking who had an inspiration for the day. One inspiration was to drive out into the country and pick berries. They got scratched and overheated and at one point Winifred was completely penned in, immobilized, by thorny branches, bellowing for a rescue party; nevertheless they said they had mightily enjoyed themselves. Another inspiration was to take my father's fishing-rods and go down to the river. They came home with a catch of rock bass, a fish we generally threw back. They organized picnics. They dressed up in old clothes, in old straw hats and my father's overalls, and took pictures of each other. They made layer cakes, and marvelous molded salads which were shaped like temples and colored like jewels.

One afternoon they put on a concert. Iris was an opera singer. She took the cloth off the dining-room table to drape herself in, and sent me out to collect hen feathers to put in her hair. She sang "The Indian Love Call," and "Women Are Fickle." Winifred was a bank-robber, with a water-pistol she had bought at the five-and-ten. Everybody had to do something. My sister and I sang, two songs: "Yellow Rose of Texas," and the Doxology. My mother, most amazingly, put on a pair of my father's trousers and stood on her head.

Audience and performers, the cousins were for each other, every waking moment. And sometimes asleep. Flora was the one who talked in her sleep. Since she was also the most ladylike and careful, the others stayed awake to ask her questions, trying to make her say something that would embarrass her. They told her she swore. They said she sat bolt upright and demanded, "Why is there no damned chalk?"

She was the one I liked least because she attempted to sharpen our minds — my sister's and mine — by throwing out mental-arithmetic questions. "If it took seven minutes to walk seven blocks, and five blocks were the same length but the other two blocks were double the length — "

"Oh, go soak your head, Flora!" said Iris, who was the rudest.

If they didn't get any inspiration, or it was too hot to do anything, they sat on the verandah drinking lemonade, fruit punch, ginger ale, iced tea, with maraschino cherries and chunks of ice chipped from the big chunk in the icebox. Sometimes my mother prettied up the glasses by dipping the rims in beaten egg whites, then in sugar. The cousins would say they were prostrated, they were good for nothing; but their complaints had a gratified sound, as if the heat of summer itself had been created to add drama to their lives.

Drama enough already.

In the larger world, things had happened to them. Accidents, proposals, encounters with lunatics and enemies. Iris could have been rich. A millionaire's widow, a crazy old woman with a wig like a haystack, had been wheeled into the hospital one day, clutching a carpetbag. And what was in the carpetbag but jewels, real jewels, emeralds and diamonds and pearls as big as pullet eggs. Nobody but Iris could do a thing with her. It was Iris who persuaded her at last to throw the wig into the garbage (it was crawling with fleas), and let the jewels go into the bank vault. So attached did this old woman become to Iris that she wanted to remake her will, she wanted to leave Iris the jewels and the stocks and the money and the apartment houses. Iris would not allow it. Professional ethics ruled it out.

"You are in a position of trust. A nurse is in a position of trust."

Then she told how she had been proposed to by an actor, dying from a life of dissipation. She allowed him to swig from a Listerine bottle because she didn't see what difference it would make. He was a stage actor, so we wouldn't recognize the name even if she told us, which she wouldn't.

She had seen other big names, too, celebrities, the top society of Philadelphia. Not at their best.

Winifred said that she had seen things too. The real truth, the real horrible truth about some of those big wheels and socialites came out when you got a look at their finances.

We lived at the end of a road running west from Dalgleish over some scrubby land where there were small wooden houses and flocks of chickens and children. The land rose to a decent height where we were and then sloped in wide fields and pastures, decorated with elm trees, down to the curve of the river. Our house was decent too, an old brick house of a fair size, but it was drafty and laid out in an inconvenient way and the trim needed paint. My mother planned to fix it up and change it all around, as soon as we got some money.

My mother did not think much of the town of Dalgleish. She was often harking back, to the town of Fork Mills, in the Ottawa Valley, where she and the cousins had gone to high school, the town their grandfather had come to from England; and to England itself, which of course she had never seen. She praised Fork Mills for its stone houses, its handsome and restrained public buildings (quite different, she said, from Huron County's, where the idea had been to throw up some brick monstrosity and stick a tower on it), for its paved streets, the service in its stores, the better quality of things for sale and the better class of people. The people who thought so highly of themselves in Dalgleish would be laughable to the leading families of Fork Mills. But then, the leading families of Fork Mills would themselves be humbled if they came into contact with certain families of England, to whom my mother was connected.

Connection. That was what it was all about. The cousins were a show in themselves, but they also provided a connection. A connection with the real, and prodigal, and dangerous, world. They knew how to get on in it, they had made it take notice. They could command a classroom, a maternity ward, the public; they knew how to deal with taxi drivers and train conductors.

The other connection they provided, and my mother provided as well, was to England and history. It is a fact that Canadians of Scottish—which in Huron County we called Scotch—and Irish descent will tell you quite freely that their ancestors came out during the potato famine, with only the rags on their backs, or that they were shepherds, agricultural laborers, poor landless people. But anyone whose ancestors came from England will have some story of black sheep or younger sons, financial reverses, lost inheritances, elopements with unsuitable partners. There may be some amount of truth in this; conditions in Scotland and Ireland were such as to force wholesale emigration, while Englishmen may have chosen to leave home for more colorful, personal reasons.

This was the case with the Chaddeley family, my mother's family. Isabel and Iris were not Chaddeleys by name, but their mother had been a Chaddeley; my mother had been a Chaddeley, though she was now a Fleming; Flora and Winifred were Chaddeleys still. All were descended from a grandfather who left England as a young man for reasons they did not quite agree on. My mother believed that he had been a student at Oxford, but had lost all the money his family sent him, and had been ashamed to go home. He lost it by gambling. No, said Isabel, that was just the story; what really happened was that he got a servant girl in trouble and was compelled to marry her, and take her to Canada. The family estates were near Canterbury, said my mother. (Canterbury pilgrims, Canterbury bells.) The others were not sure of that. Flora said that they were in the west of England, and that the name Chaddeley was said to be related to Cholmondeley; there was a Lord Cholmondeley, the Chaddeleys could be a branch of that family. But there was also the possibility, she said, that it was French, it was originally *Champ de laiche*, which means field of sedge. In that case the family had probably come to England with William the Conqueror.

Isabel said she was not an intellectual and the only person she knew from English history was Mary Queen of Scots. She wanted somebody to tell her if William the Conqueror came before Mary Queen of Scots, or after?

"Sedge fields," said my father agreeably. "That wouldn't exactly make them a fortune."

"Well, I wouldn't know sedge from oats," said Iris. "But they were prosperous enough in England, according to Grandpa, they were gentry there."

"Before," said Flora, "and Mary Queen of Scots wasn't even English."

"I knew that from the name," said Isabel. "So ha-ha."

Every one of them believed, whatever the details, that there had been a great comedown, a dim catastrophe, and that beyond them, behind them, in England, lay lands and houses and ease and honor. How could they think otherwise, remembering their grandfather?

He had worked as a postal clerk, in Fork Mills. His wife, whether she was a seduced servant or not, bore him eight children, then died. As soon as the older children were out to work and contributing money to the household—there was no nonsense about educating them—the father quit work. A fight with the Postmaster was the immediate reason, but he really had no intention of working any longer; he had made up his mind to stay at home, supported by his children. He had the air of a gentleman, was widely read, and full of rhetoric and self-esteem. His children did not balk at supporting him; they sank into their commonplace jobs, but pushed their own children—they limited themselves to one or two apiece, mostly daughters—out to Business School, to Normal School, to Nurses Training. My mother and her cousins, who were these children, talked often about their selfish and wilful grandfather, hardly ever about their decent, hard-working parents. What an old snob he was, they said, but how handsome, even as an old man, what a carriage. What ready and appropriate insults he had for people, what scathing judgements he could make. Once, in faraway Toronto, on the main floor of Eaton's as a matter of fact, he was accosted by the harnessmaker's wife from Fork Mills, a harmless, brainless woman who cried, "Well, ain't it nice to meet a friend so far from home?"

"Madam," said Grandfather Chaddeley, "you are no friend of mine."

Wasn't he the limit, they said. *Madam, you are no friend of mine!* The old snob. He paraded around with his head in the air like a prize gander. Another lower-class lady—lower-class according to him—was kind enough to bring him some soup, when he had caught cold. Sitting in his daughter's kitchen, not even his own roof over his head, soaking his feet, an ailing and in fact a dying man, he still had the gall to turn his back, let his daughter do the thanking. He despised the woman, whose grammar was terrible, and who had no teeth.

"But he didn't either! By that time he had no teeth whatever!"

"Pretentious old coot."

"And a leech on his children."

"Just pride and vanity. That's the sum total of him."

But telling these stories, laughing, they were billowing with pride themselves, they were crowing. They were proud of having such a grandfather. They believed that refusing to speak to inferior people was outrageous and mean, that preserving a sense of distinction was ridiculous, particularly when your teeth were gone, but in a way they still admired him. They did. They admired his invective, which was lost on his boss, the plodding Postmaster, and his prideful behavior, which was lost on his neighbors, the democratic citizens of Canada. (Oh what a shame, said the tooth-less neighbor, the poor old fellow, he don't even reckinize me.) They might even have admired his decision to let others do the work. A gentleman, they called him. They spoke ironically, but the possession of such a grandfather continued to delight them.

I couldn't understand this, at the time or later. I had too much Scottish blood in me, too much of my father. My father would never have admitted there were inferior people, or superior people either. He was scrupulously egalitarian, making it a point not to "snivel," as he said, to anybody, not to kowtow, and not to high-hat anybody, either, to behave as if there were no differences. I took the same tack. There were times, later, when I wondered if it was a paralyzing prudence that urged this stand, as much as any finer sentiment, when I wondered if my father and I didn't harbor, in our hearts, intact and unassailable notions of superiority, which my mother and her cousins with their innocent snobbishness could never match.

It was not of much importance to me, years later, to receive a letter from the Chaddeley family, in England. It was from an elderly lady who was working on a family tree. The family did exist, in England, after all, and they did not spurn their overseas branches, they were seeking us out. My great-grandfather was known to them. There was his name on the family tree: Joseph Ellington Chaddeley. The marriage register gave his occupation as butcher's apprentice. He had married Helena Rose Armour, a servant, in 1859. So it was true that he had married a servant. But probably not true about the gaming debts at Oxford. Did gentlemen who were embarrassed at Oxford go and apprentice themselves to butchers?

It occurred to me that if he had stayed with butchering, his children might have gone to high school. He might have been a prosperous man in Fork Mills. The letter-writer did not mention the Cholmondeley connection, or the fields of sedge, or William the Conqueror. It was a decent family we belonged to, of servants and artisans, the occasional tradesman or farmer. At one time I would have been shocked to discover this, and would hardly have believed it. At another, later, time, when I was dedicated to tearing away all false notions, all illusions, I would have been triumphant. By the time the revelation came I did not care, one way or the other. I had almost forgotten about Canterbury and Oxford and Cholmondeley, and that first England I had heard of from my mother, that ancient land of harmony and chivalry, of people on horseback, and good manners (though surely my grandfather's had broken, under the strain of a cruder life), of Simon de Montfort and Lorna Doone and hounds and castles and the New Forest, all fresh and rural, ceremonious, civilized, eternally desirable.

And I had already had my eyes opened to some other things, by the visit of Cousin Iris.

That happened when I was living in Vancouver. I was married to Richard then. I had two small children. On a Saturday evening Richard answered the phone and came to get me.

"Be careful," he said. "It sounds like Dalgleish."

Richard always said the name of my native town as if it were a clot of something unpleasant, which he had to get out of his mouth in a hurry.

I went to the phone and found my relief that it was nobody from Dalgleish at all. It was Cousin Iris. There was a bit of the Ottawa Valley accent still in her speech, something rural — she would not have suspected that herself and would not have been pleased — and something loud and jolly, which had made Richard think of the voices of Dalgleish. She said that she was in Vancouver, she was retired now and she was taking a trip, and she was dying to see me. I asked her to come to dinner the next day.

"Now, by dinner, you mean the evening meal, don't you?"

"Yes."

"I just wanted to get it straight. Because when we visited at your place, remember, your folks always had dinner at noon. You called the noon meal dinner. I didn't think you still would but I wanted to get it straight."

I told Richard that a cousin of my mother's was coming to dinner. I said she was, or had been, a nurse, and that she lived in Philadelphia.

"She's all right," I said. I meant decently educated, well enough spoken, moderately well-bred. "She's travelled all over. She's really quite interesting. Being a nurse she's met all sorts of people — " I told about the millionaire's widow and the jewels in the carpetbag. And the more I talked, the more Richard discerned of my doubts and my need for reassurance, and the more noncommittal and unreassuring he became. He knew he had an advantage, and we had reached the point in our marriage where no advantage was given up easily.

I longed for the visit to go well. I wanted this for my own sake. My motives were not such as would do me credit. I wanted Cousin Iris to shine forth as a relative nobody need be ashamed of, and I wanted Richard and his money and our house to lift me forever, in Cousin Iris's eyes, out of the category of poor relation. I wanted all this accomplished with a decent subtlety and restraint and the result to be a pleasant recognition of my own value, from both sides.

I used to think that if I could produce one rich and well-behaved and important relative, Richard's attitude to me would change. A judge, a surgeon, would have done very well. I was not sure at all how Iris would serve, as a substitute. I was worried about the way Richard had said *Dalgleish*, and that vestige of the Ottawa Valley—Richard was stern about rural accents, having had so much trouble with mine—and something else in Iris's voice which I could not identify. Was she too eager? Did she assume some proprietary family claim I no longer believed was justified?

Never mind. I started thawing a leg of lamb and made a lemon meringue pie. Lemon meringue pie was what my mother made when the cousins were coming. She polished the dessert forks, she ironed the table napkins. For we owned dessert forks (I wanted to say to Richard); yes, and we had table napkins, even though the toilet was in the basement and there was no running water until after the war. I used to carry hot water to the front bedroom in the morning, so that the cousins could wash. I poured it into a jug like those I now see in antique stores, or on hall tables, full of ornamental grasses.

But surely none of this mattered to me, none of this nonsense about dessert forks? Was I, am I, the sort of person who thinks that to possess such objects is to have a civilized attitude to life? No, not at all; not exactly; yes and no. Yes and no. Background was Richard's word. *Your background.* A drop in his voice, a warning. Or was that what I heard, not what he meant? When he said Dalgleish, even when he wordlessly handed me a letter from home, I felt ashamed, as if there was something growing over me; mold, something nasty and dreary and inescapable. Poverty, to Richard's family, was like bad breath or running sores, an affliction for which the afflicted must bear one part of the blame. But it was not good manners to notice. If ever I said anything about my childhood or my family in their company there would be a slight drawing-back, as at a low-level obscenity. But it is possible that I was a bit strident and self-conscious, like the underbred character in Virginia Woolf who makes a point of not having been taken to the circus. Perhaps that was what embarrassed them. They were tactful with me. Richard could not afford to be so tactful, since he had put himself in a chancy position, marrying me. He wanted me amputated from that past which seemed to him such shabby baggage; he was on the lookout for signs that the amputation was not complete; and of course it wasn't.

My mother's cousins had never visited us again, en masse. Winifred died suddenly one winter, not more than three or four years after that memorable visit. Iris wrote to my mother that the circle was broken now and that she had suspected Winifred was diabetic, but Winifred did not want to find that out because of her love of food. My mother herself was not well. The remaining cousins visited her, but they did so separately, and of course not often, because of distances. Nearly every one of their letters referred to the grand time they had all had, that summer, and near the end of her life my mother said, "Oh, Lord, do you know what I was thinking of? The water-pistol. Remember that concert? Winifred with the water-pistol! Everybody did their stunt. What did I do?"

"You stood on your head."

"Ah yes I did."

Cousin Iris was stouter than ever, and rosy under her powder. She was breathless from her climb up the street. I had not wanted to ask Richard to go to the hotel for her. I would not say I was afraid to ask him; I simply wanted to keep things from starting off on the wrong foot, by making him do what he hadn't offered to do. I had told myself that she would take a cab. But she had come on the bus.

"Richard was busy," I said to her, lying. "It's my fault. I don't drive."

"Never mind," said Iris staunchly. "I'm all out of puff just now but I'll be all right in a minute. It's carrying the lard that does it. Serves me right."

As soon as she said *all out of puff*, and *carrying the lard*, I knew how things were going to go, with Richard. It hadn't even taken that. I knew as soon as I saw her on my doorstep, her hair, which I remembered as gray-brown, now gilt and sprayed into a foamy pile, her sumptuous peacock-blue dress decorated at one shoulder with a sort of fountain of gold spray. Now that I think of it, she looked splendid. I wish I had met her somewhere else. I wish I had appreciated her as she deserved. I wish that everything had gone differently.

"Well, now," she said jubilantly. "Haven't you done all right for yourself!" She looked at me, and the rock garden and the ornamental shrubs and the expanse of windows. Our house was in Capilano Heights on the side of Grouse Mountain. "I'll say. It's a grand place, dear."

I took her in and introduced her to Richard and she said, "Oh-ho, so you're the husband. Well, I won't ask you how's business because I can see it's good."

Richard was a lawyer. The men in his family were either lawyers or stockbrokers. They never referred to what they did at work as any kind of business. They never referred to what they did at work at all. Talking about what you did at work was slightly vulgar; talking about how you did was unforgivably so. If I had not been still so vulnerable to Richard it might have been a pleasure to see him met like this, head on.

I offered drinks at once, hoping to build up a bit of insulation in myself. I had got out a bottle of sherry, thinking that was what you offered older ladies, people who didn't usually drink. But Iris laughed and said, "Why, I'd love a gin and tonic, just like you folks."

"Remember that time we all went to visit you in Dalgleish?" she said. "It was so dry! Your mother was still a small-town girl, she wouldn't have liquor in the house. Though I always thought your father would take a drink, if you got him off. Flora was Temperance, too. But that Winifred was a devil. You know she had a bottle in her suitcase? We'd sneak into the bedroom and take a nip, then gargle with cologne. She called your place the Sahara. Here we are crossing the Sahara. Not that we didn't get enough lemonade and iced tea to float a battleship. Float four battleships, eh?"

Perhaps she had seen something when I opened the door—some surprise, or failure of welcome. Perhaps she was daunted, though at the same time immensely pleased by the house and the furnishings, which were elegant and dull and not all chosen by Richard, either. Whatever the reason, her tone when she spoke of Dalgleish and my parents was condescending. I don't think she wanted to remind me of home, and put me in my place; I think she wanted to establish herself, to let me know that she belonged here, more than there.

"Oh, this is a treat, sitting here and looking at your gorgeous view! Is that Vancouver Island?"

"Point Grey," said Richard unencouragingly.

"Oh, I should have known. We went out there on the bus yesterday. We saw the University. I'm with a tour, dear, did I tell you? Nine old maids and seven widows and three widowers. Not one married couple. But as I say, you never know, the trip's not over yet."

I smiled, and Richard said he had to move the sprinkler.

"We go to Vancouver Island tomorrow, then we're taking the boat to Alaska. Everybody said to me back home, what do you want to go to Alaska for, and I said, because I've never been there, isn't that a good enough reason? No bachelors on the tour, and do you know why? They don't live to be this old! That's a medical fact. You tell your hubby. Tell him he did the right thing. But I'm not going to talk shop. Every time I go on a trip they find out I'm a nurse and they show me their spines and their tonsils and their whatnots. They want me to poke their livers. Free diagnosis. I say enough of that. I'm retired now and I mean to enjoy life. This beats the iced tea a mile, doesn't it? But she used to go to such a lot of trouble. The poor thing. She used to frost the glasses with egg white, remember?"

I tried to get her to talk about my mother's illness, new treatments, her hospital experiences, not only because that was interesting to me, but because I thought it might calm her down and make her sound more intelligent. I knew Richard hadn't gone out at all but was lurking in the kitchen.

But she said, no shop.

"Beaten egg white, then sugar. Oh, dear. You had to drink through straws. But the fun we had there. The john in the basement and all. We did have fun."

Iris's lipstick, her bright teased hair, her iridescent dress and oversized brooch, her voice and conversation, were all part of a policy which was not a bad one: she was in favor of movement, noise, change, flashiness, hilarity, and courage. Fun. She thought other people should be in favor of these things too, and told about her efforts on the tour.

"I'm the person to get the ball rolling. Some people get downhearted on a trip. They get indigestion. They talk about their constipation. I always get their minds off it. You can always joke. You can start a singsong. Every morning I can practically hear them thinking, what crazy thing is that Chaddeley going to come up with today?"

Nothing fazed her, she said. She told about other trips. Ireland. The other women had been afraid to get down and kiss the Blarney Stone, but she said, "I've come this far and I'm going to kiss the damn thing!" and did so, while a blasphemous Irishman hung on to her ankles.

We drank; we ate; the children came in and were praised. Richard came and went. Nothing fazed her; she was right. Nothing deflected her from her stories of herself; the amount of time she could spend not talking was limited. She told about the carpetbag and the millionaire's widow all over again. She told about the dissolute actor. How many conversations she must have ridden through like this — laughing, insisting, rambling, recollecting. I wondered if this evening was something she would describe as fun. She would describe it. The house, the rugs, the dishes, the signs of money. It might not matter to her that Richard snubbed her. Perhaps she would rather be snubbed by a rich relative than welcomed by a poor one. But had she always been like this, always brash and greedy and scared; decent, maybe even admirable, but still somebody you hope you will not have to sit too long beside, on a bus or at a party? I was dishonest when I said that I wished we had met elsewhere, that I wished I had appreciated her, when I implied that Richard's judgements were all that stood in the way. Perhaps I could have appreciated her more, but I couldn't have stayed with her long.

I had to wonder if this was all it amounted to, the gaiety I remembered; the gaiety and generosity, the worldliness. It would be better to think that time had soured and thinned and made commonplace a brew that used to sparkle, that difficulties had altered us both, and not for the better. Unsympathetic places and people might have made us harsh, in efforts and opinions. I used to love to look at magazine advertisements showing ladies in chiffon dresses with capes and floating panels, resting their elbows on a ship's rail, or drinking tea beside a potted palm. I used to apprehend a life of elegance and sensibility, through them. They were a window I had on the world, and the cousins were another. In fact the cousins' flowery dresses used to remind me of them, though the cousins were so much stouter, and not pretty. Well, now that I think of it, what were those ladies talking about, in the balloons over their heads? They were discussing underarm odor, or thanking their lucky stars they were no longer chafed, because they used Kotex.

Iris collected herself, finally, and asked when the last bus ran. Richard had disappeared again, but I said that I would take her back to her hotel in a cab. She said no, she would enjoy the bus ride, truly she would, she always got into a conversation with somebody. I got out my schedule and walked her to the bus stop. She said she hoped she hadn't talked Richard's and my ears off and asked if Richard was shy. She said I had a lovely home, a lovely family, it made her feel grand to see that I had done so well in my life. Tears filled her eyes when she hugged me good-bye.

"What a pathetic old tart," said Richard, coming into the living room as I was gathering up the coffee cups. He followed me into the kitchen, recalling things she had said, pretentious things, bits of bragging. He pointed out grammatical mistakes she had made, of the would-be genteel variety. He pretended incredulity. Maybe he really felt it. Or maybe he thought it would be a good idea to start the attack immediately, before I took him to task for leaving the room, being rude, not offering a ride to the hotel.

He was still talking as I threw the Pyrex plate at his head.

There was a piece of lemon meringue pie in it. The plate missed, and hit the refrigerator, but the pie flew out and caught him on the side of the face just as in the old movies or an *I Love Lucy* show. There was the same moment of amazement as there is on the screen, the sudden innocence, for him; his speech stopped, his mouth open. For me, too, amazement, that something people invariably thought funny in those instances should be so shocking a verdict in real life.

> *Row, row, row your boat*
> *Gently down the stream.*
> *Merrily, merrily, merrily, merrily,*
> *Life is but a dream.*

I lie in bed beside my little sister, listening to the singing in the yard. Life is transformed, by these voices, by these presences, by their high spirits and grand esteem, for themselves and each other. My parents, all of us, are on holiday. The mixture of voices and words is so complicated and varied it seems that such confusion, such jolly rivalry, will go on forever, and then to my surprise—for I am surprised, even though I know the pattern of rounds—the song is thinning out, you can hear the two voices striving.

> *Merrily, merrily, merrily, merrily,*
> *Life is but a dream.*

Then the one voice alone, one of them singing on, gamely, to the finish. One voice in which there is an unexpected note of entreaty, of warning, as it hangs the five separate words on the air. *Life is*. Wait. *But a*. Now, wait. *Dream*.

Chaddeleys and Flemings

II   THE STONE IN THE FIELD

My mother was not a person who spent all her time frosting the rims of glasses and fancying herself descended from the aristocracy. She was a businesswoman really, a trader and dealer. Our house was full of things that had not been paid for with money, but taken in some complicated trade, and that might not be ours to keep. For a while we could play a piano, consult an Encyclopaedia Britannica, eat off an oak table. But one day I would come home from school and find that each of these things had moved on. A mirror off the wall could go as easily, a cruet stand, a horsehair loveseat that had replaced a sofa that had replaced a daybed. We were living in a warehouse.

My mother worked for, or with, a man named Poppy Cullender. He was a dealer in antiques. He did not have a shop. He too had a house full of furniture. What we had was just his overflow. He had dressers back-to-back and bedsprings upended against the wall. He bought things — furniture, dishes, bedspreads, doorknobs, pump handles, churns, flatirons, anything — from people living on farms or in little villages in the country, then sold what he had bought to antique stores in Toronto. The heyday of antiques had not yet arrived. It was a time when people were covering old woodwork with white or pastel paint as fast as they were able, throwing out spool beds and putting in blond maple bedroom suites, covering patchwork quilts with chenille bedspreads. It was not hard to buy things, to pick them up for next to nothing, but it was a slow business selling them, which was why they might become part of our lives for a season. Just the same, Poppy and my mother were on the right track. If they had lasted, they might have become rich and justified. As it was, Poppy kept his head above water and my mother made next to nothing, and everybody thought them deluded.

They didn't last. My mother got sick, and Poppy went to jail, for making advances on a train.

There were farmhouses where Poppy was not a welcome sight. Children hooted and wives bolted the door, as he came toiling through the yard in his greasy black clothes, rolling his eyes in an uncontrollably lewd or silly way he had and calling in a soft, pleading voice, "Ith anybody h-home?" To add to his other problems he had both a lisp and a stammer. My father could imitate him very well. There were places where Poppy found doors barred and others, usually less respectable, where he was greeted and cheered and fed, just as if he had been a harmless weird bird dropped out of the sky, valued for its very oddity. When he had experienced no welcome he did not go back; instead, he sent my mother. He must have had in his head a map of the surrounding country with every house in it, and just as some maps have dots to show you where the mineral resources are, or the places of historical interest, Poppy's map would have marked the location of every known and suspected rocking chair, pine sideboard, piece of milk glass, moustache cup. "Why don't you run out and take a look at it?" I would hear him say to my mother when they were huddled in the dining room looking at something like the maker's mark on an old pickle crock. He didn't stammer when he talked to her, when he talked business; his voice though soft was not humble and indicated that he had his own satisfactions, maybe his own revenge. If I had a friend with me, coming in from school, she would say, "Is that Poppy *Cullender*?" She would be amazed to hear him talking like an ordinary person and amazed to find him inside somebody's house. I disliked his connection with us so much that I wanted to say no.

Not much was made, really, of Poppy's sexual tendencies. People may have thought he didn't have any. When they said he was queer, they just meant queer; odd, freakish, disturbing. His stammer and his rolling eyes and his fat bum and his house full of throwaways were all rolled up into that one word. I don't know if he was very courageous, trying to make a life for himself in a place like Dalgleish where random insults and misplaced pity would be what was always coming at him, or whether he was just not very realistic. Certainly it was not realistic to make such suggestions to a couple of baseball players on the Stratford train.

I never knew what my mother made of his final disastrous luck, or what she knew about him. Years later she read in the paper that a teacher at the college I was going to had been arrested for fighting in a bar over a male companion. She asked me did they mean he was defending a friend, and if so, why didn't they say so? *Male companion*?

Then she said, "Poor Poppy. There were always those that were out to get him. He was very smart, in his way. Some people can't survive in a place like this. It's not permitted. No."

My mother had the use of Poppy's car, for business forays, and sometimes for a weekend, when he went to Toronto. Unless he had a trailer-load of things to take down, he travelled—unfortunately, as I have said—by train. Our own car had gone so far beyond repair that we were not able to take it out of town; it was driven into Dalgleish and back, and that was all. My parents were like many other people who had entered the Depression with some large possession, such as a car or a furnace, which gradually wore out and couldn't be fixed or replaced. When we could take it on the roads we used to go to Goderich once or twice in a summer, to the lake. And occasionally we visited my father's sisters who lived out in the country.

My mother always said that my father had a very odd family. It was odd because there had been seven girls and then one boy;

and it was odd because six of those eight children still lived together, in the house where they were born. One sister had died young, of typhoid fever, and my father had got away. And those six sisters were very odd in themselves, at least in the view of many people, in the time they lived in. They were leftovers, really; my mother said so; they belonged in another generation.

I don't remember that they ever came to visit us. They didn't like to come to a town as big as Dalgleish, or to venture so far from home. It would have been a drive of fourteen or fifteen miles, and they had no car. They drove a horse and buggy, a horse and cutter in the wintertime, long after everyone else had ceased to do so. There must have been occasions when they had to drive into town, because I saw one of them once, in the buggy, on a town street. The buggy had a great high top on it, like a black bonnet, and whichever aunt it was was sitting sideways on the seat, looking up as seldom as it is possible to do while driving a horse. Public scrutiny seemed to be causing her much pain, but she was stubborn; she held herself there on the seat, cringing and stubborn, and she was as strange a sight, in her way, as Poppy Cullender was in his. I couldn't really think of her as my aunt; the connection seemed impossible. Yet I could remember an earlier time, when I had been out to the farm—maybe more than one time, for I had been so young it was hard to remember—and I had not felt this impossibility and had not understood the oddity of these relatives. It was when my grandfather was sick in bed, dying I suppose, with a big brown paper fan hanging over him. It was worked by a system of ropes which I was allowed to pull. One of my aunts was showing me how to do this, when my mother called my name from downstairs. Then the aunt and I looked at each other exactly as two children look at each other when an adult is calling. I must have sensed something unusual about this, some lack of what was expected, even necessary, in the way of balance, or barriers; else I would not have remembered it.

One other time with an aunt. I think the same one, but maybe another, was sitting with me on the back steps of the farmhouse, with a six-quart basket of clothespegs on the step beside us. She was making dolls for me, mannikins, out of the round-headed pegs. She used a black crayon and a red, to make their mouths and eyes, and she brought bits of yarn out of her apron pocket, to twist around to make the hair and clothes. And she talked to me; I am certain she talked.

"Here's a lady. She went to church with her wig on, see? She was proud. What if a wind comes up? It would blow her wig right off. See? You blow.

"Here's a soldier. See he only has the one leg? His other leg was blown off by a cannonball at the battle of Waterloo. Do you know what a cannonball is, that shoots out of a big gun? When they have a battle? Boom!"

Now we were going out to the farm, in Poppy's car, to visit the aunts. My father said no, he wouldn't drive another man's car — meaning he wouldn't drive Poppy's, wouldn't sit where Poppy had sat — so my mother drove. That made the whole expedition feel uncertain, the weight wrongly distributed. It was a hot Sunday late in the summer.

My mother was not altogether sure of the way, and my father waited until the last moment to reassure her. This was understood to be teasing, and yet was not altogether free of reservations or reproof.

"Is it here we turn? Is it one further? I will know when I see the bridge."

The route was complicated. Around Dalgleish most roads were straight, but out here the roads twisted around hills or buried themselves in swamps. Some dwindled to a couple of ruts with a row of plantain and dandelions running between. In some places wild berrybushes sent creepers across the road. These high, thick bushes, dense and thorny, with leaves of a shiny green that seemed almost black, reminded me of the waves of the sea that were pushed back for Moses.

There was the bridge, like two railway cars joined together, stripped to their skeletons, one lane wide. A sign said it was unsafe for trucks.

"We'll never make it," my father said, as we bumped on to the bridge floor. "There he is. Old Father Maitland."

My sister said, "Where? Who? Where is he?"

"The Maitland *River*," my mother said.

We looked down, where the guard-rails had fallen out of the side of the bridge, and saw the clear brown water flowing over big dim stones, between cedar banks, breaking into sunny ripples further on. My skin was craving for it.

"Do they ever go swimming?" I said. I meant the aunts. I thought that if they did, they might take us.

"Swimming?" said my mother. "I can't picture it. Do they?" she asked my father.

"I can't picture it either."

The road was going uphill, out of the gloomy cedar bush on the river bank. I started saying the aunts' names.

"Susan. Clara. Lizzie. Maggie. Jennet was the one who died."

"Annie," said my father. "Don't forget Annie."

"Annie. Lizzie. I said her. Who else?"

"Dorothy," said my mother, shifting gears with an angry little spurt, and we cleared the top of the hill, leaving the dark bush hollow behind. Up here were pasture hills covered with purple-flowering milkweed, wild pea blossom, black-eyed Susans. Hardly any trees here, but lots of elderberry bushes, blooming all along the road. They looked as if they were sprinkled with snow. One bald hill reached up higher than any of the others.

"Mount Hebron," my father said. "That is the highest point of land in Huron County. Or so I always was told."

"Now I know where I am all right," my mother said. "We'll see it in a moment, won't we?"

And there it was, the big wooden house with no trees near it, the barn and the flowering brown hills behind. The drive shed was the original barn, built of logs. The paint on the house was not white as I had absolutely believed but yellow, and much of it had peeled away.

Out in front of the house, in a block of shade which was quite narrow at this time of day, several figures were sitting on straight-backed chairs. On the wall of the house, behind them, hung the scoured milk-pails and parts of the separator.

They were not expecting us. They had no telephone, so we hadn't been able to let them know we were coming. They were just sitting there in the shade, watching the road where scarcely another car went by all afternoon.

One figure got up, and ran around the side of the house. "That'll be Susan," my father said. "She can't face company."

"She'll come back when she realizes it's us," my mother said. "She won't know the strange car."

"Maybe. I wouldn't count on it."

The others stood, and stiffly readied themselves, hands clasped in front of their aprons. When we got out of the car and were recognized, one or two of them took a few steps forward, then stopped, and waited for us to approach them.

"Come on," my father said, and led us to each in turn, saying only the name in recognition of the meeting. No embraces, no touch of hands or laying together of cheeks.

"Lizzie. Dorothy. Clara."

It was no use, I could never get them straight. They looked too much alike. There must have been a twelve- or fifteen-year age span, but to me they all looked about fifty, older than my parents but not really old. They were all lean and fine-boned, and might at one time have been fairly tall, but were stooped now, with hard work and deference. Some had their hair cut short in a plain, childish style; some had it braided and twisted on top of their heads. Nobody's hair was entirely black or entirely gray. Their faces were pale, eyebrows thick and furry, eyes deep-set and bright; blue-gray or green-gray or gray. They looked a good deal like my father though he did not stoop, and his face had opened up in a way that theirs had not, to make him a handsome man.

They looked a good deal like me. I didn't know it at the time and wouldn't have wanted to. But suppose I stopped doing anything to my hair, now, stopped wearing makeup and plucking my eyebrows, put on a shapeless print dress and apron and stood around hanging my head and hugging my elbows? Yes. So when my mother and her cousins looked me over, anxiously turned me to the light, saying, "Is she a Chaddeley? What do you think?" it was the Fleming face they were seeing, and to tell the truth it was a face that wore better than theirs. (Not that they were claiming to be pretty; to look like a Chaddeley was enough.)

One of the aunts had hands red as a skinned rabbit. Later in the kitchen this one sat in a chair pushed up against the woodbox, half hidden by the stove, and I saw how she kept stroking these hands and twisting them up in her apron. I remembered that I had seen such hands before, on one of the early visits, long ago, and my mother had told me that it was because this aunt — was it always the same one? — had been scrubbing the floor and the table and chairs with lye, to keep them white. That was what lye did to your hands. And after this visit, too, on the way home my mother was to say in a tone of general accusation, sorrow, and disgust, "Did you see those hands? They must have got a Presbyterian dispensation to let them scrub on Sundays."

The floor was pine and it was white, gleaming, but soft-looking, like velvet. So were the chairs and the table. We all sat around the kitchen, which was like a small house tacked on to the main house; back and front doors opposite each other, windows on three sides. The cold black stove shone, too, with polishing. Its trim was like mirrors. The room was cleaner and barer than any I have ever been in. There was no sign of frivolity, no indication that the people who lived here ever sought entertainment. No radio; no newspapers or magazines; certainly no books. There must have been a Bible in the house, and there must have been a calendar, but these were not to be seen. It was hard now even to believe in the clothespin dolls, the crayons and the yarn. I wanted to ask which of them had made the dolls; had there really been a wigged lady and a one-legged soldier? But though I was not usually shy, a peculiar paralysis overcame me in this room, as if I understood for the first time how presumptuous any question might be, how hazardous any opinion.

Work would be what filled their lives, not conversation; work would be what gave their days shape. I know that now. Drawing the milk down through the rough teats, slapping the flatiron back and forth on the scorched-smelling ironing board, swishing the scrub-water in whitening arcs across the pine floor, they would be mute, and maybe content. Work would not be done here as it was in our house, where the idea was to get it over with. It would be something that could, that must, go on forever.

What was to be said? The aunts, like those who engage in a chat with royalty, would venture no remarks of their own, but could answer questions. They offered no refreshments. It was clear that only a great effort of will kept them all from running away and hiding, like Aunt Susan, who never did reappear while we were there. What was felt in that room was the pain of human contact. I was hypnotized by it. The fascinating pain; the humiliating necessity.

My father did have some idea of how to proceed. He started out on the weather. The need for rain, the rain in July that spoiled the hay, last year's wet spring, floods long past, the prospects or non-prospects of a rainy fall. This talk steadied them, and he asked about the cows, the driving horse whose name was Nelly and the workhorses Prince and Queen, the garden; did the blight get on their tomatoes?

"No it didn't."

"How many quarts did you do down?"

"Twenty-seven."

"Did you make any chili sauce? Did you make some juice?"

"Juice and chili sauce. Yes."

"So you won't starve next winter. You'll be falling into flesh, next."

Giggles broke from a couple of them and my father took heart, continued teasing. He inquired whether they were doing much dancing these days. He shook his head as he pretended to recall their reputation for running around the country to dances, smoking, cutting up. He said they were a bad lot, they wouldn't get married because they'd rather flirt; why, he couldn't hold up his head for the shame of them.

My mother broke in then. She must have meant to rescue them, thinking it cruel to tease them in this way, dwelling on just what they had never had, or been.

"That is a lovely piece of furniture," she said. "That sideboard. I always have admired it."

Flappers, my father said, that's what they were, in their prime.

My mother went over to look at the kitchen dresser, which was pine, and very heavy and tall. The knobs on all the doors and drawers were not quite round but slightly irregular, either from the making, or from all the hands that had pulled on them.

"You could have an antique dealer come in here and offer you a hundred dollars for that," my mother said. "If that ever happens, don't take it. The table and chairs as well. Don't let anybody smooth-talk you into selling them before you find out what they're really worth. I know what I'm talking about." Without asking permission she examined the dresser, fingered the knobs, looked around at the back. "I can't tell you what it's worth myself but if you ever want to sell it I will get it appraised by the best person I can find. That's not all," she said, stroking the pine judiciously. "You have a fortune's worth of furniture in this house. You sit tight on it. You have the old furniture that was made around here, and there's hardly any of that left. People threw it out, around the turn of the century, they bought Victorian things when they started getting prosperous. The things that didn't get thrown out are worth money and they're going to be worth more. I'm telling you."

So she was. But they could not take such telling. They could no more understand her than if she had been spouting lunacy. Possibly the word antique was not known to them. She was talking about their kitchen dresser but she was talking about it in terms they had no understanding of. If a dealer came into the house and offered them money? Nobody came into their house. Selling the dresser was probably as hard for them to imagine as selling the kitchen wall. None of them would look at anything but their aproned laps.

"So I guess that's lucky, for the ones that never got prosperous," my father said, to ease things, but they could not answer him, either. They would know the meaning of prosperous but they would never have used such a word, would never have got their tongues around it, nor their minds around the idea of getting that way. They would have noticed that some people, their neighbors even, were spending money, on tractors and combines and milking machines as well as on cars and houses, and I think this must have seemed to them a sign of an alarming, not enviable, lack of propriety and self-control. They would pity people for it, in a way, the same way they might pity girls who did run around to dances, and smoke and flirt and get married. They might pity my mother, too. My mother looked at their lives and thought of how they could be brightened, opened up. Suppose they sold some furniture and got hydro in the house, bought a washing machine, put linoleum on the floor, bought a car and learned to drive it? Why not? my mother would ask, seeing life all in terms of change and possibility. She imagined they would yearn for things, not only material things but conditions, abilities, which they did not even bother to deplore, did not think to reject, being so perfectly encased in what they had and were, so far beyond imagining themselves otherwise.

When my father was in the hospital for the last time he became very good-humored and loquacious under the influence of the pills they were giving him, and he talked to me about his life and his family. He told me how he had left home. Actually there were two leave-takings. The first occurred the summer he was fourteen. His father had sent him out to split some chunks of wood. He broke the ax-handle, and his father cursed him out and went after him with a pitchfork. His father was known for temper, and hard work. The sisters screamed, and my father, the fourteen-year-old boy, took off down the lane running as hard as he could.

"Could they scream?"

"What? Oh yes. Then. Yes they could."

My father intended to run only as far as the road, hang around, come back when his sisters let him know the coast was clear. But he did not stop running until he was halfway to Goderich, and then he thought he might as well go the rest of the way. He got a job on a lake-boat. He spent the rest of the season working on the boat, and the month before Christmas, after the shipping season ended, he worked in a flour mill. He could do the work there, but he was underage; they were afraid of the inspector, so they let him go. He wanted to go home anyway, for Christmas. He was homesick. He bought presents for his father and his sisters. A watch was what he got for the old man. That and his ticket took every cent he had.

A few days after Christmas he was out in the barn, putting down hay, and his father came looking for him.

"Have you got any money?" his father wanted to know.

My father said he hadn't.

"Well, do you think then me and your sisters are going to spend all summer and fall looking up the arseholes of cows, for you to come home and sponge off us in the winter?"

That was the second time my father left home.

He shook with laughter in the hospital bed, telling me.

"Looking up the arseholes of cows!"

Then he said the funny thing was the old man himself had left home when he was a kid, after a fight with his own father. The father lit into him for using the wheelbarrow.

"It was this way. They always carried the feed to the horses, pail by pail. In the winter, when the horses were in the stalls. So my father took the notion to carry it to them in the wheelbarrow. Naturally it was a lot quicker. But he got beat. For laziness. That was the way they were, you know. Any change of any kind was a bad thing. Efficiency was just laziness, to them. That's the peasant thinking for you."

"Maybe Tolstoy would agree with them," I said. "Gandhi too."

"Drat Tolstoy and Gandhi. They never worked when they were young."

"Maybe not."

"But it's a wonder how those people had the courage once, to get them over here. They left everything. Turned their backs on everything they knew and came out here. Bad enough to face the North Atlantic, then this country that was all wilderness. The work they did, the things they went through. When your great-grand-father came to the Huron Tract he had his brother with him, and his wife and her mother, and his two little kids. Straightaway his brother was killed by a falling tree. Then the second summer his wife and her mother and the two little boys got the cholera, and the grandmother and both the children died. So he and his wife were left alone, and they went on clearing their farm and started up another family. I think the courage got burnt out of them. Their religion did them in, and their upbringing. How they had to toe the

line. Also their pride. Pride was what they had when they had no
more gumption."

"Not you," I said. "You ran away."

"I didn't run far."

In their old age the aunts rented the farm, but continued to live on
it. Some got cataracts in their eyes, some got arthritis, but they
stayed on and looked after each other, and died there, all except the
last one, Aunt Lizzie, who had to go to the County Home. They
lived a long time. They were a hardier clan, after all, than the
Chaddeleys, none of whom reached seventy. (Cousin Iris died
within six months of seeing Alaska.) I used to send a card at
Christmas, and I would write on it: *to all my aunts, love and a
Merry Christmas*. I did that because I could not remember which of
them were dead and which were alive. I had seen their gravestone
when my mother was buried. It was a modest pillar with all their
names and dates of birth on it, a couple of dates of death filled in
(Jennet, of course, and probably Susan), the rest left blank. By
now more dates would be finished.

They would send me a card too. A wreath or a candle on it,
and a few sentences of information.

*A good winter so far, not much snow. We are all well except
Clara's eyes not getting any better. Best wishes of the Season.*

I thought of them having to go out and buy the card, go to the
Post Office, buy the stamp. It was an act of faith for them to write
and send those sentences to any place as unimaginable as Vancouver, to someone of their own blood leading a life so strange to
them, someone who would read the card with such a feeling of
bewilderment and unexplainable guilt. It did make me guilty and
bewildered to think that they were still there, still attached to me.
But any message from home, in those days, could let me know I
was a traitor.

In the hospital, I asked my father if any of his sisters had ever
had a boyfriend.

"Not what you could call that. No. There used to be a joke
about Mr. Black. They used to say he built his shack there because
he was sweet on Susan. I don't think so. He was just a one-legged
fellow that built a shack down in a corner of the field across the

road, and he died there. All before my time. Susan was the oldest, you know, she was twenty or twenty-one years old when I was born."

"So, you don't think she had a romance?"

"I wouldn't think so. It was just a joke. He was an Austrian or some such thing. Black was just what he was called, or maybe he called himself. She wouldn't have been let near him. He was buried right there under a big boulder. My father tore the shack down and used the lumber to build our chicken-house."

I remembered that, I remembered the boulder. I remembered sitting on the ground watching my father who was fixing fence-posts. I asked him if this could be a true memory.

"Yes it could. I used to go out and fix the fences when the old man was sick in bed. You wouldn't have been very big."

"I was sitting watching you, and you said to me, do you know what that big stone is? That's a gravestone. I don't remember asking you whose. I must have thought it was a joke."

"No joke. That would be it. Mr. Black was buried underneath there. That reminds me of another thing. You know I told you how the grandmother and the little boys died? They had the three bodies in the house at the one time. And they had nothing to make the shrouds out of but the lace curtains they had brought from the old country. I guess it would be a hasty business when it was cholera and in the summer. So that was what they buried them in."

"Lace curtains."

My father looked shy, as if he had given me a present, and said brusquely, "Well, that's the kind of a detail I thought might be interesting to you."

Some time after my father died I was reading some old newspapers on a microfilm reader in the Toronto Library; this was in connection with a documentary script I was working on, for television. The name Dalgleish caught my eye and then the name Fleming, which I have gone so long without.

HERMIT DIES NEAR DALGLEISH

It is reported that Mr. Black, a man about forty-five years old, Christian name unknown, has died on the farm of Mr. Thomas

Fleming, where he has been living for the last three years in a shack which Mr. Fleming allowed him to construct in the corner of a field. He cultivated a few potatoes, subsisting mainly on those and on fish and small game. He was believed to come from some European country but gave the name Black and did not reveal his history. At some point in his life he had parted company with one of his legs, leading some to speculate that he might have been a soldier. He was heard to mutter to himself in a foreign language.

About three weeks ago Mr. Fleming, not having seen any smoke from the recluse's shack, investigated, and found the man very ill. He was suffering from a cancer of the tongue. Mr. Fleming wished to remove him to his own house for care but Mr. Black would not agree, though he finally allowed himself to be taken to Mr. Fleming's barn, where he remained, the weather being mild, and nursing care being provided by the young Misses Fleming, who reside at home. There he died, and was buried at his own request next to his hermit's shack, taking the mystery of his life with him.

I began to think that I would like to see the stone, I would like to see if it was still there. No one related to me lived in that country any more. I drove up on a Sunday in June and was able to bypass Dalgleish completely; the highway had been changed. I expected to have some trouble finding the farm, but I was on it before I could have believed it possible. It was no longer an out-of-the-way place. The back roads had been straightened; there was a new, strong, two-lane concrete bridge; half of Mount Hebron had been cut away for gravel; and the wild-pasture fields had been planted in corn.

The log drive-shed was gone. The house had been covered in pale-green aluminum siding. There were several wide new windows. The cement slab in front, where my aunts had sat on their straight-backed chairs to watch the road, had been turned into a patio, with tubs of salvia and geraniums, a metal table with an awning, and the usual folding furniture with bright plastic webbing.

All this made me doubtful, but I knocked on the door anyway. A young, pregnant woman answered. She asked me into the kitchen, which was a cheerful room with linoleum that looked something like red and brown bricks, and built-in cupboards that looked very much like maple. Two children were watching a television picture whose colors seemed drained by the brightness of the day outside, and a businesslike young husband was working at an adding machine, seemingly unbothered by the noise of the television as his children were unbothered by the sunlight. The young woman stepped over a large dog to turn off a tap at the sink.

They were not impatient of my story, as I had thought they might be. In fact they were interested and helpful, and not entirely in the dark about the stone I was looking for. The husband said that the land across the road had not been sold to his father, who had bought this farm from my aunts; it had been sold previously. He thought it was over there that the stone was. He said his father had told him there was a man buried over there, under a big stone, and they had even gone for a walk once, to look at it, but he hadn't thought of it in years. He said he would go and look for it now.

I had thought we would walk, but we drove down the lane in his car. We got out, and carefully entered a cornfield. The corn was just about to my knees, so the stone should have been in plain sight. I asked if the man who owned this field would mind, and the farmer said no, the fellow never came near it, he hired somebody else to work it for him.

"He's a fellow that has a thousand acres in corn in Huron County alone."

I said that a farmer was just like a businessman nowadays, wasn't he? The farmer seemed pleased that I had said this and began to explain why it was so. Risks had to be undertaken. Expenses were sky-high. I asked him if he had one of those tractors with the air-conditioned cabs and he said yes, he had. If you did well, he said, the rewards, the financial rewards, could be considerable, but there were trials and tribulations most people didn't know a thing about. Next spring, if all went well, he and his wife were going on their first holiday. They were going to Spain. The children wanted them to forget their holiday and put in a swimming pool, but his idea was to travel. He owned two farms now and was thinking of buying a third. He was just sitting working out some figures when I knocked on the door. In a way, he couldn't afford to buy it. In another way, he couldn't afford not to.

While carrying on this conversation we were walking up and down the corn rows looking for the stone. We looked in the corners of the field and it was not there. He said that of course the corner of a field then was not necessarily the corner of a field now. But the truth probably was that when the field got put in corn the stone was in the way, so they would have hauled it out. He said we could go over to the rock-pile near the road and see if we recognized it.

I said we wouldn't bother, I wasn't so sure I would know it, on a rock-pile.

"Me either," he said. He sounded disappointed. I wondered what he had expected to see, or feel.

I wondered the same thing about myself.

If I had been younger, I would have figured out a story. I would have insisted on Mr. Black's being in love with one of my aunts, and on one of them — not necessarily the one he was in love with — being in love with him. I would have wished him to confide in them, in one of them, his secret, his reason for living in a shack in Huron County, far from home. Later, I might have believed that he wanted to, but hadn't confided this, or his love either. I would have made a horrible, plausible connection between that silence of his, and the manner of his death. Now I no longer believe that people's secrets are defined and communicable, or their feelings full-blown and easy to recognize. I don't believe so. Now, I can only say, my father's sisters scrubbed the floor with lye, they stooked the oats and milked the cows by hand. They must have taken a quilt to the barn for the hermit to die on, they must have let water dribble from a tin cup into his afflicted mouth. That was their life. My mother's cousins behaved in another way; they dressed up and took pictures of each other; they sallied forth. However they behaved they are all dead. I carry something of them around in me. But the boulder is gone, Mount Hebron is cut down for gravel, and the life buried here is one you have to think twice about regretting.

Dulse

At the end of the summer Lydia took a boat to an island off the southern coast of New Brunswick, where she was going to stay overnight. She had just a few days left until she had to be back in Ontario. She worked as an editor, for a publisher in Toronto. She was also a poet, but she did not refer to that unless it was something people knew already. For the past eighteen months she had been living with a man in Kingston. As far as she could see, that was over.

She had noticed something about herself, on this trip to the Maritimes. It was that people were no longer so interested in getting to know her. It wasn't that she had created such a stir, before, but something had been there that she could rely on. She was forty-five, and had been divorced for nine years. Her two children had started on their own lives, though there were still retreats and confusions. She hadn't got fatter or thinner, her looks had not deteriorated in any alarming way, but nevertheless she had stopped being one sort of woman and had become another, and she had noticed it on this trip. She was not surprised because she was in a new, strange condition at the time. She made efforts, one after the other. She set little blocks on top of one another and she had a day. Sometimes she almost could not do this. At other times the very deliberateness, the seeming arbitrariness, of what she was doing, the way she was living, exhilarated her.

She found a guest-house overlooking the docks, with their stacks of lobster traps, and the few scattered stores and houses that made up the village. A woman of about her own age was cooking dinner. This woman took her to a cheap, old-fashioned room upstairs. There were no other guests around, though the room next door was open and seemed to be occupied, perhaps by a child. Whoever it was had left several comic books on the floor beside the bed.

She went for a walk up the steep lane behind the guest-house. She occupied herself by naming shrubs and weeds. The goldenrod and wild aster were in bloom, and Japanese boxwood, a rarity in Ontario, seemed commonplace here. The grass was long and coarse and the trees were small. The Atlantic coast, which she had never seen before, was just as she had expected it to be. The bending grass; the bare houses; the sea light. She started wondering what it would be like to live there, whether the houses were still cheap or if people from the outside had started to buy them up. Often on this trip she had busied herself with calculations of this kind, and also with ideas of how she could make a living in some new way, cut off from everything she had done before. She did not think of making a living writing poetry, not only because the income would be so low but because she thought, as she had thought innumerable times in her life, that probably she would not write any more poems. She was thinking that she could not cook well enough to do it for pay but she could clean. There was at least one other guest-house besides the one where she was staying, and she had seen a sign advertising a motel. How many hours' cleaning could she get if she cleaned all three places, and how much an hour did cleaning pay?

There were four small tables in the dining room, but only one man was sitting there, drinking tomato juice. He did not look at her. A man who was probably the husband of the woman she had met earlier came in from the kitchen. He had a grayish-blond beard, and a downcast look. He asked Lydia's name and took her to the table where the man was sitting. The man stood up, stiffly, and

Lydia was introduced. The man's name was Mr. Stanley and Lydia took him to be about sixty. Politely, he asked her to sit down.

Three men in work clothes came in and sat down at another table. They were not noisy in any self-important or offensive way, but just coming in and disposing themselves around the table, they created an enjoyable commotion. That is, they enjoyed it, and looked as if they expected others to. Mr. Stanley bowed in their direction. It really was a little bow, not just a nod of the head. He said good evening. They asked him what there was for supper, and he said he believed it was scallops, with pumpkin pie for dessert.

"These gentlemen work for the New Brunswick Telephone Company," he said to Lydia. "They are laying a cable to one of the smaller islands, and they stay here during the week."

He was older than she had thought at first. It did not show in his voice, which was precise and American, or in the movements of his hands, but in his small, separate, brownish teeth, and in his eyes, which had a delicate milky skin over the light-brown iris.

The husband brought their food, and spoke to the workmen. He was an efficient waiter, but rather stiff and remote, rather like a sleep-walker, in fact, as if he did not perform this job in his real life. The vegetables were served in large bowls, from which they helped themselves. Lydia was glad to see so much food: broccoli, mashed turnips, potatoes, corn. The American took small helpings of everything and began to eat in a very deliberate way, giving the impression that the order in which he lifted forkfuls of food to his mouth was not haphazard, that there was a reason for the turnip to follow the potatoes, and for the deep-fried scallops, which were not large, to be cut neatly in half. He looked up a couple of times as if he thought of saying something, but he did not do it. The workmen were quiet now, too, laying into the food.

Mr. Stanley spoke at last. He said, "Are you familiar with the writer Willa Cather?"

"Yes." Lydia was startled, because she had not seen anybody reading a book for the past two weeks; she had not even noticed any paperback racks.

"Do you know, then, that she spent every summer here?"

"Here?"

"On this island. She had her summer home here. Not more than a mile away from where we are sitting now. She came here for eighteen years, and she wrote many of her books here. She wrote in a room that had a view of the sea, but now the trees have grown up and blocked it. She was with her great friend, Edith Lewis. Have you read *A Lost Lady*?"

Lydia said that she had.

"It is my favorite of all her books. She wrote it here. At least, she wrote a great part of it here."

Lydia was aware of the workmen listening, although they did not glance up from their food. She felt that even without looking at Mr. Stanley or each other they might manage to communicate an indulgent contempt. She thought she did not care whether or not she was included in this contempt, but perhaps it was for that reason that she did not find anything much to say about Willa Cather, or tell Mr. Stanley that she worked for a publisher, let alone that she was any sort of writer herself. Or it could have been just that Mr. Stanley did not give her much of a chance.

"I have been her admirer for over sixty years," he said. He paused, holding his knife and fork over his plate. "I read and reread her, and my admiration grows. It simply grows. There are people here who remember her. Tonight, I am going to see a woman, a woman who knew Willa, and had conversations with her. She is eighty-eight years old but they say she has not forgotten. The people here are beginning to learn of my interest and they will remember someone like this and put me in touch.

"It is a great delight to me," he said solemnly.

All the time he was talking, Lydia was trying to think what his conversational style reminded her of. It didn't remind her of any special person, though she might have had one or two teachers at college who talked like that. What it made her think of was a time when a few people, just a few people, had never concerned themselves with being democratic, or ingratiating, in their speech; they spoke in formal, well-thought-out, slightly self-congratulating sentences, though they lived in a country where their formality, their pedantry, could bring them nothing but mockery. No, that was not the whole truth. It brought mockery, and an uncomfortable admiration. What he made Lydia think of, really, was the old-fashioned culture of provincial cities long ago (something she of course had never known, but sensed from books); the high-mindedness, the propriety; hard plush concert seats and hushed libraries. And his adoration of the chosen writer was of a piece with this; it was just as out-of-date as his speech. She thought that he could not be a teacher; such worship was not in style for teachers, even of his age.

"Do you teach literature?"

"No. Oh, no. I have not had that privilege. No. I have not even studied literature. I went to work when I was sixteen. In my day there was not so much choice. I have worked on newspapers."

She thought of some absurdly discreet and conservative New England paper with a fusty prose style.

"Oh. Which paper?" she said, then realized her inquisitiveness must seem quite rude, to anyone so circumspect.

"Not a paper you would have heard of. Just the daily paper of an industrial town. Other papers in the earlier years. That was my life."

"And now, would you like to do a book on Willa Cather?" This question seemed not so out of place to her, because she was always talking to people who wanted to do books about something.

"No," he said austerely. "My eyes do not permit me to do any reading or writing beyond what is necessary."

That was why he was so deliberate about his eating.

"No," he went on, "I don't say that at one time I might not have thought of that, doing a book on Willa. I would have written something just about her life here on the island. Biographies have been done, but not so much on that phase of her life. Now I have given up the idea. I do my investigating just for my own pleasure. I take a camp chair up there, so I can sit underneath the window where she wrote and looked at the sea. There is never anybody there."

"It isn't being kept up? It isn't any sort of memorial?"

"Oh, no indeed. It isn't kept up at all. The people here, you know, while they were very impressed with Willa, and some of them recognized her genius — I mean the genius of her personality, for they would not be able to recognize the genius of her work—others of them thought her unfriendly and did not like her. They took offense because she was unsociable, as she had to be, to do her writing."

"It could be a project," Lydia said. "Perhaps they could get some money from the government. The Canadian government and the Americans too. They could preserve the house."

"Well, that isn't for me to say." He smiled; he shook his head. "I don't think so. No."

He did not want any other worshippers coming to disturb him in his camp chair. She should have known that. What would this private pilgrimage of his be worth if other people got into the act, and signs were put up, leaflets printed; if this guest-house, which was now called Sea View, had to be renamed Shadows on the Rock? He would let the house fall down and the grass grow over it, sooner than see that.

After Lydia's last attempt to call Duncan, the man she had been living with in Kingston, she had walked along the street in Toronto, knowing that she had to get to the bank, she had to buy some food, she had to get on the subway. She had to remember directions, and the order in which to do things: to open her checkbook, to move forward when it was her turn in line, to choose one kind of bread over another, to drop a token in the slot. These seemed to be the most difficult things she had ever done. She had immense difficulty reading the names of the subway stations, and getting off at the right one, so that she could go to the apartment where she was staying. She would have found it hard to describe this difficulty. She knew perfectly well which was the right stop, she knew which stop it came after; she knew where she was. But she could not make the connection between herself and things outside herself, so that getting up and leaving the car, going up the steps, going along the street, all seemed to involve a bizarre effort. She thought afterwards that she had been seized up, as machines are said to be. Even at the time she had an image of herself. She saw herself as something like an egg carton, hollowed out in back.

When she reached the apartment she sat down on a chair in the hall. She sat for an hour or so, then she went to the bathroom, undressed, put on her nightgown, and got into bed. In bed she felt triumph and relief, that she had managed all the difficulties and got herself to where she was supposed to be and would not have to remember anything more.

She didn't feel at all like committing suicide. She couldn't have managed the implements, or aids, she couldn't even have thought which to use. It amazed her to think that she had chosen the loaf of bread and the cheese, which were now lying on the floor in the hall. How had she imagined she was going to chew and swallow them?

After dinner Lydia sat out on the verandah with the woman who had cooked the meal. The woman's husband did the cleaning up.

"Well, of course we have a dishwasher," the woman said. "We have two freezers and an oversize refrigerator. You have to make an investment. You get the crews staying with you, you have to feed them. This place soaks up money like a sponge. We're going to put in a swimming pool next year. We need more attractions. You have to run to stay in the same place. People think what an easy nice life. Boy."

She had a strong, lined face, and long straight hair. She wore jeans and an embroidered smock and a man's sweater.

"Ten years ago I was living in a commune in the States. Now I'm here. I work sometimes eighteen hours a day. I have to pack the crew's lunch yet tonight. I cook and bake, cook and bake. John does the rest."

"Do you have someone to clean?"

"We can't afford to hire anybody. John does it. He does the laundry—everything. We had to buy a mangle for the sheets. We had to put in a new furnace. We got a bank loan. I thought that was funny, because I used to be married to a bank manager. I left him."

"I'm on my own now, too."

"Are you? You can't be on your own forever. I met John, and he was in the same boat."

"I was living with a man in Kingston, in Ontario."

"Were you? John and I are extremely happy. He used to be a

minister. But when I met him he was doing carpentry. We both had sort of dropped out. Did you talk to Mr. Stanley?"

"Yes."

"Had you ever heard of Willa Cather?"

"Yes."

"That'd make him happy. I don't read hardly at all, it doesn't mean anything to me. I'm a visual person. But I think he's a wonderful character, old Mr. Stanley. He's a real old scholar."

"Has he been coming here for a long time?"

"No, he hasn't. This is just his third year. He says he's wanted to come here all his life. But he couldn't. He had to wait till some relative died, that he was looking after. Not a wife. A brother maybe. Anyway he had to wait. How old do you think he is?"

"Seventy? Seventy-five?"

"That man is eighty-one. Isn't that amazing? I really admire people like that. I really do. I admire people that keep going."

"The man I was living with—that is, the man I used to live with, in Kingston," said Lydia, "was putting some boxes of papers in the trunk of his car once, this was out in the country, at an old farmhouse, and he felt something nudge him and he glanced down. It was about dusk, on a pretty dark day. So he thought this was a big friendly dog, a big black dog giving him a nudge, and he didn't pay much attention. He just said go on, now, boy, go away now, good boy. Then when he got the boxes arranged he turned around. And he saw it was a bear. It was a black bear."

She was telling this later that same evening, in the kitchen.

"So what did he do then?" said Lawrence, who was the boss of the telephone work crew. Lawrence and Lydia and Eugene and Vincent were playing cards.

Lydia laughed. "He said, *excuse me*. That's what he claims he said."

"Papers all he had in the boxes? Nothing to eat?"

"He's a writer. He writes historical books. This was some material he needed for his work. Sometimes he has to go and scout out material from people who are very strange. That bear hadn't come out of the bush. It was a pet, actually, that had been let off its chain, for a joke. There were two old brothers there, that he got the papers from, and they just let it off its chain to give him a scare."

"That's what he does, collects old stuff and writes about it?" Lawrence said. "I guess that's interesting."

She immediately regretted having told this story. She had brought it up because the men were talking about bears. But there wasn't much point to it unless Duncan told it. He could show you himself, large and benign and civilized, with his courtly apologies to the bear. He could make you see the devilish old men behind their tattered curtains.

"You'd have to know Duncan," was what she almost said. And hadn't she told this simply to establish that she had known Duncan—that she had recently had a man, and an interesting man, an amusing and adventurous man? She wanted to assure them that she was not always alone, going on her aimless travels. She had to show herself attached. A mistake. They were not likely to think a man adventurous who collected old papers from misers and eccentrics, so that he could write books about things that had happened a hundred years ago. She shouldn't even have said that Duncan was a man she had lived with. All that could mean, to them, was that she was a woman who had slept with a man she was not married to.

Lawrence the boss was not yet forty, but he was successful. He was glad to tell about himself. He was a free-lance labor contractor and owned two houses in St. Stephen. He had two cars and a truck and a boat. His wife taught school. Lawrence was getting a thick waist, a trucker's belly, but he still looked alert and vigorous. You could see that he would be shrewd enough, in most situations, for his purposes; sure enough, ruthless enough. Dressed up, he might turn flashy. And certain places and people might be capable of making him gloomy, uncertain, contentious.

Lawrence said it wasn't all true—all the stuff they wrote about the Maritimes. He said there was plenty of work for people who weren't afraid to work. Men or women. He said he was not against women's lib, but the fact was, and always would be, that there was work men did better than women and work women did better than men, and if they would both settle down and realize that they'd be happier.

His kids were cheeky, he said. They had it too soft. They got everything — that was the way nowadays, what could you do? The other kids got everything, too. Clothes, bikes, education, records. He hadn't had anything handed to him. He had got out and worked, driven trucks. He had got to Ontario, got as far as Saskatchewan. He had only got to grade ten in school but he hadn't let that hold him back. Sometimes he wished, though, that he did have more of an education.

Eugene and Vincent, who worked for Lawrence, said they had never got past grade eight, when that was as far as you could go in the country schools. Eugene was twenty-five and Vincent was fifty-two. Eugene was French-Canadian from northern New Brunswick. He looked younger than his age. He had a rosy color, a downy, dreamy, look — a masculine beauty that was nevertheless soft-edged, sweet-tempered, bashful. Hardly any men or boys have that look nowadays. Sometimes you see it in an old photograph — of a bridegroom, a basketball player: the thick water-combed hair, the blooming boy's face on the new man's body. Eugene was not very bright, or perhaps not very competitive. He lost money at the game they were playing. It was a card game that the men called Skat. Lydia remembered playing it when she was a child, and calling it Thirty-one. They played for a quarter a game.

Eugene permitted Vincent and Lawrence to tease him about losing at cards, about getting lost in Saint John, about women he liked, and about being French-Canadian. Lawrence's teasing amounted to bullying. Lawrence wore a carefully good-natured expression, but he looked as if something hard and heavy had settled inside him — a load of self-esteem that weighed him down instead of buoying him up. Vincent had no such extra weight, and though he too was relentless in his teasing — he teased Lawrence as well as Eugene — there was no sense of cruelty or danger. You could see that his natural tone was one of rumbling, easy mockery. He was sharp and sly but not insistent; he would always be able to say the most pessimistic things and not sound unhappy.

Vincent had a farm — it was his family's farm, where he had grown up, near St. Stephen. He said you couldn't make enough to keep you nowadays, just from farming. Last year he put in a potato crop. There was frost in June, snow in September. Too short a season by a long shot. You never knew, he said, when you might get it like that. And the market is all controlled now, it is all run by the big fellows, the big interests. Everybody does what he can, rather than trust to farming. Vincent's wife works too. She took a course and learned to do hair. His sons are not hardworking like their parents. All they want to do is roar around in cars. They get married and the first thing their wives want is a new stove. They want a stove that practically cooks the dinner by itself and puts it on the table.

It didn't use to be that way. The first time Vincent ever had boots of his own—new boots that hadn't been worn by anybody before him—was when he joined the army. He was so pleased he walked backwards in the dirt to see the prints they made, fresh and whole. Later on, after the war, he went to Saint John to look for work. He had been working at home on the farm for a while and he had worn out his army clothes—he had just one pair of decent pants left. In a beer parlor in Saint John a man said to him, "You want to pick up a good pair of pants cheap?" Vincent said yes, and the man said, "Follow me." So Vincent did. And where did they end up? At the undertaker's! For the fact was that the family of a dead man usually bring in a suit of clothes to dress him in, and he only needs to be dressed from the waist up, that's all that shows in the coffin. The undertaker sold the pants. That was true. The army gave Vince his first pair of new boots and a corpse donated the best pair of pants he ever wore, up to that time.

Vincent had no teeth. This was immediately apparent, but it did not make him look unattractive; it simply deepened his look of secrecy and humor. His face was long and his chin tucked in, his glance unchallenging but unfooled. He was a lean man, with useful muscles, and graying black hair. You could see all the years of hard work on him, and some years of it ahead, and the body just equal to it, until he turned into a ropy-armed old man, shrunken, uncomplaining, hanging on to a few jokes.

While they played Skat the talk was boisterous and interrupted all the time by exclamations, joking threats to do with the game, laughter. Afterwards it became more serious and personal.

They had been drinking a local beer called Moose, but when the game was over Lawrence went out to the truck and brought in some Ontario beer, thought to be better. They called it "the imported stuff." The couple who owned the guest-house had long ago gone to bed, but the workmen and Lydia sat on in the kitchen, just as if it belonged to one of them, drinking beer and eating dulse, which Vincent had brought down from his room. Dulse was a kind of seaweed, greenish-brown, salty and fishy-tasting. Vincent said it was what he ate last thing at night and first thing in the morning — nothing could beat it. Now that they had found out it was so good for you, they sold it in the stores, done up in little wee packages at a criminal price.

The next day was Friday, and the men would be leaving the island for the mainland. They talked about trying to get the two-thirty boat instead of the one they usually caught, at five-thirty, because the forecast was for rough weather; the tail end of one of the tropical hurricanes was due to hit the Bay of Fundy before night.

"But the ferries won't run if it's too rough, will they?" said Lydia. "They won't run if it's dangerous?" She thought that she would not mind being cut off, she wouldn't mind not having to travel again in the morning.

"Well, there's a lot of fellows waiting to get off the island on a Friday night," Vincent said.

"Wanting to get home to their wives," said Lawrence sardonically. "There's always crews working over here, always men away from home." Then he began to talk in an unhurried but insistent way about sex. He talked about what he called the immorality on the island. He said that at one time the authorities had been going to put a quarantine around the whole island, on account of the V.D. Crews came over here to work and stayed at the motel, the Ocean Wave, and there'd be parties there all night every night, with drinking and young girls turning up offering themselves for sale. Girls fourteen and fifteen — oh, thirteen years of age. On the island, he said, it was getting so a woman of twenty-five could practically be a grandmother. The place was famous. Those girls would do anything for a price, sometimes for a beer.

"And sometimes for nothing," said Lawrence. He luxuriated in the telling.

They heard the front door open.

"Your old boyfriend," Lawrence said to Lydia.

She was bewildered for a moment, thinking of Duncan.

"The old fellow at the table," said Vincent.

Mr. Stanley did not come into the kitchen. He crossed the living room and climbed the stairs.

"Hey? Been down to the Ocean Wave?" said Lawrence softly, raising his head as if to call through the ceiling. "Old bugger wouldn't know what to do with it," he said. "Wouldn't've known fifty years ago any better than now. I don't let any of my crews go near that place. Do I, Eugene?"

Eugene blushed. He put on a solemn expression, as if he was being badgered by a teacher at school.

"Eugene, now, he don't have to," Vincent said.

"Isn't it true what I'm saying?" said Lawrence urgently, as if somebody had been disputing with him. "It's true, isn't it?"

He looked at Vincent, and Vincent said, "Yeah. Yeah." He did not seem to relish the subject as much as Lawrence did.

"You'd think it was all so innocent here," said Lawrence to Lydia. "Innocent! Oh, boy!"

Lydia went upstairs to get a quarter that she owed Lawrence from the last game. When she came out of her room into the dark hall, Eugene was standing there, looking out the window.

"I hope it don't storm too bad," he said.

Lydia stood beside him, looking out. The moon was visible, but misty.

"You didn't grow up near the water?" she said.

"No, I didn't."

"But if you get the two-thirty boat it'll be all right, won't it?"

"I sure hope so." He was quite childlike and unembarrassed about his fear. "One thing I don't like the idea of is getting drownded."

Lydia remembered that as a child she had said "drownded." Most of the adults and all the children she knew then said that.

"You won't," she said, in a firm, maternal way. She went downstairs and paid her quarter.

"Where's Eugene?" Lawrence said. "He upstairs?"

"He's looking out the window. He's worried about the storm."

Lawrence laughed. "You tell him to go to bed and forget about it. He's right in the room next to you. I just thought you ought to know in case he hollers in his sleep."

Lydia had first seen Duncan in a bookstore, where her friend Warren worked. She was waiting for Warren to go out to lunch with her. He had gone to get his coat. A man asked Shirley, the other clerk in the store, if she could find him a copy of *The Persian Letters*. That was Duncan. Shirley walked ahead of him to where the book was kept, and in the quiet store Lydia heard him saying that it must be difficult to know where to shelve *The Persian Letters*. Should it be classed as fiction or as a political essay? Lydia felt that he revealed something, saying this. He revealed a need that she supposed was common to customers in the bookstore, a need to distinguish himself, appear knowledgeable. Later on she would look back on this moment and try to imagine him again so powerless, slightly ingratiating, showing a bit of neediness. Warren came back with his coat on, greeted Duncan, and as he and Lydia went outside Warren said under his breath, "The Tin Woodman." Warren and Shirley livened up their days with nicknames for customers; Lydia had already heard of Marble-Mouth, and Chickpea and the Colonial Duchess. Duncan was the Tin Woodman. Lydia thought they must call him that because of the smooth gray overcoat he wore, and his hair, a bright gray which had obviously once been blond. He was not thin or angular and he did not look as if he would be creaky in the joints. He was supple and well-fleshed and dignified and pleasant; fair-skinned, freshly groomed, glistening.

She never told him about that name. She never told him that she had seen him in the bookstore. A week or so later she met him at a publisher's party. He did not remember ever seeing her before, and she supposed he had not seen her, being occupied with chatting to Shirley.

Lydia trusts what she can make of things, usually. She trusts what she thinks about her friend Warren, or his friend Shirley, and about chance acquaintances, like the couple who run the guesthouse, and Mr. Stanley, and the men she has been playing cards with. She thinks she knows why people behave as they do, and she puts more stock than she will admit in her own unproved theories and unjustified suspicions. But she is stupid and helpless when contemplating the collision of herself and Duncan. She has plenty to say about it, given the chance, because explanation is her habit, but she doesn't trust what she says, even to herself; it doesn't help her. She might just as well cover her head and sit wailing on the ground.

She asks herself what gave him his power. She knows who did. But she asks what, and when—when did the transfer take place, when was the abdication of all pride and sense?

She read for half an hour after getting into bed. Then she went down the hall to the bathroom. It was after midnight. The rest of the house was in darkness. She had left her door ajar, and coming back to her room, she did not turn on the hall light. The door of Eugene's room was also ajar, and as she was passing she heard a low, careful sound. It was like a moan, and also like a whisper. She remembered Lawrence saying Eugene hollered in his sleep, but this sound was not being made in sleep. She knew he was awake. He was watching from the bed in his dark room and he was inviting her. The invitation was amorous and direct and helpless-sounding as his confession of fear when he stood by the window. She went on into her own room and shut the door and hooked it. Even as she did this, she knew she didn't have to. He would never try to get in; there was no bullying spirit in him.

Then she lay awake. Things had changed for her; she refused adventures. She could have gone to Eugene, and earlier in the evening she could have given a sign to Lawrence. In the past she might have done it. She might, or she might not have done it, depending on how she felt. Now it seemed not possible. She felt as if she were muffled up, wrapped in layers and layers of dull knowledge, well protected. It wasn't altogether a bad thing—it left your mind unclouded. Speculation can be more gentle, can take its time, when it is not driven by desire.

She thought about what those men would have been like, as lovers. It was Lawrence who would have been her reasonable choice. He was nearest to her own age, and predictable, and probably well used to the discreet encounter. His approach was vulgar, but that would not necessarily have put her off. He would be cheerful, hearty, prudent, perhaps a bit self-congratulatory, attentive in a businesslike way, and he would manage in the middle of his attentions to slip in a warning: a joke, a friendly insult, a reminder of how things stood.

Eugene would never feel the need to do that, though he would have a shorter memory even than Lawrence (much shorter, for Lawrence, though not turning down opportunities, would carry afterward the thought of some bad consequence, for which he must keep ready a sharp line of defense). Eugene would be no less experienced than Lawrence; for years, girls and women must have been answering the kind of plea Lydia had heard, the artless confession. Eugene would be generous, she thought. He would be a grateful, self-forgetful lover, showing his women such kindness that when he left they would never make trouble. They would not try to trap him; they wouldn't whine after him. Women do that to the men who have held back, who have contradicted themselves, promised, lied, mocked. These are the men women get pregnant by, send desperate letters to, preach their own superior love to, take their revenge on. Eugene would go free, he would be an innocent, happy prodigy of love, until he decided it was time to get married. Then he would marry a rather plain, maternal sort of girl, perhaps a bit older than himself, a bit shrewder. He would be faithful, and good to her, and she would manage things; they would raise a large, Catholic family.

What about Vincent? Lydia could not imagine him as she easily imagined the others: their noises and movements and bare shoulders and pleasing warm skin; their power, their exertions, their moments of helplessness. She was shy of thinking any such things about him. Yet he was the only one whom she could think of now with real interest. She thought of his courtesy and reticence and humor, his inability to better his luck. She liked him for the very things that made him different from Lawrence and ensured that all his life he would be working for Lawrence—or for somebody like Lawrence—never the other way round. She liked him also for the things that made him different from Eugene: the irony, the patience, the self-containment. He was the sort of man she had known when she was a child living on a farm not so different from his, the sort of man who must have been in her family for hundreds of years. She knew his life. With him she could foresee doors opening, to what she knew and had forgotten; rooms and landscapes opening; *there*. The rainy evenings, a country with creeks and graveyards, and chokecherry and finches in the fence-corners. She had to wonder if this was what happened, after the years of appetite and greed—did you drift back into tender-hearted fantasies? Or was it just the truth about what she needed and wanted; should she have fallen in love with, and married, a man like Vincent, years ago; should she have concentrated on the part of her that would have been content with such an arrangement, and forgotten about the rest?

That is, should she have stayed in the place where love is managed for you, not gone where you have to invent it, and reinvent it, and never know if these efforts will be enough?

Duncan spoke about his former girlfriends. Efficient Ruth, pert Judy, vivacious Diane, elegant Dolores, wifely Maxine. Lorraine the golden-haired, full-breasted beauty; Marian the multilingual; Caroline the neurotic; Rosalie who was wild and gypsy-like; gifted, melancholy Louise; serene socialite Jane. What description would do now for Lydia? Lydia the poet. Morose, messy, unsatisfactory Lydia. The unsatisfactory poet.

One Sunday, when they were driving in the hills around Peterborough, he talked about the effects of Lorraine's beauty. Perhaps the voluptuous countryside reminded him. It was almost like a joke, he said. It was almost silly. He stopped for gas in a little town and Lydia went across the street to a discount store that was open Sundays. She bought makeup in tubes off a rack. In the cold and dirty toilet of the gas station she attempted a transformation, slapping buff-colored liquid over her face and rubbing green paste on her eyelids.

"What have you done to your face?" he said when she came back to the car.

"Makeup. I put some makeup on so I'd look more cheerful."

"You can see where the line stops, on your neck."

At such times she felt strangled. It was frustration, she said to the doctor later. The gap between what she wanted and what she could get. She believed that Duncan's love — love for her — was somewhere inside him, and that by gigantic efforts to please, or fits of distress which obliterated all those efforts, or tricks of indifference, she could claw or lure it out.

What gave her such an idea? He did. At least he indicated that he could love her, that they could be happy, if she could honor his privacy, make no demands upon him, and try to alter those things about her person and behavior which he did not like. He listed these things precisely. Some were very intimate in nature and she howled with shame and covered her ears and begged him to take them back or to say no more.

"There is no way to have a discussion with you," he said. He said he hated hysterics, emotional displays, beyond anything, yet she thought she saw a quiver of satisfaction, a deep thrill of relief, that ran through him when she finally broke under the weight of his calm and detailed objections.

"Could that be?" she said to the doctor. "Could it be that he wants a woman close but is so frightened of it he has to try to wreck her? Is that oversimplified?" she said anxiously.

"What about you?" said the doctor. "What do you want?"

"For him to love me?"

"Not for you to love him?"

She thought about Duncan's apartment. There were no curtains; he was higher than the surrounding buildings. No attempt had been made to arrange things to make a setting; nothing was in relation to anything else. Various special requirements had been attended to. A certain sculpture was in a corner behind some filing cabinets because he liked to lie on the floor and look at it in shadow. Books were in piles beside the bed, which was crossways in the room in order to catch the breeze from the window. All disorder was actually order, carefully thought out and not to be interfered with. There was a beautiful little rug at the end of the hall, where he sat and listened to music. There was one great, ugly armchair, a masterpiece of engineering, with all its attachments for the head and limbs. Lydia asked about his guests — how were they accommodated? He replied that he did not have any. The apartment was for himself. He was a popular guest, witty and personable, but not a host, and this seemed reasonable to him, since social life was other people's requirement and invention.

Lydia brought flowers, and there was nowhere to put them except in a jar on the floor by the bed. She brought presents from her trips to Toronto: records, books, cheese. She learned pathways around the apartment and found places where she could sit. She discouraged old friends, or any friends, from phoning or coming to see her, because there was too much she couldn't explain. They saw Duncan's friends sometimes, and she was nervous with them, thinking they were adding her to a list, speculating. She didn't like to see how much he gave them of that store of presents — anecdotes, parodies, flattering wit — which were also used to delight her. He could not bear dullness. She felt that he despised people who were not witty. You needed to be quick to keep up with him, in conversation, you needed energy. Lydia saw herself as a dancer on her toes, trembling delicately all over, afraid of letting him down on the next turn.

"Do you mean you think I don't love him?" she said to the doctor.

"How do you know you do?"

"Because I suffer so when he's fed up with me. I want to be wiped off the earth. It's true. I want to hide. I go out on the streets and every face I look at seems to despise me for my failure."

"Your failure to make him love you."

Now Lydia must accuse herself. Her self-absorption equals Duncan's, but is more artfully concealed. She is in competition with him, as to who can love best. She is in competition with all other women, even when it is ludicrous for her to be so. She cannot stand to hear them praised or know they are well remembered. Like many women of her generation she has an idea of love which is ruinous but not serious in some way, not respectful. She is greedy. She talks intelligently and ironically and in this way covers up her indefensible expectations. The sacrifices she made with Duncan — in living arrangements, in the matter of friends, as well as in the rhythm of sex and the tone of conversations — were violations, committed not seriously but flagrantly. That is what was not respectful, that was what was indecent. She made him a present of such power, then complained relentlessly to herself and finally to him, that he had got it. She was out to defeat him.

That is what she says to the doctor. But is it the truth?

"The worst thing is not knowing what is true about any of this. I spend all my waking hours trying to figure out about him and me and I get nowhere. I make wishes. I even pray. I throw money into those wishing wells. I think that there's something in him that's an absolute holdout. There's something in him that has to get rid of me, so he'll find reasons. But he says that's rubbish, he says if I could stop over-reacting we'd be happy. I have to think maybe he's right, maybe it is all me."

"When are you happy?"

"When he's pleased with me. When he's joking and enjoying himself. No. No. I'm never happy. What I am is relieved, it's as if I'd overcome a challenge, it's more triumphant than happy. But he can always pull the rug out."

"So, why are you with somebody who can always pull the rug out?"

"Isn't there always somebody? When I was married it was me. Do you think it helps to ask these questions? Suppose it's just pride? I don't want to be alone, I want everybody to think I've got such a desirable man? Suppose it's the humiliation, I want to be humiliated? What good will it do me to know that?"

"I don't know. What do you think?"

"I think these conversations are fine when you're mildly troubled and interested but not when you're desperate."

"You're desperate?"

She felt suddenly tired, almost too tired to speak. The room where she and the doctor were talking had a dark-blue carpet, blue-

and-green-striped upholstery. There was a picture of boats and fishermen on the wall. Collusion somewhere, Lydia felt. Fake reassurance, provisional comfort, earnest deceptions.

"No."

It seemed to her that she and Duncan were monsters with a lot of heads, in those days. Out of the mouth of one head could come insult and accusation, hot and cold, out of another false apologies and slimy pleas, out of another just such mealy, reasonable, true-and-false chat as she had practised with the doctor. Not a mouth would open that had a useful thing to say, not a mouth would have the sense to shut up. At the same time she believed — though she didn't know she believed it — that these monster heads with their cruel and silly and wasteful talk could all be drawn in again, could curl up and go to sleep. Never mind what they'd said; never mind. Then she and Duncan with hope and trust and blank memories could reintroduce themselves, they could pick up the undamaged delight with which they'd started, before they began to put each other to other uses.

When she had been in Toronto a day she tried to retrieve Duncan, by phone, and found that he had acted quickly. He had changed to an unlisted number. He wrote to her in care of her employer, that he would pack and send her things.

Lydia had breakfast with Mr. Stanley. The telephone crew had eaten and gone off to work before daylight.

She asked Mr. Stanley about his visit with the woman who had known Willa Cather.

"Ah," said Mr. Stanley, and wiped a corner of his mouth after a bite of poached egg. "She was a woman who used to run a little restaurant down by the dock. She was a good cook, she said. She must have been, because Willa and Edith used to get their dinners from her. She would send it up with her brother, in his car. But sometimes Willa would not be pleased with the dinner — perhaps it would not be quite what she wanted, or she would think it was not cooked as well as it might be — and she would send it back. She would ask for another dinner to be sent." He smiled, and said in a confidential way, "Willa could be imperious. Oh, yes. She was not perfect. All people of great abilities are apt to be a bit impatient in daily matters."

Rubbish, Lydia wanted to say, she sounds a proper bitch.

Sometimes waking up was all right, and sometimes it was very bad. This morning she had wakened with the cold conviction of a mistake — something avoidable and irreparable.

"But sometimes she and Edith would come down to the café," Mr. Stanley continued. "If they felt they wanted some company, they would have dinner there. On one of these occasions Willa had a long talk with the woman I was visiting. They talked for over an hour. The woman was considering marriage. She had to consider whether to make a marriage that she gave me to understand was something of a business proposition. Companionship. There was no question of romance, she and the gentleman were not young and foolish. Willa talked to her for over an hour. Of course she did not advise her directly to do one thing or the other, she talked to her in general terms very sensibly and kindly and the woman still remembers it vividly. I was happy to hear that but I was not surprised."

"What would she know about it, anyway?" Lydia said.

Mr. Stanley lifted his eyes from his plate and looked at her in grieved amazement.

"Willa Cather lived with a woman," Lydia said.

When Mr. Stanley answered he sounded flustered, and mildly upbraiding.

"They were devoted," he said.

"She never lived with a man."

"She knew things as an artist knows them. Not necessarily by experience."

"But what if they don't know them?" Lydia persisted. "What if they don't?"

He went back to eating his egg as if he had not heard that. Finally he said, "The woman considered Willa's conversation was very helpful to her."

Lydia made a sound of doubtful assent. She knew she had been rude, even cruel. She knew she would have to apologize. She went to the sideboard and poured herself another cup of coffee.

The woman of the house came in from the kitchen.

"Is it keeping hot? I think I'll have a cup, too. Are you really going today? Sometimes I think I'd like to get on a boat and go too. It's lovely here and I love it but you know how you get."

They drank their coffee standing by the sideboard. Lydia did not want to go back to the table, but knew that she would have to. Mr. Stanley looked frail and solitary, with his narrow shoulders, his neat bald head, his brown checked sports jacket which was slightly too large. He took the trouble to be clean and tidy, and it must have been a trouble, with his eyesight. Of all people he did not deserve rudeness.

"Oh, I forgot," the woman said.

She went into the kitchen and came back with a large brown-paper bag.

"Vincent left you this. He said you liked it. Do you?"

Lydia opened the bag and saw long, dark, ragged leaves of dulse, oily-looking even when dry.

"Well," she said.

The woman laughed. "I know. You have to be born here to have the taste."

"No, I do like it," said Lydia. "I was getting to like it."

"You must have made a hit."

Lydia took the bag back to the table and showed it to Mr. Stanley. She tried a conciliatory joke.

"I wonder if Willa Cather ever ate dulse?"

"Dulse," said Mr. Stanley thoughtfully. He reached into the bag and pulled out some leaves and looked at them. Lydia knew he was seeing what Willa Cather might have seen. "She would most certainly have known about it. She would have known."

But was she lucky or was she not, and was it all right with that woman? How did she live? That was what Lydia wanted to say. Would Mr. Stanley have known what she was talking about? If she had asked how did Willa Cather live, would he not have replied that she did not have to find a way to live, as other people did, that she was Willa Cather?

What a lovely, durable shelter he had made for himself. He could carry it everywhere and nobody could interfere with it. The day may come when Lydia will count herself lucky to do the same. In the meantime, she'll be up and down. "Up and down," they used to say in her childhood, talking of the health of people who weren't going to recover. "Ah. She's up and down."

Yet look how this present slyly warmed her, from a distance.

The Turkey Season

To Joe Radford

When I was fourteen I got a job at the Turkey Barn for the Christmas season. I was still too young to get a job working in a store or as a part-time waitress; I was also too nervous.

I was a turkey gutter. The other people who worked at the Turkey Barn were Lily and Marjorie and Gladys, who were also gutters; Irene and Henry, who were pluckers; Herb Abbott, the foreman, who superintended the whole operation and filled in wherever he was needed. Morgan Elliott was the owner and boss. He and his son, Morgy, did the killing.

Morgy I knew from school. I thought him stupid and despicable and was uneasy about having to consider him in a new and possibly superior guise, as the boss's son. But his father treated him so roughly, yelling and swearing at him, that he seemed no more than the lowest of the workers. The other person related to the boss was Gladys. She was his sister, and in her case there did seem to be some privilege of position. She worked slowly and went home if she was not feeling well, and was not friendly to Lily and Marjorie, although she was, a little, to me. She had come back to live with Morgan and his family after working for many years in Toronto, in a bank. This was not the sort of job she was used to. Lily and Marjorie, talking about her when she wasn't there, said

she had had a nervous breakdown. They said Morgan made her
work in the Turkey Barn to pay for her keep. They also said, with
no worry about the contradiction, that she had taken the job
because she was after a man, and that the man was Herb Abbott.

All I could see when I closed my eyes, the first few nights
after working there, was turkeys. I saw them hanging upside
down, plucked and stiffened, pale and cold, with the heads and
necks limp, the eyes and nostrils clotted with dark blood; the
remaining bits of feathers—those dark and bloody, too—seemed
to form a crown. I saw them not with aversion but with a sense of
endless work to be done.

Herb Abbott showed me what to do. You put the turkey down
on the table and cut its head off with a cleaver. Then you took the
loose skin around the neck and stripped it back to reveal the crop,
nestled in the cleft between the gullet and the windpipe.

"Feel the gravel," said Herb encouragingly. He made me
close my fingers around the crop. Then he showed me how to work
my hand down behind it to cut it out, and the gullet and windpipe as
well. He used shears to cut the vertebrae.

"Scrunch, scrunch," he said soothingly. "Now, put your
hand in."

I did. It was deathly cold in there, in the turkey's dark insides.

"Watch out for bone splinters."

Working cautiously in the dark, I had to pull the connecting
tissues loose.

"Ups-a-daisy." Herb turned the bird over and flexed each leg.
"Knees up, Mother Brown. Now." He took a heavy knife and
placed it directly on the knee knuckle joints and cut off the shank.

"Have a look at the worms."

Pearly-white strings, pulled out of the shank, were creeping
about on their own.

"That's just the tendons shrinking. Now comes the nice
part!"

He slit the bird at its bottom end, letting out a rotten smell.

"Are you educated?"

I did not know what to say.

"What's that smell?"

"Hydrogen sulfide."

"Educated," said Herb, sighing. "All right. Work your fingers around and get the guts loose. Easy. Easy. Keep your fingers together. Keep the palm inwards. Feel the ribs with the back of your hand. Feel the guts fit into your palm. Feel that? Keep going. Break the strings — as many as you can. Keep going. Feel a hard lump? That's the gizzard. Feel a soft lump? That's the heart. O.K.? O.K. Get your fingers around the gizzard. Easy. Start pulling this way. That's right. That's right. Start to pull her out."

It was not easy at all. I wasn't even sure what I had was the gizzard. My hand was full of cold pulp.

"Pull," he said, and I brought out a glistening, liverish mass.

"Got it. There's the lights. You know what they are? Lungs. There's the heart. There's the gizzard. There's the gall. Now, you don't ever want to break that gall inside or it will taste the entire turkey." Tactfully, he scraped out what I had missed, including the testicles, which were like a pair of white grapes.

"Nice pair of earrings," Herb said.

Herb Abbott was a tall, firm, plump man. His hair was dark and thin, combined straight back from a widow's peak, and his eyes seemed to be slightly slanted, so that he looked like a pale Chinese or like pictures of the Devil, except that he was smooth-faced and benign. Whatever he did around the Turkey Barn — gutting, as he was now, or loading the truck, or hanging the carcasses — was done with efficient, economical movements, quickly and buoyantly. "Notice about Herb — he always walks like he had a boat moving underneath him," Marjorie said, and it was true. Herb worked on the lake boats, during the season, as a cook. Then he worked for Morgan until after Christmas. The rest of the time he helped around the poolroom, making hamburgers, sweeping up, stopping fights before they got started. That was where he lived; he had a room above the poolroom on the main street.

In all the operations at the Turkey Barn it seemed to be Herb who had the efficiency and honor of the business continually on his mind; it was he who kept everything under control. Seeing him in the yard talking to Morgan, who was a thick, short man, red in the face, an unpredictable bully, you would be sure that it was Herb who was the boss and Morgan the hired help. But it was not so.

If I had not had Herb to show me, I don't think I could have learned turkey gutting at all. I was clumsy with my hands and had been shamed for it so often that the least show of impatience on the part of the person instructing me could have brought on a dithering paralysis. I could not stand to be watched by anybody but Herb. Particularly, I couldn't stand to be watched by Lily and Marjorie, two middle-aged sisters, who were very fast and thorough and competitive gutters. They sang at their work and talked abusively and intimately to the turkey carcasses.

"Don't you nick me, you old bugger!"

"Aren't you the old crap factory!"

I had never heard women talk like that.

Gladys was not a fast gutter, though she must have been thorough; Herb would have talked to her otherwise. She never sang and certainly she never swore. I thought her rather old, though she was not as old as Lily and Marjorie; she must have been over thirty. She seemed offended by everything that went on and had the air of keeping plenty of bitter judgments to herself. I never tried to talk to her, but she spoke to me one day in the cold little washroom off the gutting shed. She was putting pancake makeup on her face. The color of the makeup was so distinct from the color of her skin that it was as if she were slapping orange paint over a whitewashed, bumpy wall.

She asked me if my hair was naturally curly.

I said yes.

"You don't have to get a permanent?"

"No."

"You're lucky. I have to do mine up every night. The chemicals in my system won't allow me to get a permanent."

There are different ways women have of talking about their looks. Some women make it clear that what they do to keep themselves up is for the sake of sex, for men. Others, like Gladys, make the job out to be a kind of housekeeping, whose very difficulties they pride themselves on. Gladys was genteel. I could see her in the bank, in a navy-blue dress with the kind of detachable white collar you can wash at night. She would be grumpy and correct.

Another time, she spoke to me about her periods, which were profuse and painful. She wanted to know about mine. There was an uneasy, prudish, agitated expression on her face. I was saved by Irene, who was using the toilet and called out, "Do like me, and you'll be rid of all your problems for a while." Irene was only a few years older than I was, but she was recently—tardily— married, and heavily pregnant.

Gladys ignored her, running cold water on her hands. The hands of all of us were red and sore-looking from the work. "I can't use that soap. If I use it, I break out in a rash," Gladys said. "If I bring my own soap in here, I can't afford to have other people using it, because I pay a lot for it—it's a special anti-allergy soap."

I think the idea that Lily and Marjorie promoted—that Gladys was after Herb Abbott—sprang from their belief that single people ought to be teased and embarrassed whenever possible, and from their interest in Herb, which led to the feeling that somebody ought to be after him. They wondered about him. What they wondered was: How can a man want so little? No wife, no family, no house. The details of his daily life, the small preferences, were of interest. Where had he been brought up? (Here and there and all over.) How far had he gone in school? (Far enough.) Where was his girlfriend? (Never tell.) Did he drink coffee or tea if he got the choice? (Coffee.)

When they talked about Gladys's being after him they must have really wanted to talk about sex—what he wanted and what he got. They must have felt a voluptuous curiosity about him, as I did. He aroused this feeling by being circumspect and not making the jokes some men did, and at the same time by not being squeamish or gentlemanly. Some men, showing me the testicles from the turkey, would have acted as if the very existence of testicles were somehow a bad joke on me, something a girl could be taunted about; another sort of man would have been embarrassed and would have thought he had to protect me from embarrassment. A man who didn't seem to feel one way or the other was an oddity—

as much to older women, probably, as to me. But what was so welcome to me may have been disturbing to them. They wanted to jolt him. They even wanted Gladys to jolt him, if she could.

There wasn't any idea then — at least in Logan, Ontario, in the late forties — about homosexuality's going beyond very narrow confines. Women, certainly, believed in its rarity and in definite boundaries. There were homosexuals in town, and we knew who they were: an elegant, light-voiced, wavy-haired paperhanger who called himself an interior decorator; the minister's widow's fat, spoiled only son, who went so far as to enter baking contests and had crocheted a tablecloth; a hypochondriacal church organist and music teacher who kept the choir and his pupils in line with screaming tantrums. Once the label was fixed, there was a good deal of tolerance for these people, and their talents for decorating, for crocheting, and for music were appreciated — especially by women. "The poor fellow," they said. "He doesn't do any harm." They really seemed to believe — the women did — that it was the penchant for baking or music that was the determining factor, and that it was this activity that made the man what he was — not any other detours he might take, or wish to take. A desire to play the violin would be taken as more a deviation from manliness than would a wish to shun women. Indeed, the idea was that any manly man would wish to shun women but most of them were caught off guard, and for good.

I don't want to go into the question of whether Herb was homosexual or not, because the definition is of no use to me. I think that probably he was, but maybe he was not. (Even considering what happened later, I think that.) He is not a puzzle so arbitrarily solved.

The other plucker, who worked with Irene, was Henry Streets, a neighbor of ours. There was nothing remarkable about him except that he was eighty-six years old and still, as he said of himself, a devil for work. He had whiskey in his thermos, and drank it from time to time through the day. It was Henry who had said to me, in our kitchen, "You ought to get yourself a job at the Turkey Barn. They need another gutter." Then my father said at once, "Not her,

Henry. She's got ten thumbs," and Henry said he was just joking — it was dirty work. But I was already determined to try it—I had a great need to be successful in a job like this. I was almost in the condition of a grownup person who is ashamed of never having learned to read, so much did I feel my ineptness at manual work. Work, to everybody I knew, meant doing things I was no good at doing, and work was what people prided themselves on and measured each other by. (It goes without saying that the things I was good at, like schoolwork, were suspect or held in plain contempt.) So it was a surprise and then a triumph for me not to get fired, and to be able to turn out clean turkeys at a rate that was not disgraceful. I don't know if I really understood how much Herb Abbott was responsible for this, but he would sometimes say, "Good girl," or pat my waist and say, "You're getting to be a good gutter—you'll go a long ways in the world," and when I felt his quick, kind touch through the heavy sweater and bloody smock I wore, I felt my face glow and I wanted to lean back against him as he stood behind me. I wanted to rest my head against his wide, fleshy shoulder. When I went to sleep at night, lying on my side, I would rub my cheek against the pillow and think of that as Herb's shoulder.

I was interested in how he talked to Gladys, how he looked at her or noticed her. This interest was not jealousy. I think I wanted something to happen with them. I quivered in curious expectation, as Lily and Marjorie did. We all wanted to see the flicker of sexuality in him, hear it in his voice, not because we thought it would make him seem more like other men but because we knew that with him it would be entirely different. He was kinder and more patient than most women, and as stern and remote, in some ways, as any man. We wanted to see how he could be moved.

If Gladys wanted this, too, she didn't give any signs of it. It is impossible for me to tell with women like her whether they are as thick and deadly as they seem, not wanting anything much but opportunities for irritation and contempt, or if they are all choked up with gloomy fires and useless passions.

Marjorie and Lily talked about marriage. They did not have much good to say about it, in spite of their feeling that it was a state nobody should be allowed to stay out of. Marjorie said that shortly after her marriage she had gone into the woodshed with the intention of swallowing Paris green.

"I'd have done it," she said. "But the man came along in the grocery truck and I had to go out and buy the groceries. This was when we lived on the farm."

Her husband was cruel to her in those days, but later he suffered an accident—he rolled the tractor and was so badly hurt he would be an invalid all his life. They moved to town, and Marjorie was the boss now.

"He starts to sulk the other night and say he don't want his supper. Well, I just picked up his wrist and held it. He was scared I was going to twist his arm. He could see I'd do it. So I say, 'You *what*?' And he says, 'I'll eat it.' "

They talked about their father. He was a man of the old school. He had a noose in the woodshed (not the Paris green woodshed—this would be an earlier one, on another farm), and when they got on his nerves he used to line them up and threaten to hang them. Lily, who was the younger, would shake till she fell down. This same father had arranged to marry Marjorie off to a crony of his when she was just sixteen. That was the husband who had driven her to the Paris green. Their father did it because he wanted to be sure she wouldn't get into trouble.

"Hot blood," Lily said.

I was horrified, and asked, "Why didn't you run away?"

"His word was law," Marjorie said.

They said that was what was the matter with kids nowadays—it was the kids that ruled the roost. A father's word should be law. They brought up their own kids strictly, and none had turned out bad yet. When Marjorie's son wet the bed she threatened to cut off his dingy with the butcher knife. That cured him.

They said ninety per cent of the young girls nowadays drank, and swore, and took it lying down. They did not have daughters, but if they did and caught them at anything like that they would beat them raw. Irene, they said, used to go to the hockey games with her ski pants slit and nothing under them, for convenience in the snowdrifts afterward. Terrible.

I wanted to point out some contradictions. Marjorie and Lily themselves drank and swore, and what was so wonderful about the strong will of a father who would insure you a lifetime of unhappiness? (What I did not see was that Marjorie and Lily were not unhappy altogether — could not be, because of their sense of consequence, their pride and style.) I could be enraged then at the lack of logic in most adults' talk — the way they held to their pronouncements no matter what evidence might be presented to them. How could these women's hands be so gifted, so delicate and clever — for I knew they would be as good at dozens of other jobs as they were at gutting; they would be good at quilting and darning and painting and papering and kneading dough and setting out seedlings — and their thinking so slapdash, clumsy, infuriating?

Lily said she never let her husband come near her if he had been drinking. Marjorie said since the time she nearly died with a hemorrhage she never let her husband come near her, period. Lily said quickly that it was only when he'd been drinking that he tried anything. I could see that it was a matter of pride not to let your husband come near you, but I couldn't quite believe that "come near" meant "have sex." The idea of Marjorie and Lily being sought out for such purposes seemed grotesque. They had bad teeth, their stomachs sagged, their faces were dull and spotty. I decided to take "come near" literally.

The two weeks before Christmas was a frantic time at the Turkey Barn. I began to go in for an hour before school as well as after school and on weekends. In the morning, when I walked to work, the street lights would still be on and the morning stars shining. There was the Turkey Barn, on the edge of a white field, with a row of big pine trees behind it, and always, no matter how cold and still it was, these trees were lifting their branches and sighing and straining. It seems unlikely that on my way to the Turkey Barn, for an hour of gutting turkeys, I should have experienced such a sense of promise and at the same time of perfect, impenetrable mystery in the universe, but I did. Herb had something to do with that, and so did the cold snap — the series of hard, clear mornings. The truth is, such feelings weren't hard to come by then. I would get them but not know how they were to be connected with anything in real life.

One morning at the Turkey Barn there was a new gutter. This was a boy eighteen or nineteen years old, a stranger named Brian. It seemed he was a relative, or perhaps just a friend, of Herb Abbott's. He was staying with Herb. He had worked on a lake boat last summer. He said he had got sick of it, though, and quit.

What he said was, "Yeah, fuckin' boats, I got sick of that."

Language at the Turkey Barn was coarse and free, but this was one word never heard there. And Brian's use of it seemed not careless but flaunting, mixing insult and provocation. Perhaps it was his general style that made it so. He had amazing good looks: taffy hair, bright-blue eyes, ruddy skin, well-shaped body — the sort of good looks nobody disagrees about for a moment. But a single, relentless notion had got such a hold on him that he could not keep from turning all his assets into parody. His mouth was wet-looking and slightly open most of the time, his eyes were half shut, his expression a hopeful leer, his movements indolent, exaggerated, inviting. Perhaps if he had been put on a stage with a microphone and a guitar and let grunt and howl and wriggle and excite, he would have seemed a true celebrant. Lacking a stage, he was unconvincing. After a while he seemed just like somebody with a bad case of hiccups — his insistent sexuality was that monotonous and meaningless.

If he had toned down a bit, Marjorie and Lily would probably have enjoyed him. They could have kept up a game of telling him to shut his filthy mouth and keep his hands to himself. As it was, they said they were sick of him, and meant it. Once, Marjorie took up her gutting knife. "Keep your distance," she said. "I mean from me and my sister and that kid."

She did not tell him to keep his distance from Gladys, because Gladys wasn't there at the time and Marjorie would probably not have felt like protecting her anyway. But it was Gladys Brian particularly liked to bother. She would throw down her knife and go into the washroom and stay there ten minutes and come out with a stony face. She didn't say she was sick anymore and go home, the way she used to. Marjorie said Morgan was mad at Gladys for sponging and she couldn't get away with it any longer.

Gladys said to me, "I can't stand that kind of thing. I can't stand people mentioning that kind of thing and that kind of — gestures. It makes me sick to my stomach."

I believed her. She was terribly white. But why, in that case, did she not complain to Morgan? Perhaps relations between them were too uneasy, perhaps she could not bring herself to repeat or describe such things. Why did none of us complain — if not to Morgan, at least to Herb? I never thought of it. Brian seemed just something to put up with, like the freezing cold in the gutting shed and the smell of blood and waste. When Marjorie and Lily did threaten to complain, it was about Brian's laziness.

He was not a good gutter. He said his hands were too big. So Herb took him off gutting, told him he was to sweep and clean up, make packages of giblets, and help load the truck. This meant that he did not have to be in any one place or doing any one job at a given time, so much of the time he did nothing. He would start sweeping up, leave that and mop the tables, leave that and have a cigarette, lounge against the table bothering us until Herb called him to help load. Herb was very busy now and spent a lot of time making deliveries, so it was possible he did not know the extent of Brian's idleness.

"I don't know why Herb don't fire you," Marjorie said. "I guess the answer is he don't want you hanging around sponging on him, with no place to go."

"I know where to go," said Brian.

"Keep your sloppy mouth shut," said Marjorie. "I pity Herb. Getting saddled."

On the last school day before Christmas we got out early in the afternoon. I went home and changed my clothes and came into work at about three o'clock. Nobody was working. Everybody was in the gutting shed, where Morgan Elliott was swinging a cleaver over the gutting table and yelling. I couldn't make out what the yelling was about, and thought someone must have made a terrible mistake in his work; perhaps it had been me. Then I saw

Brian on the other side of the table, looking very sulky and mean, and standing well back. The sexual leer was not altogether gone from his face, but it was flattened out and mixed with a look of impotent bad temper and some fear. That's it, I thought; Brian is getting fired for being so sloppy and lazy. Even when I made out Morgan saying "pervert" and "filthy" and "maniac," I still thought that was what was happening. Marjorie and Lily, and even brassy Irene, were standing around with downcast, rather pious looks, such as children get when somebody is suffering a terrible bawling out at school. Only old Henry seemed able to keep a cautious grin on his face. Gladys was not to be seen. Herb was standing closer to Morgan than anybody else. He was not interfering but was keeping an eye on the cleaver. Morgy was blubbering, though he didn't seem to be in any immediate danger.

Morgan was yelling at Brian to get out. "And out of this town —I mean it—and don't you wait till tomorrow if you still want your arse in one piece! Out!" he shouted, and the cleaver swung dramatically towards the door. Brian started in that direction but, whether he meant to or not, he made a swaggering, taunting motion of the buttocks. This made Morgan break into a roar and run after him, swinging the cleaver in a stagy way. Brian ran, and Morgan ran after him, and Irene screamed and grabbed her stomach. Morgan was too heavy to run any distance and probably could not have thrown the cleaver very far, either. Herb watched from the doorway. Soon Morgan came back and flung the cleaver down on the table.

"All back to work! No more gawking around here! You don't get paid for gawking! What are you getting under way at?" he said, with a hard look at Irene.

"Nothing," Irene said meekly.

"If you're getting under way get out of here."

"I'm not."

"All right, then!"

We got to work. Herb took off his blood-smeared smock and put on his jacket and went off, probably to see that Brian got ready to go on the suppertime bus. He did not say a word. Morgan and his son went out to the yard, and Irene and Henry went back to the adjoining shed, where they did the plucking, working knee-deep in the feathers Brian was supposed to keep swept up.

"Where's Gladys?" I said softly.

"Recuperating," said Marjorie. She, too, spoke in a quieter voice than usual, and "recuperating" was not the sort of word she and Lily normally used. It was a word to be used about Gladys, with a mocking intent.

They didn't want to talk about what had happened, because they were afraid Morgan might come in and catch them at it and fire them. Good workers as they were, they were afraid of that. Besides, they hadn't seen anything. They must have been annoyed that they hadn't. All I ever found out was that Brian had either done something or shown something to Gladys as she came out of the washroom and she had started screaming and having hysterics.

Now she'll likely be laid up with another nervous breakdown, they said. And he'll be on his way out of town. And good riddance, they said, to both of them.

I have a picture of the Turkey Barn crew taken on Christmas Eve. It was taken with a flash camera that was someone's Christmas extravagance. I think it was Irene's. But Herb Abbott must have been the one who took the picture. He was the one who could be trusted to know or to learn immediately how to manage anything new, and flash cameras were fairly new at the time. The picture was taken about ten o'clock on Christmas Eve, after Herb and Morgy had come back from making the last delivery and we had washed off the gutting table and swept and mopped the cement floor. We had taken off our bloody smocks and heavy sweaters and gone into the little room called the lunchroom, where there was a table and a heater. We still wore our working clothes: overalls and shirts. The men wore caps and the women kerchiefs, tied in the wartime style. I am stout and cheerful and comradely in the picture, transformed into someone I don't ever remember being or pretending to be. I look years older than fourteen. Irene is the only one who has taken off her kerchief, freeing her long red hair. She peers out from it with a meek, sluttish, inviting look, which would match her reputation but is not like any look of hers I remember.

Yes, it must have been her camera; she is posing for it, with that look, more deliberately than anyone else is. Marjorie and Lily are smiling, true to form, but their smiles are sour and reckless. With their hair hidden, and such figures as they have bundled up, they look like a couple of tough and jovial but testy workmen. Their kerchiefs look misplaced; caps would be better. Henry is in high spirits, glad to be part of the work force, grinning and looking twenty years younger than his age. Then Morgy, with his hangdog look, not trusting the occasion's bounty, and Morgan very flushed and bosslike and satisfied. He has just given each of us our bonus turkey. Each of these turkeys has a leg or a wing missing, or a malformation of some kind, so none of them are salable at the full price. But Morgan has been at pains to tell us that you often get the best meat off the gimpy ones, and he has shown us that he's taking one home himself.

We are all holding mugs or large, thick china cups, which contain not the usual tea but rye whiskey. Morgan and Henry have been drinking since suppertime. Marjorie and Lily say they only want a little, and only take it at all because it's Christmas Eve and they are dead on their feet. Irene says she's dead on her feet as well but that doesn't mean she only wants a little. Herb has poured quite generously not just for her but for Lily and Marjorie, too, and they do not object. He has measured mine and Morgy's out at the same time, very stingily, and poured in Coca-Cola. This is the first drink I have ever had, and as a result I will believe for years that rye-and-Coca-Cola is a standard sort of drink and will always ask for it, until I notice that few other people drink it and that it makes me sick. I didn't get sick that Christmas Eve, though; Herb had not given me enough. Except for an odd taste, and my own feeling of consequence, it was like drinking Coca-Cola.

I don't need Herb in the picture to remember what he looked like. That is, if he looked like himself, as he did all the time at the Turkey Barn and the few times I saw him on the street—as he did all the times in my life when I saw him except one.

The time he looked somewhat unlike himself was when Morgan was cursing out Brian and, later, when Brian had run off down the road. What was this different look? I've tried to remember, because I studied it hard at the time. It wasn't much different. His face looked softer and heavier then, and if you had to describe the expression on it you would have to say it was an expression of shame. But what would he be ashamed of? Ashamed of Brian, for the way he had behaved? Surely that would be late in the day; when had Brian ever behaved otherwise? Ashamed of Morgan, for carrying on so ferociously and theatrically? Or of himself, because he was famous for nipping fights and displays of this sort in the bud and hadn't been able to do it here? Would he be ashamed that he hadn't stood up for Brian? Would he have expected himself to do that, to stand up for Brian?

All this was what I wondered at the time. Later, when I knew more, at least about sex, I decided that Brian was Herb's lover, and that Gladys really was trying to get attention from Herb, and that that was why Brian had humiliated her—with or without Herb's connivance and consent. Isn't it true that people like Herb—dignified, secretive, honorable people—will often choose some-body like Brian, will waste their helpless love on some vicious, silly person who is not even evil, or a monster, but just some importunate nuisance? I decided that Herb, with all his gentleness and carefulness, was avenging himself on us all—not just on Gladys but on us all—with Brian, and that what he was feeling when I studied his face must have been a savage and gleeful scorn. But embarrassment as well—embarrassment for Brian and for himself and for Gladys, and to some degree for all of us. Shame for all of us—that is what I thought then.

Later still, I backed off from this explanation. I got to a stage of backing off from the things I couldn't really know. It's enough for me now just to think of Herb's face with that peculiar, stricken look; to think of Brian monkeying in the shade of Herb's dignity; to think of my own mystified concentration on Herb, my need to catch him out, if I could ever get the chance, and then move in and stay close to him. How attractive, how delectable, the prospect of intimacy is, with the very person who will never grant it. I can still feel the pull of a man like that, of his promising and refusing. I would still like to know things. Never mind facts. Never mind theories, either.

When I finished my drink I wanted to say something to Herb. I stood beside him and waited for a moment when he was not listening to or talking with anyone else and when the increasingly rowdy conversation of the others would cover what I had to say.

"I'm sorry your friend had to go away."

"That's all right."

Herb spoke kindly and with amusement, and so shut me off from any further right to look at or speak about his life. He knew what I was up to. He must have known it before, with lots of women. He knew how to deal with it.

Lily had a little more whiskey in her mug and told how she and her best girlfriend (dead now, of liver trouble) had dressed up as men one time and gone into the men's side of the beer parlor, the side where it said "Men Only," because they wanted to see what it was like. They sat in a corner drinking beer and keeping their eyes and ears open, and nobody looked twice or thought a thing about them, but soon a problem arose.

"Where were we going to go? If we went around to the other side and anybody seen us going into the ladies', they would scream bloody murder. And if we went into the men's somebody'd be sure to notice we didn't do it the right way. Meanwhile the beer was going through us like a bugger!"

"What you don't do when you're young!" Marjorie said.

Several people gave me and Morgy advice. They told us to enjoy ourselves while we could. They told us to stay out of trouble. They said they had all been young once. Herb said we were a good crew and had done a good job but he didn't want to get in bad with any of the women's husbands by keeping them there too late. Marjorie and Lily expressed indifference to their husbands, but Irene announced that she loved hers and that it was not true that he had been dragged back from Detroit to marry her, no matter what people said. Henry said it was a good life if you didn't weaken. Morgan said he wished us all the most sincere Merry Christmas.

When we came out of the Turkey Barn it was snowing. Lily said it was like a Christmas card, and so it was, with the snow whirling around the street lights in town and around the colored lights people had put up outside their doorways. Morgan was giving Henry and Irene a ride home in the truck, acknowledging age and pregnancy and Christmas. Morgy took a shortcut through the field, and Herb walked off by himself, head down and hands in his pockets, rolling slightly, as if he were on the deck of a lake boat. Marjorie and Lily linked arms with me as if we were old comrades.

"Let's sing," Lily said. "What'll we sing?"

" 'We Three Kings'?" said Marjorie. " 'We Three Turkey Gutters'?"

" 'I'm Dreaming of a White Christmas.' "

"Why dream? You got it!"

So we sang.

Accident

Frances is loitering by a second-floor window of the high school in Hanratty, on an afternoon in early December. It is 1943. Frances' outfit is fashionable for that year: a dark plaid skirt and fringed, triangular shawl of the same material, worn over the shoulders with the ends tucked in at the waist; a creamy satin blouse—real satin, a material soon to disappear — with many little pearl buttons down the front and up the sleeves. She never used to wear such clothes when she came to teach music at the high school; any old sweater and skirt was good enough. This change has not gone unnoticed.

She has no business on the second floor. Her glee club is singing downstairs. She has been working them hard, getting them ready for the Christmas concert. "He Shall Feed His Flock" is their hard piece. Then "The Huron Carol" (one complaint from a parent who said he understood it was written by a priest), "Hearts of Oak" because there had to be something patriotic, times being what they were, and "The Desert Song," their choice. Now they are singing "The Holy City." A great favorite, that one, especially with big-breasted moony girls and choir ladies. High-school girls could irritate the life out of Frances. They wanted the windows closed, they wanted the windows opened. They felt drafts, they were faint from the heat. They were tender toward their bodies, moving in a trance of gloomy self-love, listening for heart flutters, talking of twinges. The start of being women. Then what happened to them? The big fronts and rears, the bland importance, milkiness, dopiness, stubbornness. Smell of corsets, sickening revelations. Sacrificial looks they would get in the choir. It was all a dreary sort of sex. *He walks with me and he talks with me and he tells me I am his own.*

She has left them on their own, pretended she is going to the teachers' washroom. All she does there is turn on the light and look with relief at her own unrapt, unswollen face, her long bright face, with its rather large nose, clear brown eyes and short bush of dark-reddish hair, uncontrollably curly. Frances likes her own looks, is usually cheered by her own face in the mirror. Most women, at least in books, seem to have a problem about their looks, thinking themselves less pretty than they really are. Frances has to admit she may have an opposite problem. Not that she thinks herself pretty; just that her face seems lucky to her, and encouraging. She remembers sometimes a girl at the conservatory, Natalie somebody, who played the violin. Frances was amazed to learn that people sometimes confused her with this Natalie, who was pale, frizzy-haired, bony-faced; she was even more amazed to learn, through a network of friends and confidantes, that it bothered Natalie as much as it did her. And when she broke her engagement to Paul, another student at the conservatory, he said to her in a harsh, matter-of-fact voice without any of the courtliness or sentimentality he had previously felt obliged to use toward her, "Well, do you really think you can do that much better? You're not the greatest beauty, you know."

She turns out the light and instead of going back to the glee club she goes upstairs. In the winter mornings the school is dreary; not enough heat yet, everybody yawning and shivering, country children who have left home before light rubbing crusty bits of sleep from the corners of their eyes. But by this time of day, by midafternoon, Frances feels a comforting hum about the place, a more agreeable drowsiness, with the dark wainscoting soaking up the light, and the silent cloakrooms stuffed with drying woolen

coats and scarves and boots and skates and hockey sticks. Through
the open transoms flow some orderly instructions; French dicta-
tion; confident facts. And along with all this order and acquies-
cence there is a familiar pressure, of longing or foreboding, that
strange lump of something you can feel sometimes in music or a
landscape, barely withheld, promising to burst and reveal itself,
but it doesn't, it dissolves and goes away.

Frances is directly opposite the door of the science room.
That transom is open, too, and she can hear clinking sounds, low
voices, shifting of stools. He must have them doing an experiment.
Absurdly, shamefully, she feels the sweat in her palms, the ham-
mering in her chest, that she has felt before a piano examination or
recital. That air of crisis, the supposed possibilities of triumph or
calamity that she could manufacture, for herself and others, now
seems trumped up, foolish, artificial. But what about this, her
affair with Ted Makkavala? She is not so far gone that she cannot
see how foolish that would seem to anybody looking on. Never
mind. If foolish means risky and imprudent, she does not care.
Perhaps all she has ever wanted was a chance to take chances. But
the thought comes to her sometimes that a love affair can be, not
artificial, yet somehow devised and deliberate, an occasion provided, just as those silly performances were: a rickety invention.
That is an idea she can't take a chance with; she puts it out of sight.

A student's voice, a girl's, puzzled and complaining (another
thing about high-school girls — they whine when they don't understand; boys' grunting contempt is better). Ted's low voice answering, explaining. Frances can't hear his words. She thinks of him
bending attentively, performing some ordinary action such as
lowering the flame of a Bunsen burner. She likes to think of him as
diligent, patient, self-contained. But she knows, word has reached
her, that his classroom behavior is different from what he has led
her or anyone to believe. It is his habit to speak rather scornfully of
his job, of his students. If asked what sort of discipline he favors,
he will say, oh, nothing much, maybe a knuckle sandwich, maybe
a good swift kick in the arse. The truth is, he gets his students'
attention by all sorts of tricks and cajolery; he makes use of props
such as dunce hats and birthday whistles; he carries on in a highly

melodramatic way over their stupidity, and once burned their test papers one by one in the sink. *What a character*, Frances has heard students say of him. She does not like hearing them say that. She is sure they say it of her, too; she herself is not above using extravagant tactics, tearing her fingers through her bushy hair lamenting *no-no-no-no* when they sing badly. But she would rather he did not have to do such things. She shies away sometimes from mention of him, from hearing what people have to say. He's very friendly, they say, and she thinks she hears some puzzlement, some scorn; why does he take such pains? She has to wonder, too; she knows what he thinks of this town and the people in it. Or what he says he thinks.

The door is opening, giving Frances a shock. There is nothing she wants less than for Ted to find her here, listening, spying. But it isn't Ted, thank God, it's the school secretary, a plump, serious woman who has been secretary here forever, since Frances was a student herself, and before that. She is devoted to the school, and to the Bible class she runs at the United Church.

"Hello there, dear; getting a bit of air?"

The window Frances is standing beside is of course not open, has even been taped around the cracks. But Frances makes a humorous assenting face, says, "Playing hooky," to acknowledge being out of her classroom, and the secretary goes calmly downstairs, her kind voice floating back.

"Your glee club sounds lovely today. I always like the Christmas music."

Frances goes back to her classroom and sits on the desk, smiling into the singing faces. They have got through "The Holy City" and all by themselves got on "The Westminster Carol." They do look silly, but how can they help it? Singing is silly altogether. She never thinks that they will notice her smile and mention it afterward, sure she has been out to meet Ted in the hall. It is in imagining her affair to be a secret that Frances shows, most clearly, a lack of small-town instincts, a trust and recklessness she is unaware of; this is what people mean when they say of her that it sure shows that she has been away. She was only four years away, at the conservatory; the truth was, she always lacked caution. Tall, fine-boned, with narrow shoulders, she has the outsider's quick movements, preoccupied look, high-pitched, urgent voice, the outsider's innocent way of supposing herself unobserved as she dashes from one place to another around town, arms full of music books, calling across the street some message relating to the fluctuating and it would seem nearly impossible arrangements of her life.

Tell Bonnie not to come until 3:30!
Did you get the keys? I left them in the office!

She showed that even when she was little, and was so determined to learn to play the piano, even though they didn't have one, in the apartment over the hardware store where she lived with her mother and brother (her mother a widow, poorly paid, who worked downstairs). Somehow the thirty-five cents a week had been found, but the only piano she saw was the teacher's. At home, she practiced on a keyboard penciled on the windowsill. There was some composer — Handel, was it? — who used to practice on the harpsichord in the attic with the door closed, so his father would not know what a grip music had got on him. (How he managed to sneak a harpsichord in there was an interesting question.) If Frances had become a famous pianist, the windowsill keyboard — overlooking the alley, the roof of the curling rink — would have become another such legend.

"Don't think you're any genius," was another thing Paul had said to her, "because you're not." Had she thought that? She thought the future had something remarkable in store for her. She didn't even think it very clearly, just behaved as if she thought it. She came home, started teaching music. Mondays at the high school, Wednesdays at the public school, Tuesdays and Thursdays at little schools out in the country. Saturdays for organ practice and private pupils; Sundays she played in the United Church.

"Still bumbling around this great cultural metropolis," she would scrawl on her Christmas cards to old friends from the conservatory, the idea being that once her mother died, once she was free, she would embark on the separate, dimly imagined, immeasurably more satisfying life that was still waiting for her. The messages she got back had often the same distracted and disbelieving tone. *Another baby and my hands are in the diaper pail more often than on the keyboard as you can well imagine.* They were all in their early thirties. An age at which it is sometimes hard to admit that what you are living is your life.

Wind is bending the trees outside and snow is blurring them. A minor blizzard is going on, nothing to take much notice of in this part of the country. On the windowsill is an ink pitcher of battered brass with a long spout, a familiar object that makes Frances think of the Arabian nights, or something like that; something whose promise, or suggestion, is foreign, reticent, delightful.

"Hello, how are you?" said Ted when she met him in the hall after four. Then he said in a lower voice, "Supply room. I'll be right there."

"Fine," said Frances. "*Fine.*" She went to lock up some music books and close the piano. She fussed and dawdled around until all the students were gone, then ran upstairs, into the science room, into a large, windowless closet opening off it, which was Ted's supply room. He was not there yet.

The room was a sort of pantry, lined with shelves on which sat bottles of various chemicals—copper sulfate was the only one she would have known without the label, she remembered the beautiful color—Bunsen burners, flasks, test tubes, a human skeleton and a cat's, some bottled organs, or maybe organisms; she didn't look too closely and anyway the room was dark.

She was afraid that the janitor might come in, or even some students working under Ted's direction on some project involving mold or frog spawn (though it would surely be the wrong time of year for that). What if they should come back to check on something? When she heard footsteps her heart began banging away; when she realized they were Ted's it did not quiet down but seemed to shift into another gear, so that it was pounding not from fright but from strong, overpowering expectation, which, however delightful, was as hard on her, physically, as fear; it seemed enough to suffocate her.

She heard him lock the door.

She had two ways of looking at him, all in the moment it took him to appear in the doorway of the supply room, then pull that door nearly shut, so they were almost in the dark. First, she saw him as if it was a year ago, and he was someone who had nothing to do with her. Ted Makkavala, the science teacher, not in the war, though he was under forty; he did have a wife and three children, and perhaps he had a heart murmur, or something like that; he did look tired. A tall, slightly stooping, dark-haired, dark-skinned man, with an irritable, humorous expression, eyes both tired and bright. It could be supposed he had a similar sighting of her, standing there looking irresolute and alarmed, with her coat over her arm and her boots in her hand, since she had thought it unwise to leave them in the teachers' cloakroom. There was a moment's chance they would not be able to make the switch, to see each other differently; they wouldn't remember how the crossover was managed or grace wouldn't be granted them, and if that could be so, what were they doing in this place?

As he drew the door shut she saw him again, the side of his face and the slant of the cheekbones, a marvelous, polished, Tartarish slant; she perceived the act of drawing the door closed as stealthy and ruthless, and she knew there was no chance in the world they would not make the switch. It was already made.

Then, as usual. Licks and pressures, tongues and bodies, teasing and hurting and comforting. Invitations, attentions. She used to wonder, in her days with Paul, if the whole thing could be a fraud, an Emperor's clothes sort of thing, if nobody really felt what they pretended, and certainly she and Paul did not. There had been a dreadful air of apology and constraint and embarrassment about the whole business, the worst of it being the moans and endearments and reassurances they had to offer. But no, it wasn't a fraud, it was all true, it surpassed everything; and the signs that it could happen—the locked eyes, the shiver along the spine, all that elemental foolishness—those were true, too.

"How many other people know about this?" she said to Ted.

"Oh, not very many, maybe a dozen or so."

"It'll never catch on, I don't suppose."

"Well. It'll never be popular with the masses."

The space between the shelves was narrow. There was so

much breakable equipment. And why had she not had sense enough to put down her boots and her coat? The truth was she had not expected so much or such purposeful embracing. She had thought he wanted to tell her something.

He opened the door slightly, to give them a bit more light. He took her boots from her and set them outside the door. Then he took her coat. But instead of setting it down outside he was opening it out and spreading it on the bare boards of the floor. The first time she had seen him do something like that was last spring. In the cold, still-leafless woods he had taken off his windbreaker and spread it inadequately on the ground. She had been powerfully moved by this simple preparatory act, by the way he spread the jacket open and patted it down, without any questions, any doubts or hurry. She had not been sure, until he did that, what was going to happen. Such a gentle, steady, fatalistic look he had. She was stirred by the memory as he knelt in this narrow space and spread out her coat. At the same time she was thinking: if he wants to do it now, does it mean he can't come on Wednesday? Wednesday night was when they regularly met, in the church after Frances' choir practice. Frances would stay on in the church, playing the organ, until everyone had gone home. At about eleven o'clock she would go down and turn out the lights and wait at the back door, the Sunday-school door, to let him in. They had thought of this when the weather turned cold. What he told his wife she did not know.

"Take everything off."

"We can't here," said Frances, though she knew they would. They always took all their clothes off, even that first time in the woods; she had never believed she could feel the cold so little.

Only once before here, in the school, in this same room, and that had been in the summer holidays, just after dark. All the woodwork in the science room had been freshly painted and there had been no warning signs up — why should there be, nobody was expected to get in. The smell was strong enough, when they finally noticed. They had twisted around somehow so that their legs were in this doorway, and they both got smeared with the paint from the door frame. Fortunately Ted had been wearing shorts that evening — an odd sight in town, at the time — and had been able to tell Greta the truth, that he had smeared his leg when he went to do something in the science room, without having to explain how his legs were bare. Frances did not have to explain since her mother was beyond noticing such things. She did not clean the crescent of paint off (it was just above her ankle); she let it wear away, and enjoyed looking at it and knowing it was there, just as she enjoyed the dark bruises, the bite marks, on her upper arms and shoulders, that she could easily have covered with long sleeves but often did not. Then people would say to her, "How did you get that nasty bruise?" and she would say, "You know, I don't know! I bruise so easily. Every time I look at myself, there's a bruise!" Her sister-in-law Adelaide, her brother's wife, was the only one who would know what it was, and would find occasion to say something.

"Oh-oh, you been out with that tomcat again. Haven't you, eh? Haven't you?" She would laugh and even put her finger to the mark.

Adelaide was the only person Frances had told. Ted said he had told nobody, and she believed him. He did not know that she had told Adelaide. She wished she had not. She did not like Adelaide well enough to make a confidante of her. It was all vulgar, discreditable; she had done it just to have somebody to parade in front of. When Adelaide said *tomcat*, in that crude, taunting, aroused and unconsciously jealous way, Frances was gratified and excited, though of course ashamed. She would be frantic if she thought Ted had made similar confidences about her.

The night they got the paint on themselves was such a hot night, the whole town was cranky and drooping and waiting for rain, which came toward morning, with a thunderstorm. Frances looking back at this time always thought of lightning, a crazy and shattering, painful kind of lust. She used to think of each time separately, would go over them in her mind. There was a peculiar code, a different feeling, for each time. The time in the science room like lightning and wet paint. The time in the car in the rain in the middle of the afternoon, with sleepy rhythms, so pleased and sleepy they were then that it seemed they could hardly be bothered to do the next thing. That time had a curved, smooth feeling for her, in memory; the curve came from the sheets of rainwater on the windshield, looking like looped-back curtains.

Since they were meeting regularly in the church, the pattern did not change so much, one time was much like another.

"Everything," Ted said confidently. "It's all right."

"The janitor."

"It's all right. He's finished here."

"How do you know?"

"I asked him to finish up so I could work here."

"Work," said Frances, giggling, struggling out of her blouse and her brassiere. He had undone the buttons down the front, but there were still six buttons on each of the sleeves. She liked the idea of his planning it, she liked to think of determined lustfulness working in him this afternoon while he was busy directing his class. And in another way she did not like it at all; she giggled to cover some dismay or disappointment that she would not listen to. She kissed the straight line of hairs that ran like a stem up his belly, from the pubic roots to the fine symmetrical bush on his chest. His body was a great friend of hers, no matter what. There was the dark, flat mole, tear-shaped, probably more familiar to her (and to Greta?) than it was to him. The discreet bellybutton, the long stomach-ulcer scar, the appendectomy scar. The wiry pubic bush and the ruddy cheerful penis, upright and workmanlike. The little tough hairs in her mouth.

Then came some knocking at the door.

"Ssh. It's all right. They'll go away."

"Mr. Makkavala!"

It was the secretary.

"Ssh. She'll go away."

The secretary was standing out in the hall wondering what to do. She was fairly sure that Ted was in there, and that Frances was with him. Like almost everybody else in town, she had known about them for some time. (Among the few people who apparently did not know were Ted's wife, Greta, and Frances' mother. Greta was such an unsociable woman that nobody had found a way to tell her. People had tried in various ways to tell old Mrs. Wright, but she did not seem to take it in.)

"Mr. Makkavala!"

Directly in front of Frances' eyes that workman was losing color, was drooping, and looking gentle and forlorn.

"Mr. Makkavala! I'm sorry. Your son's been killed!"

Ted's son Bobby, who was twelve years old, had not been killed, but the secretary did not know that. She had been told that there had been an accident, a terrible accident in front of the post office; the O'Hare boy and the Makkavala boy killed. Bobby was very badly hurt and was taken to London, by ambulance, immediately. It took nearly four hours to get there, because of the snowstorm. Ted and Greta followed in their car.

They sat in the waiting room of Victoria Hospital. Ted noticed the old queen, the grumpy widow, in a stained-glass window. Like a saint, and what an unsatisfactory one. Rival, he supposed, for the plaster St. Joseph they had in the other hospital, stretching out his arms ready to topple on you. One as bad as the other. He thought of telling Frances. When something amused or enraged him—a number of things did both, and at the same time—he thought of telling Frances. That seemed to satisfy him, as another man might be satisfied by writing a letter to the editor.

He thought of phoning her, not to tell her about Queen Victoria, not now, but to let her know what had happened, that he was in London. He had not told her, either, that he would not be able to see her on Wednesday night. He had meant to tell her afterward. Afterward. It didn't matter now. Everything was changed. And he couldn't phone her from here; the phones were in plain view of the waiting room.

Greta said that she had noticed a cafeteria, or a sign with arrows pointing to a cafeteria. It was after nine o'clock, and they had not had any supper.

"You have to eat," said Greta, not addressing Ted in particular, but speaking out of her fund of general principles. Probably at this moment she would like to have spoken Finnish. She did not speak Finnish to Ted. He knew only a few words, had grown up in a home where there was an insistence on English. Greta's home was the opposite. There was no one in Hanratty she could speak Finnish to; that was one of her problems. The phone bill was their main extravagance, because Ted did not feel that he could object to her long, dreary-sounding but apparently revitalizing conversations with her mother and sisters.

They picked up ham and cheese sandwiches, and coffee. Greta took a piece of raisin pie. Her hand hovered over it a minute before picking it up, maybe just in hesitation about what kind of pie she wanted. Or maybe she was shy about eating pie at this time, and in front of her husband. When they were sitting down it occurred to Ted that now was the time to excuse himself, go back to the phones, call Frances.

He watched Greta's heavy white face, her pale eyes, as she applied herself devoutly, perhaps hopefully, to the food. She ate to keep her panic down, just as he thought about Queen Victoria and St. Joseph. He was just going to excuse himself, and get up, when he received out of nowhere the idea that if he went to phone Frances, his son would die. By not phoning her, by not even thinking about her, by willing her to stop existing in his life, he could increase Bobby's chances, hold off his death. What a flood of nonsense this was, what superstition, coming over him when he didn't expect it. And it was impossible to stop, impossible to disregard. What if worse was coming? What if the next idea to present itself was one of those senseless bargains? Believe in God, the Lutheran God, promise to go back to church, do it at once, *now*, and Bobby would not die. Give up Frances, give her up for good, and Bobby would not die.

Give up Frances.

How stupid and unfair it was, and yet how easy, to set Frances on one side, tainted, and on the other his hurt child, his poor crushed child whose look, the one time he had opened his eyes, had shown a blinded question, the claim of his twelve-year-old life. Innocence and corruption; Bobby; Frances; what simplification; what nonsense. What powerful nonsense.

Bobby died. His ribs were crushed, a lung was punctured.

The main puzzle to the doctors was why he had not died sooner. But before midnight, he died.

Much later, Ted told Frances, not only about the idiotic queen but about the meal in the cafeteria, about his thoughts of phoning her, and why he had not done so; his thoughts of bargains; everything. He did not tell her as a confession, but as a matter of interest, an illustration of the way the most rational mind could relapse and grovel. He did not imagine that what he was telling her could be upsetting, when he had, after all, decided so thoroughly in her favor.

Frances waited a few moments, alone in the supply room, dressed, buttoned, booted, with her coat on. She didn't think about anything. She looked at the skeletons. The human skeleton looked smaller than a man, while the cat's skeleton looked larger, longer than a cat.

She got out of the school without meeting anybody. She got into her car. Why had she taken her coat and boots out of the cloakroom, so that it would look as if she had gone home, when anybody could see her car still sitting here?

Frances drove an old car, a 1936 Plymouth. A picture that surfaced in many people's minds, after she was gone, was of Frances at the wheel of her stalled car, trying one thing after another (she would already be late for somewhere) while it coughed and stuttered and refused her. Or—as now—with the window down, her bare head stuck out in the falling snow, trying to get her spinning wheels out of a drift, with an expression on her face that said she had never expected that car to do anything but balk and confound her, but would fight it just the same to her last breath.

She did get out, at last, and drove down the hill toward the main street. She didn't know what had happened to Bobby, what sort of accident. She had not heard what was said, after Ted had left her. On the main street the stores were warmly lighted. There were horses as well as cars along the street (at this time the township roads were not plowed out); they clouded the air with their comforting breath. More people than usual, it seemed to her, were standing around talking, or not talking, just unwilling to separate. Some storekeepers had come outside and were standing there, too, in their shirtsleeves, in the snow. The post office corner seemed to be blocked off, and that was the direction people were looking in.

She parked behind the hardware store, and ran up the long outdoor steps, which she had shovelled free of snow and ice that morning, and was going to have to shovel again. She felt as if she was running to a hiding place. But she wasn't; Adelaide was there.

"Frances, is that you?"

Frances took off her coat in the back hall, checked her blouse buttons. She put her boots on the rubber mat.

"I was just telling Grandma. She never knew anything about it. She never heard the ambulance."

There was a basket of clean laundry on the kitchen table, an old pillowcase over it to keep off the snow. Frances came into the kitchen prepared to cut Adelaide short but knew she couldn't when she saw that laundry. At the times when Frances was busiest, around Christmas, or spring recital, Adelaide would come and take their laundry to her house, and come back with everything pressed and bleached and starched. She had four children, but she was always helping other people out, baking and shopping for them, looking after extra babies, running in and out of houses where there was trouble. Pure generosity. Pure blackmail.

"Fred Beecher's car was full of blood," Adelaide said, turning to Frances. "He had the trunk open, he had the baby buggy in it that he was taking over to his sister-in-law's, and the trunk of his car was full of blood. It was full of blood."

"Was it Fred Beecher?" said Frances, because there was no getting away from it now, she would have to be told. "Did Fred Beecher hit — the Makkavala boy?" She knew Bobby's name, of course, she knew all Ted's children's names and faces, but she had developed an artificial vagueness in speaking of any of them — of Ted, too — so that even now she had to say *the Makkavala boy*.

"Don't you know about it either?" Adelaide said. "Where were you? Weren't you at the high school? Didn't they come and get him?"

"I heard they did," said Frances. She saw that Adelaide had

made tea. She badly wanted a cup, but was afraid to touch the cups or the teapot, because her hands were shaking. "I heard his son was killed."

"He wasn't the one killed, it was the other one was killed. The O'Hare boy. It was two of them in it. The O'Hare boy was instantly killed. It was awful. The Makkavala boy won't live. They took him to London in the ambulance. He won't live."

"Oh, oh," said Frances' mother, seated at the table, her book open in front of her. "Oh, oh. Think of the poor mother." But she had heard it all once.

"It wasn't Fred Beecher hit them, that wasn't it at all," said Adelaide to Frances in rather a scolding way. "They tied their sled on to the back of his car. He didn't even know they done it. They must've tied it on when he was slowed down in front of the school with all the kids just let out and then on the hill a car was coming behind and it skidded and run into them. It run the sled right under Fred's car."

Old Mrs. Wright made an assenting, moaning noise.

"They must've been warned. All the kids been warned and they been doing it for years and it was just bound to happen. It was so awful," Adelaide said, staring at Frances as if to will more reaction out of her. "All the ones that saw it says they will never forget. Fred Beecher went and threw up in the snow. Right in front of the post office. Oh, the blood."

"Terrible," said Frances' mother. Her interest had quite faded. She was probably thinking about supper. From about three o'clock in the afternoon on, her interest in supper mounted. When Frances was late, as she was tonight, or when somebody dropped in during the late afternoon, thinking, no doubt, that she would be glad of a visitor, she would become more and more agitated, thinking that supper was going to be delayed. She would try to control herself, she would become very affable, eager to respond, rummaging in her collection of social phrases, tossing them out one after another, in her hope that the visitor would soon be satisfied and would go away.

"Did you get the pork chops?" she said to Frances.

Of course, Frances had forgotten. She had promised breaded

pork chops and she had not gone to the butcher shop, she had forgotten.

"I'll go back."

"Oh, don't bother."

"She had too much on her mind with the accident," Adelaide said. "We had a pork-chop casserole last night, it was one you do in the oven with creamed corn, and was it ever good."

"Well. Frances does them in bread crumbs."

"Oh, I do that, too. That way's good, too. Sometimes you feel like a change. I saw the O'Hare boy's father coming out of the undertaker's. It was awful to see him. He looked sixty years old."

"Viewing the body," said Frances' mother. "An omelette would do just as good."

"Would it?" said Frances, who could not bear to think of going back out on the street.

"Oh, yes. And save on the ration coupons."

"Aren't they the devil, the ration coupons? He wouldn't be viewing it yet. Not with the work that'll have to be done on it. He'd be picking out the casket."

"Oh. Likely."

"No, he wouldn't be fixed up yet. He'd still be on the slab."

The way Adelaide said that, *on the slab*, was so emphatic, so full of energy, it was just as if she had slapped a big wet fish down in front of them. She had an uncle who was an undertaker, in another town, and she was proud of this connection, of her insider's knowledge. Sure enough, she began to talk about this uncle's work with accident victims, of a boy who had been scalped and how her uncle had restored his appearance, going to the barbershop and getting snips of hair from the wastebasket, mixing to get exactly the right color, working all night. The boy's family couldn't believe he could look so natural. It's an art, said Adelaide, when they know their business like he does.

Frances thought she must tell Ted about this. She often told Ted things Adelaide had said. Then she remembered.

"Of course, they can have the casket closed if they want to," said Adelaide, having explained again how inferior this undertaker was to her uncle. "Was that the Makkavalas' only son?" she asked Frances.

"I think he was."

"I feel sorry for them. And they haven't got any family here. She doesn't even speak too good English, does she? Of course the O'Hares being Catholics, they've got four or five more. You know, the priest came and did the business on him, even if he was stone dead."

"Oh, oh," said Frances' mother disapprovingly. There was not much hostility to Catholics in this disapproval, really; it was a courtesy Protestants were bound to pay to each other.

"I won't have to go to the funeral parlor, will I?" A worried, stubborn look settled on Frances' mother's face whenever there was a chance she might have to go near sick or dead people. "What were their names?"

"O'Hare . . ."

"Oh, yes. Catholics."

"And Makkavala."

"I don't know them. Do I? Are they foreigners?"

"Finnish. From Northern Ontario."

"I thought so. I thought it sounded foreign. I don't have to go."

Frances did have to go out again. She had to go to the library, in the evening, to get her mother's books. Every week she brought her mother three new books from the library. Her mother liked the sight of a good thick book. A lot of reading in that one, she would say, just as she would say there was a lot of wear in a coat or blanket. Indeed, the book was just like a warm, thick eiderdown that she could pull over herself, snuggle into. When she got toward the end, and her covering was getting thinner and thinner, she would count the pages left and say, "Did you get me another book? Oh, yes. There it is. I remember. Well, I still have that one when I finish this one."

But there always came the time when she had finished the last book and had to wait while Frances went to the library and got three more. (Fortunately, Frances was able to repeat the same book after a short interval, say three or four months; her mother would sink in all over again, even giving out bits of information about the setting and the characters, as if she had never met them before.)

Frances would tell her mother to listen to the radio while she was waiting, but although her mother never refused to do anything she was told, the radio did not seem to comfort her. While she was coverless, so to speak, she might go into the living room and pull an old book out of the bookcase — *Jacob Faithful*, it might be, or *Lorna Doone* — and sit crouched over on the low stool, hanging on to and reading it. Other times she might just shuffle around from room to room. Never lifting her feet except for a threshold, hanging on to the furniture, and blundering against the walls, blind because she hadn't turned the light on, weak because she never walked now, overtaken by a fearful restlessness, a sort of slow-motion frenzy, that could get her when she didn't have books or food or sleeping pills to keep it away.

Frances was disgusted with her mother tonight for saying, "How about my library books?" She was disgusted with her mother's callousness, her self-absorption, her feebleness, her survival, her wretched little legs and her arms on which the skin hung like wrinkled sleeves. But her mother was not more callous than she was herself. She went past the post office corner where there was no sign of an accident now, just fresh snow, snow blowing up the street from the south, from London (he would have to come back, no matter what happened he would have to come back). She felt fury at that child, at his stupidity, his stupid risk, his showing off, his breaking through into other people's lives, into her life. She could not stand the thought of anybody right now. The thought of Adelaide, for instance. Adelaide, before she left, had followed Frances into the bedroom where Frances was taking off her satin blouse, because she could not cook supper in it. She had it open in front, she was undoing the sleeve buttons; she was standing in front of Adelaide just as she had stood in front of Ted a while before.

"Frances," said Adelaide in a tense whisper, "are you feeling all right?"

"Yes."

"You don't think it was paying back for you and him?"

"What?"

"God paying him back," said Adelaide. Excitement, satisfaction, self-satisfaction shone out of her. Before her marriage to Frances' stubborn and innocent younger brother, she had enjoyed a year or two of sexual popularity, or notoriety, puns being frequently made on her name. Her figure was stocky and maternal, her eyes slightly crossed. Frances could not understand what had driven her into such a friendship, or alliance, or whatever it could be called. Sitting in Adelaide's kitchen on the nights when Clark was out coaching the junior hockey team, spiking their coffee with Clark's precious whiskey (they watered what was left), with the diapers drying beside the stove, some cheap metal toy-train tracks and a hideous, eyeless, armless doll on the table in front of them, they had talked about sex and men. A shameful relief, a guilty indulgence, a bad mistake. God had not entered into Adelaide's conversation at that time. She had never heard the word *penis*, tried it but couldn't get used to it. *Pecker*, she said. *Whipped out his pecker*, she said, with the same disturbing gusto as she said *on the slab*.

"You don't look all right, I'll tell you that," she said to Frances. "You look like it knocked you silly. You look sick."

"Go home," said Frances.

How was she going to have to pay for that?

Two men were putting Christmas lights on the blue spruce trees in front of the post office. Why were they doing it at this hour? They must have got started before the accident, then had to leave it. They must have spent the time off getting drunk, at least one of them must have. Cal Callaghan had got himself tangled up in a string of lights. The other man, Boss Creer, who had got his name because he would never be boss of anything, stood by waiting for Cal to get himself out of his difficulties in his own time. Boss Creer did not know how to read or write, but he knew how to be comfortable. The back of their truck was full of wreaths of artificial holly and ropes of red and green stuff still to be hung. Frances, because of her involvement with concerts and recitals and almost everything in the way of public festivity the town could think up, had got to know where the trappings were kept and she knew that these decorations lay year after year in the attic of the Town Hall, forgotten, then remembered and hauled out when somebody on the town council said, "Well, now. We had better think what we are going to do about Christmas." Leaving these two fools to get the ropes and lights up somehow, and the wreaths hung, Frances was despising them. The incompetence, the ratty wreaths and ropes, the air of ordinary drudgery, all set in motion by some irrational sense of seasonal obligation. At another time, she might have found it touching, faintly admirable. She might have tried to explain to Ted, who could never understand her feeling of loyalty to Hanratty. He said he could live in a city, or in the woods, in the kind of frontier settlement he came from, but not in a place like this, such a narrow place, crude without the compensations of the wilderness, cramped without any urban variety or life.

But here he was.

She remembered feeling this same disgust with everything last summer. Ted and Greta and the children had gone away, for three weeks, up to Northern Ontario to visit their relatives. For the first two weeks of the three, Frances had gone to a cottage on Lake Huron, the same cottage she always rented. She took her mother, who sat reading under the Balm of Gilead tree. Frances was all right there. In the cottage there was an old edition of the Encyclopaedia Britannica and she read in it, over and over, the out-of-date article on Finland. She lay on the porch of the cottage at night and heard the lake on the shore and thought of Northern Ontario, where she had never been. Wilderness. But when she had to come back to town and he was not there she had a very bad time. Every morning she walked to the post office and there was nothing from him. She would stand looking out the post office window at the Town Hall, where there was a great red-and-white thermometer recording the progress of a Victory Bond drive. She could no longer place him in Northern Ontario, in his relatives' houses, getting drunk and eating enormous meals. He had gone away. He could be anywhere, outside this town; he had stopped existing for her, except in the ridiculous agony of memory. She did hate everybody then; she could hardly bring out a civil answer. She hated the people, the heat, the Town Hall, the Victory Bond thermometer, the sidewalks, the buildings, the voices. She was afraid to think about this afterward, she did not want to think how the decent, inoffensive shapes of houses or the tolerable tone of greetings could depend on the existence of one person, whom she had not known a year before, how his presence in the same town, even when she could not see or hear from him, made the necessary balance for her own.

The first night he got back was the night they got into the school and rubbed against the fresh paint. She thought then that doing without him had been worth it, was only the price to pay. She forgot what it was like, just as they said you forgot the pain of having a baby, from one time to the next.

Now she could remember. That was only a rehearsal; that was something she had concocted, to torture herself. Now it would be real. He would come back to Hanratty but he would not come back to her. Because he was with her when it happened he would hate her; at least, he would hate the thought of her, because it always made him think of the accident. And suppose somehow the child survived, crippled. That would be no better, not for Frances. They would want to get away from here. He had told her Greta did not like it, that was one of the few things he had told her about Greta. Greta was lonely, she didn't feel at home in Hanratty. How much less was she going to like it now? What Frances had imagined last summer would be the reality this summer. He would be somewhere outside, reunited with his wife whom he probably held in his arms at this minute, comforting her, talking to her in their own language. He said he did not talk to her in Finnish. Frances had asked him. She could tell he did not like her asking. He said that he spoke hardly any Finnish. She did not believe him.

The origin of the Finno-Ugrian tribes is shrouded in mystery, Frances had read. That statement pleased her; she had not thought that an encyclopedia could admit such a thing. The Finns were called the Tavastians and the Karelians, and they had remained pagans until well into the thirteenth century. They believed in a god of the air, a god of the forests, a god of the water. Frances learned the names of these gods and surprised Ted with them. *Ukko*. *Tapio*. *Ahti*. These names were news to him. The ancestors he knew were not those peaceable pagans, the Magyar forest-dwellers, who in some places, according to the encyclopedia, still offered sacrifices to ghosts; they were the nineteenth-century nationalists, socialists, radicals. His family had been banished from Finland. It was not the northern forest, the pines and birch, but the meeting halls and newspaper offices of Helsinki, the lecture rooms and reading rooms, that Ted had been taught to be nostalgic for. No pagan ceremonies lingered in his mind (rubbish, he said, when Frances told him about sacrifices to ghosts), but a time of secret printing presses, after-dark distribution of leaflets, doomed demonstrations and honorable jail sentences. Against the Swedes, they demonstrated and propagandized, against the Russians. But if your family were Communists wouldn't they be in favor of the Russians, said Frances stupidly, with the dates all wrong; he was talking of a time before the revolution. Not that it was any different now. Russia had invaded Finland; Finland was officially aligned with Germany. Ted's loyalties had nowhere to turn. They were certainly not going to turn to Canada, where he said he was now considered an enemy alien and was under surveillance by the R.C.M.P. Frances could hardly believe such a thing. And he sounded proud of it.

When they were out walking in the fall, in the dry woods, he had told her plenty of things she should have been ashamed not to know; about the Spanish Civil War, the purges in Russia. She listened, but her attention kept sneaking out, under cover of her reasonable questions and replies, to fasten on a fence post or a groundhog hole. She caught the drift. He believed that a general bankruptcy existed, and that the war, which was generally believed to be an enormous but temporary crisis, was actually just a natural aspect of this condition. Whenever she pointed out any hopeful possibility he explained how she was wrong, why by now all systems were doomed and one cataclysm would follow another until—

"What?"

"Until there's a total smashup."

How contented he seemed, saying that. How could she argue against a vision that seemed to yield him such peace and satisfaction?

"You are so dark," she said, turning his hand over in her own. "I didn't know any northern Europeans were so dark."

He told her that there were the two kinds of looks in Finland, the Magyar and the Scandinavian looks, dark and fair, and how they did not seem to mingle but kept themselves distinct, showing up generation after generation unaltered, in the same district, in the same family.

"Greta's family is a perfect example," he said. "Greta is absolutely Scandinavian. She has big bones, long bones, she's dolichocephalic — "

"What?"

"Long-headed. She's fair-skinned and blue-eyed and fair-haired. Then her sister Kartrud is olive-skinned and slightly slant-eyed, very dark. The same thing in our family. Bobby is like Greta. Margaret is like me. Ruth-Ann is like Greta."

Frances was both chilled and curious to hear him speak of Greta, of *our family*. She never asked, never spoke of them. In the beginning, he did not speak of them either. Two things he said that stayed with her. One was that he and Greta had been married while he was still at the university, on scholarships; she had stayed up north with her family until he graduated and got a job. That made Frances wonder if Greta had been pregnant; was that why he had married her? The other thing he said — in an unemphatic way, and while he and Frances were talking about places to meet — was that he had never been unfaithful before. Frances had supposed this all along, due to her innocence or conceit; she had never for a moment supposed she could be part of a procession. But the word unfaithful (he did not even say unfaithful to Greta) suggested a bond. It put Greta under a spotlight for them, showed her sitting somewhere waiting; cool and patient, decent, wronged. It did her honor; he did her honor.

At the beginning, that was all. But now in their conversations doors were opening, to swing quickly shut again. Frances caught glimpses, which she shrank from and desired. Greta had to have the car to take Ruth-Ann to the doctor; Ruth-Ann had an earache, she had cried all night. Ted and Greta together were papering the front hall. The whole family had fallen sick after eating some questionable sausages. Frances caught more than glimpses. She caught the Makkavala family's colds. She began to feel she lived with them in a bizarre and dreamlike intimacy.

She had asked one question.

"What was the wallpaper like? That you and your wife put on the hall?"

He had to think.

"It's striped. It's white and silver stripes."

The choice of wallpaper made Greta seem harder, shrewder, more ambitious, than she seemed on the street or shopping in the Superior Grocery Store, in her soft, dowdy, flowered dresses, her loose checked slacks, a bandana over her hair. A big, fair, freckled housewife, who once bumped Frances' arm with her grocery basket and said, "Excuse me." The only words Frances had ever heard her say. A thickly accented, cold and timid voice. The voice Ted heard every day of his life, the body he slept beside every night. Frances' knees weakened and trembled, there in the Superior Grocery Store in front of the shelves of Kraft Dinner and pork and beans. Just to be so close to this big, mysterious woman, so innocent and powerful, was blurring her mind and making her shake in her shoes.

On Saturday morning Frances found a note in her mailbox, asking her to let Ted into the church that night. She was as nervous all day as she had been when waiting to meet him for the first time, in Beattie's Bush. She waited, in the dark, by the Sunday-school-room door. It was a bad night, Saturday, either the minister or the janitor was likely to be there, and both had been, earlier, when Frances was distractedly playing the organ. They had gone home, she hoped for good.

They usually made love here in the dark, but tonight Frances thought they would need a light on, they would need to talk. She led the way at once to a Sunday-school classroom behind the choir loft. It was a long, narrow, stuffy room with no outside windows. The Sunday-school chairs had been stacked in one corner. There was a strange thing on the teacher's table — an ash tray with two cigarette stubs in it. Frances held it up.

"Somebody else must come here, too."

She had to talk about something besides the accident, because she was sure she could never say the right thing about that.

"Whole relay of lovers," said Ted, to her relief. "I wouldn't be surprised." He named some possible pairs. The school secretary and the principal. Frances' sister-in-law and the minister of this church. But he spoke drearily.

"We'll have to set up a schedule."

They didn't bother taking the chairs down, but sat on the floor with their backs against the wall, under a picture of Jesus walking by the Sea of Galilee.

"I have never put in such a week in my life," Ted said. "I don't know where to start. We came back from London Tuesday, and Wednesday, Greta's family descended on us. They drove all night, two nights. I don't know how they did it. They commandeered a snowplow to go ahead of them for about fifty miles in one place. Those women are capable of anything. The father's just a shadow. The women are terrors. Kartrud is the worst. She has eight children of her own and she's never stopped running her sisters and her sisters' families and anybody else who'll allow her. Greta is just useless against her."

He said that trouble had started right away, about the funeral. Ted had decided on a nonreligious funeral. He had made up his mind long ago that if any of his family died, he would not call in the church. The undertaker didn't like it, but agreed. Greta said it was all right. Ted wrote out a few memorial paragraphs he intended to read himself. That would be all. No hymn-singing, no prayers. There was nothing new about this. They all knew how he felt. Greta knew. Her family knew. Nevertheless, they started to carry on as if this was a new and horrifying revelation. They acted as if atheism itself was an unheard-of position. They had tried to tell him a funeral of this sort was illegal, that he could go to jail.

"They'd brought this old fellow with them, who I just assumed was some uncle or cousin or other. I haven't met them all, it's an enormous family. So after I told them my plans for the funeral they explained to me that he's their minister. A Finnish Lutheran minister they carted four hundred miles to intimidate me with. He was in bad shape, too, the poor old bugger. He'd caught cold. They were running around putting mustard plasters on him and soaking his feet and trying to keep him fit to perform. Serve them right if he'd conked out on them."

Ted was up by this time, walking back and forth in the

Sunday-school room. He said there was no way he was going to be intimidated. They could have brought the whole congregation and the Lutheran Church itself on a flatcar. He told them that. He meant to bury his own son in his own way. By this time Greta had caved in, she had gone over to their side. Not that she had an ounce of religious feeling, it was just the weeping and recriminations and the weakness in the face of her family that she always had. Nor was it left to the family. Various Hanratty busybodies got into it. The house was full of them. The United Church minister, the minister of this church, showed up at one point for a consultation with the Lutheran. Ted threw him out. Later on he found out it wasn't exactly the minister's fault, he hadn't come on his own. Kartrud had summoned him, saying there was a desperate situation, her sister was having a nervous breakdown.

"Was she?" said Frances.

"What?"

"Was she — your wife — having a nervous breakdown?"

"Anybody would be having a nervous breakdown with that pack of maniacs in the house."

The funeral was private, Ted said, but that didn't seem to prevent anybody who wanted from showing up. He himself stood up beside the casket ready to knock down anyone who interfered. His sister-in-law — with pleasure — or the ailing old minister or even Greta if they pushed her into it.

"Oh, no," said Frances involuntarily.

"I knew she wouldn't. But Kartrud might have. Or the old mother. I didn't know what was going to happen. I knew I couldn't show a moment's hesitation. It was horrible. I started to talk and the old mother started to rock and wail. I had to shout over her. The louder she got in Finnish the louder I got in English. It was insane."

While he talked he dumped the cigarette stubs from the ash tray into his hand and back, was pitching them back and forth.

Frances said, after a pause, "But Greta was his mother."

"How do you mean?"

"If she did want an ordinary funeral."

"Oh, she didn't."

"How do you know?"

"I know her. She doesn't have any opinions one way or the other. She just caved in in front of Kartrud; she always will."

He did it all for himself, Frances was thinking. He wasn't thinking of Greta for a moment. Or of Bobby. He was thinking of himself and his beliefs and not giving in to his enemies. That was what mattered to him. She could not help seeing this and she did not like it. She could not help seeing how much she did not like it. That did not mean that she had stopped liking him; at least, she had not stopped loving him. But there was a change. When she thought about it later, it seemed to her that up to that point she had been involved in something childish and embarrassing. She had managed it all for her own delight, seeing him as she wanted to, paying attention when she wanted to, not taking him seriously, although she thought she did; she would have said he was the most important thing in her life.

She wasn't going to be allowed that any more, that indolence and deception.

For the first time, she was surprised when he wanted to make love. She was not ready, she could not comprehend him yet, but he seemed too intent to notice.

The next day, Sunday, when she played for services, was the last time Frances ever played in the United Church.

On Monday Ted was called into the principal's office. What had happened was that Greta's sister Kartrud had got to know the women of Hanratty better in five days than Greta had in eighteen months, and that someone had told her about Ted and Frances. Frances thought afterward that it would have been Adelaide who told, it must have been Adelaide, but she was wrong. Adelaide presented herself at the Makkavala house, but she was not the one who told; somebody else had got there before her. In a rage already from the struggle over the funeral, and her loss there, Kartrud went to visit both the principal of the high school and the minister of the United Church. She inquired of them what steps they meant to take. Neither the minister nor the principal wanted to take any. Both of them had known about the affair, and been nervous about it, and hoped it would blow over. Ted and Frances were both valuable to them. Both of them said to Kartrud that surely now, after the death of the child, husband and wife would draw together and this other business would be forgotten. A pity to make a fuss now, they said, when the family had suffered such a loss and the damage could be mended, with the wife none the wiser. But Kartrud promised she would be the wiser. She meant to tell Greta, she said, before she left for home, she meant to persuade Greta to go with her, if something had not been done to stop this. She was a powerful woman, physically and vocally. Both men were cowed by her.

The principal said to Ted that an unfortunate matter had come to his attention, been brought to his attention. He apologized for bringing it up so soon after the bereavement but said he had no choice. He said that he hoped Ted could guess the matter he had in mind, which concerned a lady of this town who had previously had everyone's respect and he hoped would have it again. He said he imagined that Ted himself might have already decided to put an end to things. He was expecting that Ted would make some embarrassed ambiguous statement to the effect that he had, or would, put an end to things, and no matter how convincing or unconvincing this statement sounded, the principal was prepared to accept it. He was only carrying out his promise; so that Kartrud would get out of town without starting more trouble.

Ted jumped up, to the principal's amazement, and said this was harassment, and he would not put up with it. He said he knew who was behind it. He said that he would brook no interference, his relationships were entirely his own affair, and marriage was nothing anyway but an antiquated custom promoted by the authorities of the church, just like everything else they rammed down people's throats. Rather inconsistently, he followed this up by stating that he was leaving Greta anyway, he was leaving the school, his job, Hanratty; he was going to marry Frances.

No, no, the principal kept saying, have a drink of water. You don't mean that, what nonsense. You can't make up your mind when you're in a state like this.

"My mind was made up long ago," said Ted. He believed that was true.

"I could at least have asked you first," said Ted to Frances. They were sitting in the living room of the apartment, in the late afternoon. Frances had not gone to the high school that Monday; she had ordered the glee club to meet at the Town Hall, so that she could rehearse them there, get them used to the stage. She came home rather late and her mother said, "There's a man waiting for you in the front room. He said his name but I forget." Her mother also forgot to say that the minister had phoned and wanted Frances to call him back. Frances never did know that.

She thought it was probably the insurance agent. There was some problem about the fire insurance for the building. The agent had called last week and asked if he could come to see her when he was next in town. Going through the hall, she tried to clear her mind to talk to him, wondering if she would have to find another place to live. Then she saw Ted sitting by the window, with his overcoat on. He had not turned on the lights. But some light from the street came in, some red and green Christmas rainbows played on him.

She knew as soon as she saw him what had happened. She knew not in detail but in substance. How else could he be sitting here in her mother's living room in front of the old ferny wallpaper and *The Angelus*?

"This is an old-fashioned room," he said gently, as if picking up her thoughts. He had run down, he was in the strange, weakened, dreamy state that follows terrible rows or irrevocable decisions. "It's not a bit like you."

"It's my mother's room," said Frances, wanting to ask — but it wasn't the time — what sort of room would have been like her. What did she seem like, to him, how much had he really noticed about her? She drew the curtains and turned on two wall bracket lights.

"Is that your corner?" said Ted politely, as she closed the music on the piano. She closed it so it wouldn't bother him, or to protect it from him; he had no interest in music.

"It is sort of. That's Mozart," she said hurriedly, touching the cheap bust on a side table. "My favorite composer."

What an idiotic, schoolgirl sort of thing to say. She felt her apologies should not be to Ted, but to this corner of her life, the piano and Mozart and the dark print of *A View of Toledo*, which she was very fond of, and was now ready to expose and betray.

Ted began to tell her of the day's events, what the principal had said, what he had said, as well as he could remember. In the telling, his replies were somewhat cooler, more controlled and thoughtful, than they had been in fact.

"So, I said I was going to marry you, and then I thought, of all the presumption. What if she says no?"

"Oh, well. You knew I wouldn't," said Frances. "Say no."

Of course he had known that. They were going through with it, nothing could stop them. Not Frances' mother, who sat in the kitchen reading and not knowing she was under sentence of death (for that was what it amounted to; she would go to Clark and Adelaide and the confusion in their house would finish her; they would forget about her library books and she would go to bed and die). Not Ted's young daughters, who were skating this afternoon at the outdoor rink, to the blurry music "Tales from the Vienna Woods," and enjoying, in a subdued and guilty way, the attention their brother's death was bringing to them.

"Would you like coffee?" said Frances. "Oh, I don't know if we have any. We save all the ration coupons for tea. Would you like tea?"

"We save all ours for coffee. No. It's all right."

"I'm sorry."

"I don't really want anything."

"We're stunned," said Frances. "We're both stunned."

"It would have happened anyway. Sooner or later we would have decided."

"Do you think so?"

"Oh, yes, of course," said Ted impatiently. "Of course we would."

But it didn't seem so to Frances, and she wondered if he said it just because he could not bear the thought of anything being set in motion outside his control — and so wastefully, so cruelly — and because he felt bound to conceal from her how small a part she herself had played in all this. No, not a small part; an ambiguous part. There was a long chain of things, many of them hidden from her, that brought him here to propose to her in the most proper place, her mother's living room. She had been made necessary. And it was quite useless to think, would anyone else have done as well, would it have happened if the chain had not been linked exactly as it was? Because it was linked as it was, and it was not anybody else. It was Frances, who had always believed something was going to happen to her, some clearly dividing moment would come, and she would be presented with her future. She had foreseen that, and she could have foreseen some scandal; but not the weight, the disturbance, the possibility of despair, that was at the heart of it.

"We will have to be careful," she said.

He thought that she meant they must not have children, at least for a while, and he agreed, though he thought she picked an odd time to mention it. She did not mean anything like that.

Frances is greeting people, standing near her brother Clark and the coffin of her sister-in-law Adelaide in the Hanratty Funeral Home, nearly thirty years later. The Hanratty Funeral Home is a new extension of the furniture store which was next to the old hardware store. The hardware store burned down. So Frances is standing underneath where she used to live, if that can be imagined. Frances doesn't imagine it.

Her hair is an odd color. The dark hairs have gone gray but not the red, resulting in such a grizzled mixture that her daughters have persuaded her to dye it. But the shade they chose for her is a mistake. The wrong shade of hair, however, like the dashed-on lipstick, the plaid tailored suit, the enduring leanness and dis-tracted, energetic manner, only makes her seem more like herself, and many people are glad to see her.

She has been back before this, of course, but not often. She never brought Ted with her. She brought her children, who thought Hanratty was a quaint, ridiculous place, an absurd place for their parents to have lived in. She has two daughters. Ted has four daughters altogether, but no son. On each occasion, in the delivery room, Frances felt relief.

She continued to believe that Adelaide informed on her, and

she continued to be angry about it, though she saw that she might just as easily have been grateful. Now Adelaide is dead. She got very fat; she developed heart trouble.

People at the funeral home don't ask Frances about Ted but she feels this is due to old embarrassment, not ill-feeling. They ask about her children. Then Frances herself is able to bring up Ted's name, saying that the younger girl has come home from Montreal, where she is studying, to spend a few days near her father while her mother is away. Ted is in a hospital, he has emphysema. He goes into the hospital when there is a crisis, is relieved, comes home again. This will go on for a while.

Then people start talking about Ted, recalling his classroom antics, saying there had never been anyone like him, there ought to be more teachers like that, what a different kind of place school would have been. Frances laughs, agrees, thinks how she must report all this to Ted, but in a casual way, so he won't think it is being done to cheer him up. He never taught again, after Hanratty. He got a job in Ottawa, working for the government, as a biologist. It was possible to get such a job in wartime, without having advanced degrees. Frances worked as a music teacher, so that they could send money to Greta, who went back to Northern Ontario, to her family. She believes Ted has liked his job. He has been involved in great feuds and battles and talked cynically but this as far as she could see was the way of civil servants. But he has come to look on teaching as his real vocation. He talks of his teaching days more and more, as he gets older, making them into a kind of serial adventure, with mad principals, preposterous school boards, recalcitrant but finally vanquished pupils, interest sparked in most unlikely places. He is going to be glad to hear how his pupils' memories accord with his own.

She also means to tell him about Helen, Adelaide's daughter, a blocky woman in her thirties. She took Frances up for a close look at Adelaide, who is looking pinch-mouthed and reticent as she never did in life.

"See what they done, they wired her jaws shut. That's the way they do it now, they wire their jaws and it never looks natural. They used to put the little pads in and fill their lips out but they don't any more, it's too much trouble."

A pale, fat man, using two canes, comes up to Frances.

"I don't know if you remember me. I used to be Clark's and Adelaide's neighbor. Fred Beecher."

"Yes I do, I remember you," says Frances, though she cannot think for a moment how she remembers him. It comes back to her as they talk. He gives her neighborly memories of Adelaide and tells her about his own treatments for arthritis. She remembers Adelaide saying that he vomited in the snow. She says she is sorry about the pain he has, and his trouble walking, but she really wants to say she is sorry about the accident. If he had not gone out in the snow that day to take a baby carriage across town, Frances would not live in Ottawa now, she would not have her two children, she would not have her life, not the same life. That is true. She is sure of it, but it is too ugly to think about. The angle from which she has to see that can never be admitted to; it would seem monstrous. And if he hadn't gone out that day — Frances is thinking as she talks to him — where would we all be now? Bobby would be about forty years old, perhaps he would be an engineer — his childish interests, recalled now more often by Ted, made that seem likely — he would have a good job, maybe even an interesting job, a wife and children. Greta would be going to see Ted in the hospital, looking after his emphysema. Frances might still be here, in Hanratty, teaching music; or she might be elsewhere. She might have recovered, fallen in love with someone else, or she might have grown hard and solitary around her wound.

What difference, thinks Frances. She doesn't know where that thought comes from or what it means, for of course there is a difference, anybody can see that, a life's difference. She's had her love, her scandal, her man, her children. But inside she's ticking away, all by herself, the same Frances who was there before any of it.

Not altogether the same, surely.

The same.

I'll be as bad as Mother when I get old, she thinks, turning eagerly to greet somebody. Never mind. She has a way to go yet.

Bardon Bus

I think of being an old maid, in another generation. There were plenty of old maids in my family. I come of straitened people, madly secretive, tenacious, economical. Like them, I could make a little go a long way. A piece of Chinese silk folded in a drawer, worn by the touch of fingers in the dark. Or the one letter, hidden under maidenly garments, never needing to be opened or read because every word is known by heart, and a touch communicates the whole. Perhaps nothing so tangible, nothing but the memory of an ambiguous word, an intimate, casual tone of voice, a hard, helpless look. That could do. With no more than that I could manage, year after year as I scoured the milk pails, spit on the iron, followed the cows along the rough path among the alder and the black-eyed Susans, spread the clean wet overalls to dry on the fence, and the tea towels on the bushes. Who would the man be? He could be anybody. A soldier killed at the Somme or a farmer down the road with a rough-tongued wife and a crowd of children; a boy who went to Saskatchewan and promised to send for me, but never did, or the preacher who rouses me every Sunday with lashings of fear and promises of torment. No matter. I could fasten on any of them, in secret. A lifelong secret, lifelong dream-life. I could go round singing in the kitchen, polishing the stove, wiping the lamp chimneys, dipping water for the tea from the drinking-pail. The faintly sour smell of the scrubbed tin, the worn scrub-cloths. Upstairs my bed with the high headboard, the crocheted spread, and the rough, friendly-smelling flannelette sheets, the hot-water bottle to ease my cramps or be clenched between my legs. There I come back again and again to the center of my fantasy, to the moment when you give yourself up, give yourself over, to the assault which is guaranteed to finish off everything you've been before. A stubborn virgin's belief, this belief in perfect mastery; any broken-down wife could tell you there is no such thing.

Dipping the dipper in the pail, lapped in my harmless crazi-ness, I'd sing hymns, and nobody would wonder.

> *"He's the Lily of the Valley,*
> *The Bright and Morning Star.*
> *He's the Fairest of Ten Thousand to my Soul."*

2

This summer I'm living in Toronto, in my friend Kay's apartment, finishing a book of family history which some rich people are paying me to write. Last spring, in connection with this book, I had to spend some time in Australia. There I met an anthropologist whom I had known slightly, years before, in Vancouver. He was then married to his first wife (he is now married to his third) and I was married to my first husband (I am now divorced). We both lived in Fort Camp, which was the married students' quarters, at the university.

The anthropologist had been investigating language groups in northern Queensland. He was going to spend a few weeks in the city, at a university, before joining his wife in India. She was there on a grant, studying Indian music. She is the new sort of wife with serious interests of her own. His first wife had been a girl with a job, who would help him get through the university, then stay home and have children.

We met at lunch on Saturday, and on Sunday we went up the river on an excursion boat, full of noisy families, to an animal preserve. There we looked at wombats curled up like blood puddings, and disgruntled, shoddy emus, and walked under an arbor of brilliant unfamiliar flowers and had our pictures taken with koala bears. We brought each other up-to-date on our lives, with jokes, sombre passages, buoyant sympathy. On the way back we drank gin from the bar on the boat, and kissed, and made a mild spectacle of ourselves. It was almost impossible to talk because of the noise of the engines, the crying babies, the children shrieking and chasing each other, but he said, "Please come and see my house. I've got a borrowed house. You'll like it. Please, I can't wait to ask you, please come and live with me in my house."

"Should I?"

"I'll get down on my knees," he said, and did.

"Get up, behave!" I said. "We're in a foreign country."

"That means we can do anything we like."

Some of the children had stopped their game to stare at us. They looked shocked and solemn.

3

I call him X, as if he were a character in an old-fashioned novel, that pretends to be true. X is a letter in his name, but I chose it also because it seems to suit him. The letter X seems to me expansive and secretive. And using just the letter, not needing a name, is in line with a system I often employ these days. I say to myself, "Bardon Bus, No. 144," and I see a whole succession of scenes. I see them in detail; streets and houses. LaTrobe Terrace, Paddington. Schools like large, pleasant bungalows, betting shops, frangipani trees dropping their waxy, easily bruised, and highly scented flowers. It was on this bus that we rode downtown, four or five times in all, carrying our string bags, to shop for groceries at Woolworths, meat at Coles, licorice and chocolate ginger at the candy store. Much of the city is built on ridges between gullies, so there was a sense of coming down through populous but half-wild hill villages into the central part of town, with its muddy river and pleasant colonial shabbiness. In such a short time everything seemed remarkably familiar and yet not to be confused with anything we had known in the past. We felt we knew the lives of the housewives in sun-hats riding with us on the bus, we knew the insides of the shuttered, sun-blistered houses set up on wooden posts over the gullies, we knew the streets we couldn't see. This familiarity was not oppressive but delightful, and there was a slight strangeness to it, as if we had come by it in a way we didn't understand. We moved through a leisurely domesticity with a feeling of perfect security — a security we hadn't felt, or so we told each other, in any of our legal domestic arrangements, or in any of the places where we more properly belonged. We had a holiday of lightness of spirit without the holiday feeling of being at loose ends. Every day X went off to the university and I went downtown to the research library, to look at old newspapers on the microfilm reader.

One day I went to the Toowong Cemetery to look for some graves. The cemetery was more magnificent and ill-kempt than cemeteries are in Canada. The inscriptions on some of the splendid white stones had a surprising informality. "Our Wonderful Mum," and "A Fine Fellow." I wondered what this meant, about Australians, and then I thought how we are always wondering what things mean, in another country, and how I would talk this over with X.

The sexton came out of his little house, to help me. He was a young man in shorts, with a full-blown sailing ship tattooed on his chest. *Australia Felix* was its name. A harem girl on the underside of one arm, a painted warrior on top. The other arm decorated with dragons and banners. A map of Australia on the back of one hand; the Southern Cross on the back of the other. I didn't like to peer at his legs, but had an impression of complicated scenes like a vertical comic strip, and a chain of medallions wreathed in flowers, perhaps containing girls' names. I took care to get all these things straight, because of the pleasure of going home and telling X.

He too would bring things home: conversations on the bus; word derivations; connections he had found.

We were not afraid to use the word love. We lived without responsibility, without a future, in freedom, with generosity, in constant but not wearying celebration. We had no doubt that our happiness would last out the little time required. The only thing we reproached ourselves for was laziness. We wondered if we would later regret not going to the Botanical Gardens to see the lotus in bloom, not having seen one movie together; we were sure we would think of more things we wished we had told each other.

4

I dreamed that X wrote me a letter. It was all done in clumsy block printing and I thought, that's to disguise his handwriting, that's clever. But I had great trouble reading it. He said he wanted us to go on a trip to Cuba. He said the trip had been offered to him by a clergyman he met in a bar. I wondered if the clergyman might be a spy. He said we could go skiing in Vermont. He said he did not want to interfere with my life but he did want to shelter me. I loved that word. But the complications of the dream multiplied. The letter had been delayed. I tried to phone him and I couldn't get the telephone dial to work. Also it seemed I had the responsibility of a baby, asleep in a dresser drawer. Things got more and more tangled and dreary, until I woke. The word shelter was still in my head. I had to feel it shrivel. I was lying on a mattress on the floor of Kay's apartment at the corner of Queen and Bathurst streets at eight o'clock in the morning. The windows were open in the summer heat, the streets full of people going to work, the streetcars stopping and starting and creaking on the turn.

This is a cheap, pleasant apartment with high windows, white walls, unbleached cotton curtains, floorboards painted in a glossy gray. It has been a cheap temporary place for so long that nobody ever got around to changing it, so the wainscoting is still there, and the old-fashioned perforated screens over the radiators. Kay has some beautiful faded rugs, and the usual cushions and spreads, to make the mattresses on the floor look more like divans and less like mattresses. A worn-out set of bedsprings is leaning against the wall, covered with shawls and scarves and pinned-up charcoal sketches by Kay's former lover, the artist. Nobody can figure a way to get the springs out of here, or imagine how they got up here in the first place.

Kay makes her living as a botanical illustrator, doing meticulous drawings of plants for textbooks and government handbooks.

She lives on a farm, in a household of adults and children who come and go and one day are gone for good. She keeps this place in Toronto, and comes down for a day or so every couple of weeks. She likes this stretch of Queen Street, with its taverns and second-hand stores and quiet derelicts. She doesn't stand much chance here of running into people who went to Branksome Hall with her, or danced at her wedding. When Kay married, her bridegroom wore a kilt, and his brother officers made an arch of swords. Her father was a brigadier-general; she made her debut at Government House. I often think that's why she never tires of a life of risk and improvisation, and isn't frightened by the sound of brawls late at night under these windows, or the drunks in the doorway downstairs. She doesn't feel the threat that I would feel, she never sees herself slipping under.

Kay doesn't own a kettle. She boils water in a saucepan. She is ten years younger than I am. Her hips are narrow, her hair long and straight and dark and streaked with gray. She usually wears a beret and charming, raggedy clothes from the secondhand stores. I have known her six or seven years and during that time she has often been in love. Her loves are daring, sometimes grotesque.

On the boat from Centre Island she met a paroled prisoner, a swarthy tall fellow with an embroidered headband, long gray-black hair blowing in the wind. He had been sent to jail for wrecking his ex-wife's house, or her lover's house; some crime of passion Kay boggled at, then forgave. He said he was part Indian and when he had cleared up some business in Toronto he would take her to his native island off the coast of British Columbia, where they would ride horses along the beach. She began to take riding lessons.

During her break-up with him she was afraid for her life. She found threatening, amorous notes pinned to her nightgowns and underwear. She changed her locks, she went to the police, but she didn't give up on love. Soon she was in love with the artist, who had never wrecked a house but was ruled by signs from the spirit world. He had gotten a message about her before they met, knew what she was going to say before she said it, and often saw an ominous blue fire around her neck, a yoke or a ring. One day he disappeared, leaving those sketches, and a lavish horrible book on anatomy which showed real sliced cadavers, with innards, skin, and body hair in their natural colors, injected dyes of red or blue illuminating a jungle of blood vessels. On Kay's shelves you can read a history of her love affairs: books on prison riots, autobiographies of prisoners, from the period of the parolee; this book on anatomy and others on occult phenomena, from the period of the artist; books on caves, books by Albert Speer, from the time of the wealthy German importer who taught her the word *spelunker*; books on revolution which date from the West Indian.

She takes up a man and his story wholeheartedly. She learns his language, figuratively or literally. At first she may try to disguise her condition, pretending to be prudent or ironic. "Last week I met a peculiar character — " or, "I had a funny conversation with a man at a party, did I tell you?" Soon a tremor, a sly flutter, an apologetic but stubborn smile. "Actually I'm afraid I've fallen for him, isn't that terrible?" Next time you see her she'll be in deep, going to fortune-tellers, slipping his name into every other sentence; with this mention of the name there will be a mushy sound to her voice, a casting down of the eyes, an air of cherished helplessness, appalling to behold. Then comes the onset of gloom, the doubts and anguish, the struggle either to free herself or to keep him from freeing himself; the messages left with answering services. Once she disguised herself as an old woman, with a gray wig and a tattered fur coat; she walked up and down, in the cold, outside the house of the woman she thought to be her supplanter. She will talk coldly, sensibly, wittily, about her mistake, and tell discreditable things she has gleaned about her lover, then make desperate phone calls. She will get drunk, and sign up for rolfing, swim therapy, gymnastics.

In none of this is she so exceptional. She does what women do. Perhaps she does it more often, more openly, just a bit more illadvisedly, and more fervently. Her powers of recovery, her faith, are never exhausted. I joke about her, everybody does, but I defend her too, saying that she is not condemned to living with reservations and withdrawals, long-drawn-out dissatisfactions, inarticulate wavering miseries. Her trust is total, her miseries are sharp, and she survives without visible damage. She doesn't allow for drift or stagnation and the spectacle of her life is not discouraging to me.

She is getting over someone now; the husband, the estranged husband, of another woman at the farm. His name is Roy; he too is an anthropologist.

"It's really a low ebb falling in love with somebody who's lived at the farm," she says. "Really low. Somebody you know all about."

I tell her I'm getting over somebody I met in Australia, and that I plan to be over him just about when I get the book done, and then I'll go and look for another job, a place to live.

"No rush, take it easy," she says.

I think about the words "getting over." They have an encouraging, crisp, everyday sound. They are in tune with Kay's present mood. When love is fresh and on the rise she grows mystical, tentative; in the time of love's decline, and past the worst of it, she is brisk and entertaining, straightforward, analytical.

"It's nothing but the desire to see yourself reflected," she says. "Love always comes back to self-love. The idiocy. You don't want them, you want what you can get from them. Obsession and self-delusion. Did you every read those journals of Victor Hugo's daughter, I think that's who it was?"

"No."

"I never did either, but I read about them. The part I remember, the part I remember reading about, that struck me so, was where she goes out into the street after years and years of loving this man, obsessively loving him, and she meets him. She passes him in the street and she either doesn't recognize him or she does but she can't connect the real man any more with the person she loves, in her head. She can't connect him at all."

5

When I knew X in Vancouver he was a different person. A serious graduate student, still a Lutheran, stocky and resolute, rather a prig in some people's opinion. His wife was more scatterbrained; a physiotherapist named Mary, who liked sports and dancing. Of the two, you would have said she might be the one to run off. She had blond hair, big teeth; her gums showed. I watched her play baseball at a picnic. I had to go off and sit in the bushes, to nurse my baby. I was twenty-one, a simple-looking girl, a nursing mother. Fat and pink on the outside; dark judgements and strenuous ambitions within. Sex had not begun for me, at all.

X came around the bushes and gave me a bottle of beer.

"What are you doing back here?"

"I'm feeding the baby."

"Why do you have to do it here? Nobody would care."

"My husband would have a fit."

"Oh. Well, drink up. Beer's supposed to be good for your milk, isn't it?"

That was the only time I talked to him, so far as I can remember. There was something about the direct approach, the slightly clumsy but determined courtesy, my own unexpected, lightened feeling of gratitude, that did connect with his attentions to women later, and his effect on them. I am sure he was always patient, unalarming; successful, appreciative, sincere.

6

I met Dennis in the Toronto Reference Library and he asked me out to dinner.

Dennis is a friend of X's, who came to visit us in Australia. He is a tall, slight, stiff, and brightly smiling young man — not so young either, he must be thirty-five — who has an elaborately courteous and didactic style.

I go to meet him thinking he may have a message for me. Isn't it odd, otherwise, that he would want to have dinner with an older woman he has met only once before? I think he may tell me whether X is back in Canada. X told me that they would probably come back in July. Then he was going to spend a year writing his book. They might live in Nova Scotia during that year. They might live in Ontario.

When Dennis came to see us in Australia, I made a curry. I was pleased with the idea of having a guest and glad that he arrived in time to see the brief evening light on the gully. Our house like the others was built out on posts, and from the window where we ate we looked out over a gully like an oval bowl, ringed with small houses and filled with jacaranda, poinciana, frangipani, cypress, and palm trees. Leaves like fans, whips, feathers, plates; every bright, light, dark, dusty, glossy shade of green. Guinea fowl lived down there, and flocks of rackety kookaburras took to the sky at dusk. We had to scramble down a steep dirt bank under the house to get to the wash-hut, and peg the clothes on a revolving clothesline. There we encountered spider-webs draped like tent-tops, matched like lids and basins with one above and one below. We had to watch out for the one little spider that weaves a conical web and has a poison for which there is no antidote.

We showed Dennis the gully and told him this was a typical old Queensland house with the high tongue-and-groove walls and the ventilation panels over the doors filled with graceful carved vines. He did not look at anything with much interest, but talked about China, where he had just been. X said afterwards that Dennis always talked about the last place he'd been and the last people he'd seen, and never seemed to notice anything, but that he would probably be talking about us, and describing this place, to the next people he had dinner with, in the next city. He said that Dennis spent most of his life travelling, and talking about it, and that he knew a lot of people just well enough that when he showed up somewhere he had to be asked to dinner.

Dennis told us that he had seen the recently excavated Army Camp at Sian, in China. He described the rows of life-sized soldiers, each of them so realistic and unique, some still bearing traces of the paint which had once covered them and individualized them still further. Away at their backs, he said, was a wall of earth. The terra-cotta soldiers looked as if they were marching out of the earth.

He said it reminded him of X's women. Row on row and always a new one appearing at the end of the line.

"The Army marches on," he said.

"Dennis, for God's sake," said X.

"But do they really come out of the earth like that?" I said to Dennis. "Are they intact?"

"Are which intact?" said Dennis with his harsh smile. "The soldiers or the women? The women aren't intact. Or not for long."

"Could we get off the subject?" said X.

"Certainly. Now to answer your question," said Dennis, turning to me. "They are very seldom found as whole figures. Or so I understand. Their legs and torsos and heads have to be matched up, usually. They have to be put together and stood on their feet."

"It's a lot of work, I can tell you," said X, with a large sigh.

"But it's not that way with the women," I said to Dennis. I spoke with a special, social charm, almost flirtatiously, as I often do when I detect malice. "I think the comparison's a bit off. Nobody has to dig the women out and stand them on their feet. Nobody put them there. They came along and joined up of their own free will and some day they'll leave. They're not a standing army. Most of them are probably on their way to someplace else anyway."

"Bravo," said X.

When we were washing the dishes, late at night, he said, "You didn't mind Dennis saying that, did you? You didn't mind if I went along with him a little bit? He has to have his legends."

I laid my head against his back, between the shoulder blades.

"Does he? No. I thought it was funny."

"I bet you didn't know that soap was first described by Pliny and was used by the Gauls. I bet you didn't know they boiled goat's tallow with the lye from the wood ashes."

"No. I didn't know that."

7

Dennis hasn't said a word about X, or about Australia. I wouldn't have thought his asking me to dinner strange, if I had remembered him better. He asked me so he would have somebody to talk to. Since Australia, he has been to Iceland, and the Faeroe Islands. I ask him questions. I am interested, and surprised, even shocked, when necessary. I took trouble with my makeup and washed my hair. I hope that if he does see X, he will say that I was charming.

Besides his travels Dennis has his theories. He develops theories about art and literature, history, life.

"I have a new theory about the life of women. I used to feel it was so unfair the way things happened to them."

"What things?"

"The way they have to live, compared to men. Specifically with aging. Look at you. Think of the way your life would be, if you were a man. The choices you would have. I mean sexual choices. You could start all over. Men do. It's in all the novels and it's in life too. Men fall in love with younger women. Men want younger women. Men can get younger women. The new marriage, new babies, new families."

I wonder if he is going to tell me something about X's wife; perhaps that she is going to have a baby.

"It's such a coup for them, isn't it?" he says in his malicious, sympathetic way. "The fresh young wife, the new baby when other men their age are starting on grandchildren. All those men envying them and trying to figure out how to do the same. It's the style, isn't it? It must be hard to resist starting over and having that nice young mirror to look in, if you get the opportunity."

"I think I might resist it," I say cheerfully, not insistently. "I don't really think I'd want to have a baby, now."

"That's it, that's just it, though, you don't get the opportunity! You're a woman and life only goes in one direction for a woman. All this business about younger lovers, that's just froth, isn't it? Do you want a younger lover?"

"I guess not," I say, and pick my dessert from a tray. I pick a rich creamy pudding with pureed chestnuts at the bottom of it and fresh raspberries on top. I purposely ate a light dinner, leaving plenty of room for dessert. I did that so I could have something to look forward to, while listening to Dennis.

"A woman your age can't compete," says Dennis urgently. "You can't compete with younger women. I used to think that was so rottenly unfair."

"It's probably biologically correct for men to go after younger women. There's no use whining about it."

"So the men have this way of renewing themselves, they get

this refill of vitality, while the women are you might say removed from life. I used to think that was terrible. But now my thinking has undergone a complete reversal. Do you know what I think now? I think women are the lucky ones! Do you know why?"

"Why?"

"Because they are forced to live in the world of loss and death! Oh, I know, there's face-lifting, but how does that really help? The uterus dries up. The vagina dries up."

I feel him watching me. I continue eating my pudding.

"I've seen so many parts of the world and so many strange things and so much suffering. It's my conclusion now that you won't get any happiness by playing tricks on life. It's only by natural renunciation and by accepting deprivation, that we prepare for death and therefore that we get any happiness. Maybe my ideas seem strange to you?"

I can't think of anything to say.

8

Often I have a few lines of a poem going through my head, and I won't know what started it. It can be a poem or rhyme that I didn't even know I knew, and it needn't be anything that conforms to what I think is my taste. Sometimes I don't pay any attention to it, but if I do, I can usually see that the poem, or the bit of it I've got hold of, has some relation to what is going on in my life. And that may not be what seems to be going on.

For instance last spring, last autumn in Australia, when I was happy, the line that would go through my head, at a merry clip, was this:

"Even such is time, that takes in trust —"

I could not go on, though I knew trust rhymed with dust, and that there was something further along about "and in the dark and silent grave, shuts up the story of our days." I knew the poem was written by Sir Walter Raleigh on the eve of his execution. My mood did not accord with such a poem and I said it, in my head, as if it was something pretty and lighthearted. I did not stop to wonder what it was doing in my head in the first place.

And now that I'm trying to look at things soberly I should

remember what we said when our bags were packed and we were waiting for the taxi. Inside the bags our clothes that had shared drawers and closet space, tumbled together in the wash, and been pegged together on the clothesline where the kookaburras sat, were all sorted and separated and would not rub together any more.

"In a way I'm glad it's over and nothing spoiled it. Things are so often spoiled."

"I know."

"As it is, it's been perfect."

I said that. And that was a lie. I had cried once, thought I was ugly, thought he was bored.

But he said, "Perfect."

On the plane the words of the poem were going through my head again, and I was still happy. I went to sleep thinking the bulk of X was still beside me and when I woke I filled the space quickly with memories of his voice, looks, warmth, our scenes together.

I was swimming in memories, at first. Those detailed, repetitive scenes were what buoyed me up. I didn't try to escape them, didn't wish to. Later I did wish to. They had become a plague. All they did was stir up desire, and longing, and hopelessness, a trio of miserable caged wildcats that had been installed in me without my permission, or at least without my understanding how long they would live and how vicious they would be. The images, the language, of pornography and romance are alike; monotonous and mechanically seductive, quickly leading to despair. That was what my mind dealt in; that is what it still can deal in. I have tried vigilance and reading serious books but I can still slide deep into some scene before I know where I am.

On the bed a woman lies in a yellow nightgown which has not been torn but has been pulled off her shoulders and twisted up around her waist so that it covers no more of her than a crumpled scarf would. A man bends over her, naked, offering a drink of water. The woman, who has almost lost consciousness, whose legs are open, arms flung out, head twisted to the side as if she has been struck down in the course of some natural disaster — this woman rouses herself and tries to hold the glass in her shaky hands. She slops water over her breast, drinks, shudders, falls back. The man's hands are trembling, too. He drinks out of the same glass, looks at her, and laughs. His laugh is rueful, apologetic, and kind, but it is also amazed, and his amazement is not far from horror. How are we capable of all this? his laugh says, what is the meaning of it?

He says, "We almost finished each other off."

The room seems still full of echoes of the recent commotion, the cries, pleas, brutal promises, the climactic sharp announcements and the long subsiding spasms.

The room is brimming with gratitude and pleasure, a rich broth of love, a golden twilight of love. Yes, yes, you can drink the air.

You see the sort of thing I mean, that is my torment.

9

This is the time of year when women are tired of sundresses, prints, sandals. It is already fall in the stores. Thick sweaters and skirts are pinned up against black or plum-colored velvet. The young salesgirls are made up like courtesans. I've become feverishly preoccupied with clothes. All the conversations in the stores make sense to me.

"The neckline doesn't work. It's too stark. I need a flutter. Do you know what I mean?"

"Yes. I know what you mean."

"I want something very classy and very provocative. Do you know what I mean?"

"Yes. I know exactly what you mean."

For years I've been wearing bleached-out colors which I suddenly can't bear. I buy a deep-red satin blouse, a purple shawl, a dark-blue skirt. I get my hair cut and pluck my eyebrows and try a lilac lipstick, a brownish rouge. I'm appalled to think of the way I went around in Australia, in a faded wraparound cotton skirt and T-shirt, my legs bare because of the heat, my face bare too and sweating under a cotton hat. My legs with the lumps of veins showing. I'm half convinced that a more artful getup would have made a more powerful impression, more dramatic clothes might have made me less discardable. I have fancies of meeting X unexpectedly at a party or on a Toronto street, and giving him a shock, devastating him with my altered looks and late-blooming splendor. But I do think you have to watch out, even in these garish times; you have to watch out for the point at which the splendor collapses into absurdity. Maybe they are all watching out, all the old women I see on Queen Street: the fat woman with pink hair; the eighty-year-old with painted-on black eyebrows; they may all be thinking they haven't gone too far yet, not quite yet. Even the buttercup woman I saw a few days ago on the streetcar, the little, stout, sixtyish woman in a frilly yellow dress well above the knees, a straw hat with yellow ribbons, yellow pumps dyed-to-match on her little fat feet—even she doesn't aim for comedy. She sees a flower in the mirror: the generous petals, the lovely buttery light.

I go looking for earrings. All day looking for earrings which I can see so clearly in my mind. I want little filigree balls of silver, of diminishing size, dangling. I want old and slightly tarnished silver. It's a style I well remember; you'd think the secondhand stores would be sure to have them. But I can't find them, I can't find anything resembling them, and they seem more and more necessary. I go into a little shop on a side street near College and Spadina. The shop is all done up in black paper with cheap, spooky effects—for instance a bald, naked mannequin sitting on a stepladder, dangling some beads. A dress such as I wore in the fifties, a dance dress of pink net and sequins, terribly scratchy under the arms, is displayed against the black paper in a way that makes it look sinister, and desirable.

I look around for the tray of jewelry. The salesgirls are busy dressing a customer hidden from me by a three-way mirror. One salesgirl is fat and gypsyish with a face warmly colored as an apricot. The other is spiky and has a crest of white hair surrounded by black hair, like a skunk. They are shrieking with pleasure as they bring hats and beads for the customer to try. Finally everybody is satisfied and a beautiful young lady, who is not a young lady at all but a pretty boy dressed up as a lady, emerges from the shelter of the mirror. He is wearing a black velvet dress with long sleeves and a black lace yoke; black pumps and gloves; a little black hat with a dotted veil. He is daintily and discreetly made up; he has a fringe of brown curls; he is the prettiest and most ladylike person I have seen all day. His smiling face is tense and tremulous. I remember how when I was ten or eleven years old I used to dress up as a bride in old curtains, or as a lady in rouge and a feathered hat. After all the effort and contriving and my own enchantment with the finished product there was a considerable letdown. What are you supposed to do now? Parade up and down on the sidewalk? There is a great fear and daring and disappointment in this kind of display.

He has a boyish, cracking voice. He is brash and timid.

"How do I look, momma?"

"You look very nice."

10

I am at a low point. I can recognize it. That must mean I will get past it.

I am at a low point, certainly. I cannot deal with all that assails me unless I get help and there is only one person I want help from and that is X. I can't continue to move my body along the streets unless I exist in his mind and in his eyes. People have this problem frequently, and we know it is their own fault and they have to change their way of thinking, that's all. It is not an honorable problem. Love is not serious though it may be fatal. I read that somewhere and I believe it. Thank God I don't know where he is. I can't telephone him, write letters to him, waylay him on the street.

A man I had broken with used to follow me. Finally he persuaded me to go into a café and have a cup of tea with him.

"I know what a spectacle I am," he said. "I know if you did have any love left for me this would destroy it."

I said nothing.

He beat the spoon against the sugar bowl.

"What do you think of, when you're with me?"

I meant to say, "I don't know," but instead I said, "I think of how much I want to get away."

He reared up trembling and dropped the spoon on the floor.

"You're free of me," he said in a choking voice.

This is the scene both comic and horrible, stagy and real. He was in desperate need, as I am now, and I didn't pity him, and I'm not sorry I didn't.

11

I have had a pleasant dream that seems far away from my waking state. X and I and some other people I didn't know or can't remember were wearing innocent athletic underwear outfits, which changed at some point into gauzy bright white clothes, and these turned out to be not just clothes but our substances, our flesh and bones and in a sense our souls. Embraces took place which started out with the usual urgency but were transformed, by the lightness and sweetness of our substance, into a rare state of content. I can't describe it very well, it sounds like a movie-dream of heaven, all banality and innocence. So I suppose it was. I can't apologize for the banality of my dreams.

12

I go along the street to Rooneem's Bakery and sit at one of their little tables with a cup of coffee. Rooneem's is an Estonian bakery where you can usually find a Mediterranean housewife in a black dress, a child looking at the cakes, and a man talking to himself.

I sit where I can watch the street. I have a feeling X is somewhere in the vicinity. Within a thousand miles, say, within a hundred miles, within this city. He doesn't know my address but he knows I am in Toronto. It would not be so difficult to find me.

At the same time I'm thinking that I have to let go. What you have to decide, really, is whether to be crazy or not, and I haven't the stamina, the pure, seething will, for prolonged craziness.

There is a limit to the amount of misery and disarray you will put up with, for love, just as there is a limit to the amount of mess you can stand around a house. You can't know the limit beforehand, but you will know when you've reached it. I believe this.

When you start really letting go this is what it's like. A lick of pain, furtive, darting up where you don't expect it. Then a lightness. The lightness is something to think about. It isn't just relief. There's a queer kind of pleasure in it, not a self-wounding or malicious pleasure, nothing personal at all. It's an uncalled-for pleasure in seeing how the design wouldn't fit and the structure wouldn't stand, a pleasure in taking into account, all over again, everything that is contradictory and persistent and unaccommodating about life. I think so. I think there's something in us wanting to be reassured about all that, right alongside — and at war with — whatever there is that wants permanent vistas and a lot of fine talk.

I think about my white dream and how it seemed misplaced. It strikes me that misplacement is the clue, in love, the heart of the problem, but like somebody drunk or high I can't quite get a grasp on what I see.

What I need is a rest. A deliberate sort of rest, with new definitions of luck. Not the sort of luck Dennis was talking about. You're lucky to be sitting in Rooneem's drinking coffee, with people coming and going, eating and drinking, buying cakes, speaking Spanish, Portuguese, Chinese, and other languages that you can try to identify.

13

Kay is back from the country. She too has a new outfit, a dark-green schoolgirl's tunic worn without a blouse or brassiere. She has dark-green knee socks and saddle oxfords.

"Does it look kinky?"

"Yes it does."

"Does it make my arms look dusky? Remember in some old poem a woman had dusky arms?"

Her arms do look soft and brown.

"I meant to get down on Sunday but Roy came over with a friend and we all had a corn roast. It was lovely. You should come out there. You should."

"Some day I will."

"The kids ran around like beautiful demons and we drank up the mead. Roy knows how to make fertility dolls. Roy's friend is Alex Walther, the anthropologist. I felt I should have known about him but I didn't. He didn't mind. He's a nice man. Do you know what he did? After dark when we were sitting around the fire he came over to me and just sighed, and laid his head on my lap. I thought it was such a nice simple thing to do. Like a St. Bernard. I've never had anybody do that before."

Prue

Prue used to live with Gordon. This was after Gordon had left his wife and before he went back to her — a year and four months in all. Some time later, he and his wife were divorced. After that came a period of indecision, of living together off and on; then the wife went away to New Zealand, most likely for good.

Prue did not go back to Vancouver Island, where Gordon had met her when she was working as a dining-room hostess in a resort hotel. She got a job in Toronto, working in a plant shop. She had many friends in Toronto by that time, most of them Gordon's friends and his wife's friends. They liked Prue and were ready to feel sorry for her, but she laughed them out of it. She is very likable. She has what eastern Canadians call an English accent, though she was born in Canada — in Duncan, on Vancouver Island. This accent helps her to say the most cynical things in a winning and lighthearted way. She presents her life in anecdotes, and though it is the point of most of her anecdotes that hopes are dashed, dreams ridiculed, things never turn out as expected, everything is altered in a bizarre way and there is no explanation ever, people always feel cheered up after listening to her; they say of her that it is a relief to meet somebody who doesn't take herself too seriously, who is so unintense, and civilized, and never makes any real demands or complaints.

The only thing she complains about readily is her name. Prue is a schoolgirl, she says, and Prudence is an old virgin; the parents who gave her that name must have been too shortsighted even to take account of puberty. What if she had grown a great bosom, she says, or developed a sultry look? Or was the name itself a guarantee that she wouldn't? In her late forties now, slight and fair, attending to customers with a dutiful vivacity, giving pleasure to dinner guests, she might not be far from what those parents had in mind: bright and thoughtful, a cheerful spectator. It is hard to grant her maturity, maternity, real troubles.

Her grownup children, the products of an early Vancouver Island marriage she calls a cosmic disaster, come to see her, and instead of wanting money, like other people's children, they bring presents, try to do her accounts, arrange to have her house insulated. She is delighted with their presents, listens to their advice, and, like a flighty daughter, neglects to answer their letters.

Her children hope she is not staying on in Toronto because of Gordon. Everybody hopes that. She would laugh at the idea. She gives parties and goes to parties; she goes out sometimes with other men. Her attitude toward sex is very comforting to those of her friends who get into terrible states of passion and jealousy, and feel cut loose from their moorings. She seems to regard sex as a wholesome, slightly silly indulgence, like dancing and nice dinners—something that shouldn't interfere with people's being kind and cheerful to each other.

Now that his wife is gone for good, Gordon comes to see Prue occasionally, and sometimes asks her out for dinner. They may not go to a restaurant; they may go to his house. Gordon is a good cook. When Prue or his wife lived with him he couldn't cook at all, but as soon as he put his mind to it he became—he says truthfully —better than either of them.

Recently he and Prue were having dinner at his house. He had made Chicken Kiev, and crème brûlée for dessert. Like most new, serious cooks, he talked about food.

Gordon is rich, by Prue's—and most people's—standards. He is a neurologist. His house is new, built on a hillside north of the city, where there used to be picturesque, unprofitable farms. Now there are one-of-a-kind, architect-designed, very expensive houses on half-acre lots. Prue, describing Gordon's house, will say, "Do you know there are four bathrooms? So that if four people want to have baths at the same time there's no problem. It seems a bit much, but it's very nice, really, and you'd never have to go through the hall."

Gordon's house has a raised dining area — a sort of platform, surrounded by a conversation pit, a music pit, and a bank of heavy greenery under sloping glass. You can't see the entrance area from the dining area, but there are no intervening walls, so that from one area you can hear something of what is going on in the other.

During dinner the doorbell rang. Gordon excused himself and went down the steps. Prue heard a female voice. The person it belonged to was still outside, so she could not hear the words. She heard Gordon's voice, pitched low, cautioning. The door didn't close — it seemed the person had not been invited in — but the voices went on, muted and angry. Suddenly there was a cry from Gordon, and he appeared halfway up the steps, waving his arms.

"The crème brûlée," he said. "Could you?" He ran back down as Prue got up and went into the kitchen to save the dessert. When she returned he was climbing the stairs more slowly, looking both agitated and tired.

"A friend," he said gloomily. "Was it all right?"

Prue realized he was speaking of the crème brûlée, and she said yes, it was perfect, she had got it just in time. He thanked her but did not cheer up. It seemed it was not the dessert he was troubled over but whatever had happened at the door. To take his mind off it, Prue started asking him professional questions about the plants.

"I don't know a thing about them," he said. "You know that."

"I thought you might have picked it up. Like the cooking."

"She takes care of them."

"Mrs. Carr?" said Prue, naming his housekeeper.

"Who did you think?"

Prue blushed. She hated to be thought suspicious.

"The problem is that I think I would like to marry you," said

Gordon, with no noticeable lightening of his spirits. Gordon is a large man, with heavy features. He likes to wear thick clothing, bulky sweaters. His blue eyes are often bloodshot, and their expression indicates that there is a helpless, baffled soul squirming around inside this doughty fortress.

"What a problem," said Prue lightly, though she knew Gordon well enough to know that it was.

The doorbell rang again, rang twice, three times, before Gordon could get to it. This time there was a crash, as of something flung and landing hard. The door slammed and Gordon was immediately back in view. He staggered on the steps and held his hand to his head, meanwhile making a gesture with the other hand to signify that nothing serious had happened, Prue was to sit down.

"Bloody overnight bag," he said. "She threw it at me."

"Did it hit you?"

"Glancing."

"It made a hard sound for an overnight bag. Were there rocks in it?"

"Probably cans. Her deodorant and so forth."

"Oh."

Prue watched him pour himself a drink. "I'd like some coffee, if I might," she said. She went to the kitchen to put the water on, and Gordon followed her.

"I think I'm in love with this person," he said.

"Who is she?"

"You don't know her. She's quite young."

"Oh."

"But I do think I want to marry you, in a few years' time."

"After you get over being in love?"

"Yes."

"Well. I guess nobody knows what can happen in a few years' time."

When Prue tells about this, she says, "I think he was afraid I was going to laugh. He doesn't know why people laugh or throw their overnight bags at him, but he's noticed they do. He's such a proper person, really. The lovely dinner. Then she comes and throws her overnight bag. And it's quite reasonable to think of marrying me in a few years' time, when he gets over being in love. I think he first thought of telling me to sort of put my mind at rest."

She doesn't mention that the next morning she picked up one of Gordon's cufflinks from his dresser. The cufflinks are made of amber and he bought them in Russia, on the holiday he and wife took when they got back together again. They look like squares of candy, golden, translucent, and this one warms quickly in her hand. She drops it into the pocket of her jacket. Taking one is not a real theft. It could be a reminder, an intimate prank, a piece of nonsense.

She is alone in Gordon's house; he has gone off early, as he always does. The housekeeper does not come till nine. Prue doesn't have to be at the shop until ten; she could make herself breakfast, stay and have coffee with the housekeeper, who is her friend from olden times. But once she has the cufflink in her pocket she doesn't linger. The house seems too bleak a place to spend an extra moment in. It was Prue, actually, who helped choose the building lot. But she's not responsible for approving the plans — the wife was back by that time.

When she gets home she puts the cufflink in an old tobacco tin. The children bought this tobacco tin in a junk shop years ago, and gave it to her for a present. She used to smoke, in those days, and the children were worried about her, so they gave her this tin full of toffees, jelly beans, and gumdrops, with a note saying, "Please get fat instead." That was for her birthday. Now the tin has in it several things besides the cufflink—all small things, not of great value but not worthless, either. A little enamelled dish, a sterling-silver spoon for salt, a crystal fish. These are not sentimental keepsakes. She never looks at them, and often forgets what she has there. They are not booty, they don't have ritualistic significance. She does not take something every time she goes to Gordon's house, or every time she stays over, or to mark what she might call memorable visits. She doesn't do it in a daze and she doesn't seem to be under a compulsion. She just takes something, every now and then, and puts it away in the dark of the old tobacco tin, and more or less forgets about it.

Labor Day Dinner

Just before six o'clock in the evening, George and Roberta and Angela and Eva get out of George's pickup truck — he traded his car for a pickup when he moved to the country — and walk across Valerie's front yard, under the shade of two aloof and splendid elm trees that have been expensively preserved. Valerie says those trees cost her a trip to Europe. The grass underneath them has been kept green all summer, and is bordered by fiery dahlias. The house is of pale-red brick, and around the doors and windows there is a decorative outline of lighter-colored bricks, originally white. This style is often found in Grey County; perhaps it was a specialty of one of the early builders.

George is carrying the folding lawn chairs Valerie asked them to bring. Roberta is carrying a dessert, a raspberry bombe made from raspberries picked on their own farm — George's farm — earlier in the summer. She has packed it in ice cubes and wrapped it in dish towels, but she is eager to get it into the freezer. Angela and Eva carry bottles of wine. Angela and Eva are Roberta's daughters. It has been arranged between Roberta and her husband that they spend the summers with her and George and the school year in Halifax with him. Roberta's husband is in the Navy. Angela is seventeen, Eva is twelve.

These four people are costumed in a way that would suggest they were going to different dinner parties. George, who is a stocky, dark, barrel-chested man, with a daunting, professional look of self-assurance and impatience (he used to be a teacher), wears a clean T-shirt and nondescript pants. Roberta is wearing faded tan cotton pants and a loose raw-silk top of mud-brick color — a color that suits her dark hair and pale skin well enough when she is at her best, but she is not at her best today. When she made herself up in the bathroom, she thought her skin looked like a piece of waxed paper that had been crumpled into a tight ball and then smoothed out. She was momentarily pleased with her thinness and had planned to wear a slinky silver halter top she owns — a glamorous joke — but at the last minute she changed her mind. She is wearing dark glasses, and the reason is that she has taken to weeping in spurts, never at the really bad times but in between; the spurts are as unbidden as sneezes.

As for Angela and Eva, they are dramatically arrayed in outfits contrived from a box of old curtains found in the upstairs of George's house. Angela wears emerald-green damask with long, sun-faded stripes, draped so as to leave one golden shoulder bare. She has cut vine leaves out of the same damask, pasted them on cardboard, and arranged them in her hair. Angela is tall and fair-haired, and embarrassed by her recently acquired beauty. She will go to great trouble to flaunt it, as she does now, and then will redden and frown and look stubbornly affronted when somebody tells her she looks like a goddess. Eva is wearing several fragile, yellowed lace curtains draped and bunched up, and held together with pins, ribbons, and nosegays of wild phlox already drooping and scattering. One of the curtains is pinned across her forehead and flows behind her, like a nineteen-twenties bridal veil. She has put her shorts on underneath, in case anybody should glimpse underpants through the veiling. Eva is puritanical, outrageous — an acrobat, a parodist, an optimist, a disturber. Her face, under the pinned veil, is lewdly painted with green eyeshadow and dark lipstick and rouge and mascara. The violent colors emphasize her childish look of recklessness and valor.

Angela and Eva have ridden here in the back of the truck,

stretched out on the lawn chairs. It is only three miles from George's place to Valerie's, but Roberta did not think riding like that was safe—she wanted them to get down and sit on the truck bed. To her surprise, George spoke up on their behalf, saying it would be ignominious for them to have to huddle down on the floor in their finery. He said he would drive slowly and avoid bumps; so he did. Roberta was a little nervous, but she was relieved to see him sympathetic and indulgent about the very things—self-dramatization, self-display—that she had expected would annoy him. She herself has given up wearing long skirts and caftans because of what he has said about disliking the sight of women trailing around in such garments, which announce to him, he says, not only a woman's intention of doing no serious work but her persistent wish to be admired and courted. This is a wish George has no patience with and has spent some energy, throughout his adult life, in thwarting.

Roberta thought that after speaking in such a friendly way to the girls, and helping them into the truck, he might speak to her when he got into the cab, might even take her hand, brushing away her undisclosed crimes, but it did not happen. Shut up together, driving over the hot gravel roads at an almost funereal pace, they are pinned down by a murderous silence. On the edge of it, Roberta feels herself curling up like a jaundiced leaf. She knows this to be a hysterical image. Also hysterical is the notion of screaming and opening the door and throwing herself on the gravel. She ought to make an effort not to be hysterical, not to exaggerate. But surely it is hatred—what else can it be?—that George is steadily manufacturing and wordlessly pouring out at her, and surely it is a deadly gas. She tries to break the silence herself, making little clucks of worry as she tightens the towels over the bombe and then sighing—a noisy imitation sigh meant to sound tired, pleased, and comfortable. They are driving between high stands of corn, and she thinks how ugly the corn looks—a monotonous, coarse-leaved crop, a foolish army. How long has this been going on? Since yesterday morning: she felt it in him before they got out of bed. They went out and got drunk last night to try to better things, but the relief didn't last.

Before they left for Valerie's Roberta was in the bedroom, fastening her halter top, and George came in and said, "Is that what you're wearing?"

"I thought I would, yes. Doesn't it look all right?"

"Your armpits are flabby."

"Are they? I'll put on something with sleeves."

In the truck, now that she knows he isn't going to make up, she lets herself hear him say that. A harsh satisfaction in his voice. The satisfaction of airing disgust. He is disgusted by her aging body. That could have been foreseen. She starts humming something, feeling the lightness, the freedom, the great tactical advantage of being the one to whom the wrong has been done, the bleak challenge offered, the unforgivable thing said.

But suppose he doesn't think it's unforgivable, suppose in his eyes she's the one who's unforgivable? She's always the one; disasters overtake her daily. It used to be that as soon as she noticed some deterioration she would seek strenuously to remedy it. Now the remedies bring more problems. She applies cream frantically to her wrinkles, and her face breaks out in spots, like a teen-ager's. Dieting until her waist was thin enough to please produced a haggard look about her cheeks and throat. Flabby armpits—how can you exercise the armpits? What is to be done? Now the payment is due, and what for? For vanity. Hardly even for that. Just for having those pleasing surfaces once, and letting them speak for you; just for allowing an arrangement of hair and shoulders and breasts to have its effect. You don't stop in time, don't know what to do instead; you lay yourself open to humiliation. So thinks Roberta, with self-pity—what she knows to be self-pity—rising and sloshing around in her like bitter bile.

She must get away, live alone, wear sleeves.

Valerie calls to them from a darkened window under the vines, "Go on in, go in. I'm just putting on my panty hose."

"Don't put on your panty hose!" cry George and Roberta together. You would think from the sound of their voices that all the way over here they had been engaged in tender and lively conversation.

"Don't put on your *panty* hose," wail Angela and Eva.
"Oh, all right, if there's all that much prejudice against panty
hose," says Valerie behind her window. "I won't even put on a
dress. I'll come as I am."

"Not that!" cries George, and staggers, holding the lawn
chairs up in front of his face.

But Valerie, appearing in the doorway, is dressed beautifully,
in a loose gown of green and gold and blue. She doesn't have to
worry about George's opinion of long dresses. She is absolved of
blame anyway, because you could never say that Valerie is looking
to be courted or admired. She is a tall, flat-chested woman, whose
long, plain face seems to be crackling with welcome, eager
understanding, with humor and intelligence and appreciation. Her
hair is thick, gray-black, and curly. This summer she recklessly cut
it off, so that all that is left is a curly crewcut, revealing her long,
corded neck and the creases at the edge of her cheeks, and her
large, flat ears.

"I think it makes me look like a goat," she has said. "I like
goats. I love their eyes. Wouldn't it be wonderful to have those
horizontal pupils. Bizarre!"

Her children tell her she is bizarre enough already.

Here come Valerie's children now, as George and Roberta and
Angela and Eva crowd into the hall, Roberta saying that she is
dripping ice and must get this pretentious concoction into the
freezer. First Ruth, who is twenty-five and nearly six feet tall and
looks a lot like her mother. She has given up wanting to be an
actress and is learning to teach disturbed children. Her arms are
full of goldenrod and Queen Anne's lace and dahlias — weeds and
flowers all mixed up together — and she throws them on the hall
floor with a theatrical gesture and embraces the bombe.

"Dessert," she says lovingly. "Oh, bliss! Angela, you look
incredibly lovely! Eva, too. I know who Eva is. She's the Bride of
Lammermoor!"

Angela will allow, even delight in, such open praise from
Ruth, because Ruth is the person she admires most in the world —
possibly the only person she admires.

"The Bride of who?" Eva is asking happily. "The Bride of
who?"

David, Valerie's twenty-one-year-old son, a history student, is standing in the living-room doorway, smiling tolerantly and affectionately at the excitement. David is tall and lean, dark-haired and dark-skinned, like his mother and sister, but he is deliberate, low-voiced, never rash. In this household of many delicate checks and balances it is noticeable that the lively, outspoken women defer to David in some ceremonial way, seeming to ask for the gesture of his protection, though protection itself is something they are not likely to need.

When the greetings die down David says, "This is Kimberly," and introduces them each in turn to the young woman standing under his arm. She is very clean and trim, in a white skirt and a short-sleeved pink shirt. She wears glasses and no makeup; her hair is short and straight and tidy, and a pleasant light-brown color. She shakes hands with each of them and looks each of them in the eye, through her glasses, and though her manner is entirely polite, even subdued, there is a slight feeling of an official person greeting the members of an unruly, outlandish delegation.

Valerie has known both George and Roberta for years. She knew them long before they knew each other. She and George were on the staff of the same Toronto high school. George was head of the art department; Valerie was school counsellor. She knew George's wife, a jittery, well-dressed women, who was killed in a plane crash in Florida. George and his wife were separated by that time.

And, of course, Valerie knew Roberta because Roberta's husband, Andrew, is her cousin. They never cared much for each other — Valerie and Roberta's husband — and each of them has described the other to Roberta as a stick. Andrew used to say that Valerie was a queer-looking stick and utterly sexless, and when Roberta told Valerie that she was leaving him Valerie said, "Oh, good. He is such a stick." Roberta was pleased to find such sympathy and pleased that she wouldn't have to dredge up acceptable reasons; apparently Valerie thought his being a stick was reason enough. At the same time Roberta had a wish to defend her husband and to inquire how on earth Valerie could presume to know whether he was a stick or wasn't. She can't get over wishing to defend him; she feels he had such bad luck marrying her.

When Roberta moved out and left Halifax, she came and stayed with Valerie in Toronto. There she met George, and he took her off to see his farm. Now Valerie says they are her creation, the result of her totally inadvertent matchmaking.

"It was the first time I ever saw love bloom at close quarters," she says. "It was like watching an amaryllis. Astounding."

But Roberta has the idea that, much as she likes them both and wishes them well, love is really something Valerie could do without being reminded of. In Valerie's company you do wonder sometimes what all the fuss is about. Valerie wonders. Her life and her presence, more than any opinion she expresses, remind you that love is not kind or honest and does not contribute to happiness in any reliable way.

When she talked to Roberta about George (this was before she knew Roberta was in love with him), Valerie said, "He's a mysterious man, really. I think he's very idealistic, though he'd hate to hear me say that. This farm he's bought. This self-sufficient, remote, productive life in the country." She went on to talk about how he had grown up in Timmins, the son of a Hungarian shoemaker, youngest of six children and the first to finish high school, let alone go to university. "He's the sort of person who would know what to do in a street fight but doesn't know how to swim. He brought his old crabby, bent-over father down to Toronto and took care of him till he died. I think he drops women rather hard."

Roberta listened to all this with great interest and a basic disregard, because what other people knew about George already seemed inessential to her. She was full of alarm and delight. Being in love was nothing she had counted on. The most she'd hoped for was a life like Valerie's. She had illustrated a couple of children's books and thought she could get more commissions; she could rent a room out in the Beaches, in East Toronto, paint the walls white, sit on cushions instead of chairs, and learn to be self-disciplined and self-indulgent, as she thought solitary people must be.

Valerie and Roberta walk through the house, carrying a bottle of cold wine and two of Valerie's grandmother's water goblets. Roberta thinks Valerie's house is exactly what people have in mind when they say longingly "a house in the country" or, more particularly, "an old brick farmhouse." The warm, pale-red brick with the light brick trim, the vines and elms, the sanded floors and hooked rugs and white walls, the chipped wash-jug set on a massive chest of drawers in front of a dim mirror. Of course, Valerie has had fifteen years to bring this about. She and her husband bought the house as a summer place, and then when he died she sold their city house and moved to an apartment and put her money and her energy into this. George bought his house and land two years ago, having been introduced to this part of the country by Valerie, and fourteen months ago he left his teaching job and moved up here for good. On the heels of that move came his first meeting with Roberta. Last December she came to live with him. She thought that it would take them about a year to get the place fixed up, and then George could get back to doing his sculpting. A sculptor is what he really wants to be. That is why he wanted to give up teaching and live cheaply in the country — raise a lot of vegetables, keep chickens. He hasn't started on the chickens yet.

Roberta meant to keep busy illustrating books. Why hasn't she done this? No time, nowhere to work: no room, no light, no table. No clear moments of authority, now that life has got this new kind of grip on her.

What they have done so far — what George has done, mostly, while Roberta sweeps and cooks — is put a new roof on the house, put in aluminum-frame windows, pour bag after bag of dusty pebble-like insulation into the space behind the walls, fit batts of yellow, woolly-looking fibre glass against the attic roof, clean all the stovepipes and replace some of them and re-brick part of the chimney, replace the rotting eaves. After all these essential and laborious repairs the house is still unattractive on the outside, with its dark-red imitation-brick covering and its sagging porch heaped with drying new lumber and salvaged old lumber and extra batts of fibre glass and other useful debris. And it is dark and sour-smelling within. Roberta would like to rip up the linoleum and tear down the dismal wallpaper, but everything must be done in order, and George has figured out the order; it is no use ripping up and tearing down until the wiring and insulating have been finished and the shell of the house reconstructed. Lately he has been saying that before he starts on the inside of the house or puts the siding on the outside he must do a major job on the barn; if he doesn't get the beam structure propped and strengthened the whole building may come down in next winter's storms.

As well as this there is the garden: the apple and cherry trees, which have been pruned; the raspberry canes, which have been cleaned out; the lawn, which has been reseeded, reclaimed from patches of long wild grass and patches of bare ground and rubble under the shade of some ragged pines. At first Roberta kept an idea of the whole place in her mind — all the things that had been done, that were being done, and that were yet to do. Now she doesn't think of the work that way — she has no general picture of it — but stays in the kitchen and does jobs as they arise. Dealing with the produce of the garden — making chili sauce, preparing tomatoes and peppers and beans and corn for the freezer, making tomato juice, making cherry jam — has taken up a lot of her time. Sometimes she looks into the freezer and wonders who will eat all this — George and who else? She can feel her own claims shrinking.

The table is laid on the long screened verandah at the back of the house. Valerie and Roberta go out a door at the end of the verandah, down some shallow steps, and into a little brick-walled, brick-paved area that Valerie has had made this summer but does not like to call a patio. She says you can't have a patio on a farmhouse. She hasn't decided yet what she does like to call it. She hasn't decided, either, whether to get heavy wooden lawn chairs, which she likes the look of, or comfortable lightweight metal-and-plastic chairs, like those which George and Roberta brought.

They pour the wine and lift their glasses, the capacious old water goblets they love to drink wine from. They can hear Ruth and Eva and Angela laughing in Ruth's bedroom. Ruth has said they must help her get into costume, too — she is going to think of something that will outdo them all. And they can hear the swish of George's scythe, which he has brought to cut the long grass and burdocks around Valerie's little stone dairy house.

"The dairy house would make a lovely studio," Valerie says. "I should rent it to an artist. George? You? I'd rent it for the scything and a raspberry bombe. George is going to make a studio in the barn, though, isn't he?"

"Eventually," says Roberta. At present all George's work is in the front of the house, in the old parlor. Some half-finished and nearly finished pieces are there, covered up with dusty sheets, and also some blocks of wood (George works only in wood)—a big chunk of seasoned oak and pieces of kiln-dried butternut and cherry. His ripsaw, his chisels and gouges, his linseed oil and turpentine and beeswax and resins are all there, the lids dusty and screwed tight. Eva and Angela used to go around and, standing on tiptoe in the rubble and weeds, peer in the front window at the shrouded shapes.

"Ugh, they look spooky," Eva said to George. "What are they underneath?"

"Wooden doughnuts," George said. "Pop sculpt."

"Really?"

"A potato and a two-headed baby."

Next time they went to look they found a sheet tacked up over the window. This was a grayish-colored sheet, torn at the top. To anybody driving by it made the house look even more bleak and neglected.

"Do you know I had cigarettes all the time?" Valerie says. "I have half a carton. I hid them in the cupboard in my room."

She has sent David and Kimberly into town, telling them she's out of cigarettes. Valerie can't stop smoking, though she takes vitamin pills and is careful not to eat anything with red food coloring in it. "I couldn't think of anything else to say I was out of, and I had to have them clear off for a while. Now I don't dare smoke one or they'll smell it when they get back and know I was a liar. And I want one."

"Drink instead," says Roberta. When she got here she thought she couldn't talk to anybody—she was going to say her head ached and ask if she could lie down. But Valerie steadies her, as always. Valerie makes what isn't bearable interesting.

"So how are you?" Valerie says.

"Ohhh," says Roberta.

"Life would be grand if it weren't for the people," says Valerie moodily. "That sounds like a quotation, but I think I just made it up. The problem is that Kimberly is a Christian. Well, that's fine. We could use a Christian or two. For that matter, I am not an un-Christian. But she is very noticeably a Christian, don't you think? I'm amazed how mean she makes me feel."

George is enjoying the scything. For one thing, he likes working without spectators. Whenever he works at home these days, he is aware of a crowd of female spectators. Even if they're nowhere in sight, he feels as if they're watching — taking their ease, regarding his labors with mystification and amusement. He admits, if he thinks about it, that Roberta does do some work, though she has done nothing to earn money as far as he knows; she hasn't been in touch with her publishers, and she hasn't worked on ideas of her own. She permits her daughters to do nothing all day long, all summer long. Yesterday morning he got up feeling tired and disheartened — he had gone to sleep thinking of the work he had to do on the barn, and this preoccupation had seeped into his dreams, which were full of collapses, miscalculations, structural treacheries — and he went out to the deck off the kitchen, thinking to eat his eggs there and brood about the day's jobs. This deck is the only thing he has built as yet, the only change he has made in the house. He built it last spring in response to Roberta's complaints about the darkness of the house and the bad ventilation. He told her that the people who built these houses did so much work in the sun that they never thought of sitting in it.

He came out on the deck, then, carrying his plate and mug, and all three of them were already there. Angela was dressed in a sapphire-blue leotard; she was doing ballet exercises by the deck railing. Eva was sitting with her back against the wall of the house, spooning up bran flakes out of a soup bowl; she did this with such enthusiasm that many were spilled on the deck floor. Roberta, in a deck chair, had the everlasting mug of coffee clasped in both hands. She had one knee up and her back hunched, and with her dark glasses on she looked tense and mournful. He knows she weeps behind those glasses. It seems to him that she has let the children draw the sap right out of her body. She spends her time placating them, picking up after them; she has to beg them to make their beds and clean up their rooms; he has heard her pleading with them to collect their dirty dishes, so that she can wash them. Or that is what it sounds like to him. Is this the middle-class fashion of bringing up children? Here she was admiring Angela, meekly admiring her own daughter — the naked, lifted, golden leg, the disdainful profile. If either of his sisters had ventured on such a display, his mother would have belted them.

Angela lowered her leg and said, "Greetings, Master!"

"I don't see you bumping your head on the ground," said George. He usually joked with the girls no matter what he felt like. Rough joking was his habit, and it had been hugely successful in the classroom, where he had maintained a somewhat overdrawn, occasionally brutal, consistently entertaining character. He had done this with most of the other teachers as well, expressing his contempt for them so colorfully that they could not believe he meant it.

Eva loved to act out any suggestion of this sort. She stretched herself full length on the deck and knocked her head hard on the boards.

"You'll get a concussion," Roberta said.

"No, I won't. I'll just give myself a lobotomy."

"George, do you realize that in four brief days we will be gone?" said Angela. "Isn't your heart broken?"

"In twain."

"But will you let Mom take care of Diana when we're gone?" said Eva, sitting upright and feeling her head for bruises. Diana was a stray cat she was feeding in the barn.

"What do you mean, *let*?" said Roberta, and George at the same time said, "Certainly not. I'll tie her to the bedpost if she ever tries to go near the barn."

This cat is a sore point. If Angela sees the farm as a stage for herself, or sometimes as Nature — a begetter of thoughts and poems, to which she yields herself, wandering and dreaming — Eva sees it as a place to look for animals, with some of her attention left over for insects, minnows, rocks, and slugs. Both of them see it, certainly, as vacationland, spread out before them for whatever use or pleasure they can get out of it; neither sees the jobs waiting to be done under their noses. Eva has spent the summer stalking groundhogs and rabbits, trapping frogs and letting them go, catching minnows in a jar, trying to figure out how various animals could be housed in the barn. George holds her responsible — out of the very strength of her desire — for luring the deer out of the bush, so that he had to stop everything else that he was doing and build an eight-foot-high wire fence around the garden. The only animal she has managed to install in the barn is Diana, rail-thin, ugly, and half wild, whose dangling teats show that she is maintaining a family of kittens elsewhere. Much of Eva's time has been spent trying to discover the whereabouts of these kittens.

George sees the cat as a freeloader, a potential great nuisance, an invader of his property. By feeding it and encouraging it, Eva has embarked on a course of minor but significant treachery, which Roberta has implicitly supported. He knows his feelings on this matter are exaggerated, even comical; that does not help him. One of the things he has never wanted to be, and has avoided being, is a comic dad, a fulminator, a bungler. But it is Roberta's behavior that bothers him, more than Eva's. Here Roberta shows most plainly the mistake she has made in bringing up her children. In his mind he can hear Roberta talking to somebody at a party. "Eva has adopted a horrible cat, a really nasty-looking vagabond — that's her summer achievement. And Angela spends the whole day doing jetés and sulking at us." He has not actually heard Roberta say this — they have not been to any parties — but he can well imagine it. She would summon her children up for the entertainment of others; she would make them into characters, from whom nothing serious was to be expected. This seems to George not only frivolous but heartless. Roberta, who is so indulgent with her children, who worries constantly that they may find her insufficiently loving, interested, understanding, is nevertheless depriving them. She is not taking them seriously; she is not bringing them up. And what is George to do in the face of this? They are not his children. One of the reasons he has not had children is that he doubts if he could give his attention unreservedly, and for as long as would be needed, to this very question of bringing them up. As a teacher, he knows how to make a lot of noise and keep several steps ahead of them, but it is exhausting to have to do that on the home front. And it was boys, chiefly, whom he learned to outmaneuver; boys were the threat in a class. The girls he never bothered much about, beyond some careful sparring with the sexy ones. That is not in order here.

Aside from all this, he often can't help liking Angela and Eva. They seem to him confused and appealing. They think him highly amusing, which irks him sometimes and pleases him at other times. His way with people is to be very reserved or very entertaining, and he believes that his preference is to be reserved. Therefore, he likes the entertainment to be appreciated.

But when he finished his breakfast and got two six-quart baskets and went down to the garden to pick the tomatoes, nobody stirred to help him. Roberta continued her moody thinking and her coffee drinking. Angela had finished her exercises and was writing in the notebook she uses for a journal. Eva had taken off for the barn.

Angela sits down at the piano in Valerie's living room. There is no piano in George's house, and she misses one. Doesn't her mother miss one? Her mother has become a person who doesn't ask for anything.

"I have seen her change," Angela has written in her journal, "from a person I deeply respected into a person on the verge of being a nervous wreck. If this is love I want no part of it. He wants to enslave her and us all and she walks a tightrope trying to keep him from getting mad. She doesn't enjoy anything and if you gave her the choice she would like best to lie down in a dark room with a cloth over her eyes and not see anybody or do anything. This is an intelligent woman who used to believe in freedom."

She starts to play the "Turkish March," which brings to her mind the picture of a house her parents sold when she was five. There was a little shelf up near the ceiling in the dining room, where her mother had set the dessert plates for decoration. A tree, or bush, in the yard had lettuce-colored leaves as big as plates.

She has written in her journal: "I know nostalgia is a futile emotion. Sometimes I feel like tearing out some things I have written where perhaps I have been too harsh in judging certain people or situations but I have decided to leave everything because I want to have a record of what I really felt at the time. I want to have a truthful record of my whole life. How to keep oneself from lying I see as the main problem everywhere."

During the summer Angela has spent a lot of time reading. She has read *Anna Karenina*, *The Second Sex*, *Emily of New Moon*, *The Norton Anthology of Poetry*, *The Autobiography of W. B. Yeats*, *The Happy Hooker*, *The Act of Creation*, *Seven Gothic Tales*. Some of these, to be accurate, she has not read all the way through. Her mother used to read all the time, too. Angela would come home from school at noon, and again in the afternoon, and find her mother reading. Her mother read about the conquest of Mexico, she read *The Tale of Genji*. Angela marvels at how safe her mother seemed then.

Angela has one picture in her mind of Eva before Eva was born. The three of them — Angela, her mother, and her father — are on a beach. Her father is scooping out a large hole in the sand. Her father is a gifted builder of sand castles with road and irrigation systems, so Angela watches with interest any projects he undertakes. But the hole has nothing to do with a sand castle. When it is finished her mother rolls over, giggling, and fits her stomach into it. In her stomach is Eva, and the hollow is like a spoon for an egg. The beach is wide, mile after mile of white sand sloping delicately into the blue-green water. No rocky lakefront or stingy bit of cove. A radiant, generous place. Where could it have been?

She proceeds from the "Turkish March" to a try at "Eine Kleine Nachtmusik." Roberta, listening to the piano at the same time she's listening to Valerie talking humorously and despairingly about her fear of Kimberly, her dislike of intruders, her indefensible reluctance to relinquish her children, thinks, No, it wasn't a mistake. What does she mean by that? She means it wasn't a mistake to leave her husband. Whatever happens, it wasn't a mistake. It was necessary. Otherwise she wouldn't have known.

"This is a bad time for you," Valerie says judiciously. "There is just a spectacular lot of strain."

"That's what I say to myself," says Roberta. "But sometimes I think that's not it. It's not the house, it's not the children. It's just something black that rises."

"Oh, there's always something black," says Valerie, grumbling.

"I think about Andrew — what was I doing to him? Setting things up to find the failure in him, railing at him, then getting cold feet and making up. Gradually the need to get rid of him would build again, but I was always sure it was his fault — if he'd just do this or that I could love him. So horrible for him that he turned into — remember what you said he was? A stick."

"He was a stick," says Valerie. "He always was. You're not responsible for everything."

"I think about it, because I wonder if that's what George is doing to me. He wants to be rid of me, then he doesn't, then he does, then he can't admit that, even to himself; he has to set up failures. I feel I know what Andrew went through. Not that I'd go back. Never. But I see it."

"I doubt if things happen so symmetrically."

"I don't think so, either, really. I don't think you get your punishment in such a simple way. Isn't it funny how you're attracted — I am — to the idea of a pattern like that? I mean, the idea is attractive, of there being that balance. But not the experience. I'd like to avoid them."

"You forget how happy you are when you're happy."

"And vice versa. It's like childbirth."

George has finished scything and is cleaning the blade. He can hear the piano through the open windows of Valerie's house, and erratic streams of sweet, cold air are coming up from the river. He feels much better now, either because of the simple exercise or from the relief of feeling unobserved; perhaps it's just good to get away from the mountainous demands of his own place. He wonders if it's Roberta playing. The music fits in nicely with what he's doing: first the cheerful, workaday "Turkish March," to go along with the scything; now, as he stands cleaning the blade and smelling the cut grass, the subtle congratulations — even if a bit uncertainly delivered — of "Eine Kleine Nachtmusik." As always, when his mood truly lifts, when the dawn breaks, he wants to go and find Roberta and envelop her, assure her — assure himself — that no real damage has been done. He hoped to be able to do that last night when they went drinking, but he couldn't; something still held him back.

He recalls Roberta's first visit to his house. That was in late August or early September, about a year ago now. They staged an indecorous sort of picnic, cooking feasts and playing records, hauling a mattress out into the yard. Clear nights, with Roberta pointing out to him the unlikely ways the stars tie up into their constellations, and every day pure gold. Roberta saying he must get it all straight now: she is forty-three years old, which is six years too old for him; she has left her husband because everything between them seemed artificial; but she hates saying that, because it may be just cant, she isn't sure what she means, and above all, she doesn't know what she's capable of. She seemed to him courageous, truthful, without vanity. How out of this could come such touchiness, tearfulness, weariness, such a threat of collapse he cannot imagine.

But the first impression is worth respecting, he thinks.

Eva and Ruth are decorating the dinner table on the verandah. Ruth is wearing a white shirt belonging to her brother, his striped pajama bottoms, and a monumental black turban. She looks like a proud but good-natured Sikh.

"I think the table ought to be strewn," says Ruth. "Subtlety is out, Eva."

At intervals they set orange and gold dahlias and beautifully striped pepper squash, zucchini, yellow gourds, Indian corn.

Under cover of the music Eva says, "Angela has more problems living here than I do. She thinks that whenever they fight it's about her."

"Do they fight?" says Ruth softly. Then she says, "It's none of my business." She was in love with George when she was thirteen or fourteen. It was when her mother first became friends with him. She used to hate his wife, and was glad when they separated. She remembers that the wife was the daughter of a gynecologist, and that this was cited by her mother as a reason George and his wife could never get on. It was probably the father's prosperity her mother was talking about, or the way the daughter had been brought up. But to Ruth the word "gynecologist" seemed sharp and appalling, and she saw the gynecologist's daughter dressed in an outfit of cold, jagged metal.

"They have silent fights. We can tell. Angela is so self-interested she thinks everything revolves around her. That's what happens when you become an adolescent. I don't want it to happen to me."

There is a pause in Angela's playing, and Eva says sharply, "Oh, I don't want to leave! I hate leaving."

"Do you?"

"I hate to leave Diana. I don't know what will happen to her. I don't know if I'll ever see her again. I don't think I'll ever see the deer again. I hate having to leave things."

Now that the piano is silent, Eva can be heard outside, where Valerie and Roberta are sitting. Roberta hears what Eva says, and waits, expecting to hear her say something about next summer. She braces herself to hear it.

Instead, Eva says, "You know, I understand George. I don't mind about him the way Angela does. I know how to be jokey. I understand him."

Roberta and Valerie look at each other, and Roberta smiles, shakes her head, and shivers. She has been afraid, sometimes, that George would hurt her children, not physically but by some turnabout, some revelation of dislike, that they could never forget. It seems to her that she has instructed them, by example, that he is to be accommodated, his silences respected, his joking responded to. What if he should turn, within this safety, and deal them a memorable blow? If it happened, it would be she who would have betrayed them into it. And she can feel a danger. For instance, when George was pruning the apple trees she heard Angela say, "My father's got an apple tree and a cherry tree now."

(That was information. Would he take it as competition?)

"I suppose he has some minions come and prune them for him?" George said.

"He has hundreds," said Angela cheerfully. "Dwarfs. He makes them all wear little Navy uniforms."

Angela was on thin ice at that moment. But Roberta thinks now that the real danger is not to Angela, who would find a way to welcome insult, would be ready to reap some advantage. (Roberta has read parts of the journal.) It is Eva, with her claims of understanding, her hopes of all-round conciliation, who could be smashed and stranded.

Over cold apple-and-watercress soup Eva has switched back to her *enfant terrible* style to tell the table, "They went out and got drunk last night. They were polluted."

David says he hasn't heard that expression in a long time.

Valerie says, "How awful for you little ones."

"We considered phoning the Children's Aid," says Angela, looking very unchildlike in the candlelight—looking like a queen, in fact—and aware that David is watching her, though with David it's hard to say whether he's watching with approval or with reservations. It seems as if it might be approval. Kimberly has taken over his reservations.

"Did you have a dissolute time?" said Valerie. "Roberta, you never told me. Where did you go?"

"It was highly respectable," says Roberta. "We went to the Queen's Hotel in Logan. To the Lounge—that's what they call it. The posh place to drink."

"George wouldn't take you out to any old beer parlor," says Ruth. "George is a closet conservative."

"It's true," says Valerie. "George believes you should take ladies only to nice places."

"And children should be seen and not heard," says Angela.

"Not seen, either," says George.

"Which is confusing to everyone, because he comes on like a raving radical," says Ruth.

"This is a treat," says George, "getting a free analysis. Actually, it was quite dissolute, and Roberta probably doesn't remember, on account of being so polluted, as Eva says. She bewitched a fellow who did toothpick tricks."

Roberta says it was a game where you made a word out of toothpicks, then took a toothpick away or rearranged what was there and made another word, and so on.

"I hope not dirty words?" says Eva.

"I never talked like that when I was her age," Angela says. "I was your pre-permissive child."

"And after we got tired of the game, or after he did, because I was tired of it quite soon, he showed me pictures of his wife and himself on their Mediterranean cruise. He was with another lady last night, because his wife is dead now, and if he forgot where the pictures were taken this lady reminded him. She said she didn't think he'd ever get over it."

"The cruise or his wife?" says Ruth, while George is saying that he had a conversation with a couple of Dutch farmers who wanted to take him for a ride in their plane.

"I don't think I went," George adds.

"I dissuaded you," says Roberta, not looking at him.

"'Dissuaded' sounds so lovely," says Ruth. "It's so smooth. I must be thinking of suède."

Eva asks what it means.

"Persuaded not to," says Roberta. "I persuaded George not to go for a plane ride at one o'clock in the morning with the rich Dutch farmers. Instead, we all had an adventure getting the man from the Mediterranean cruise into his car so his girlfriend could drive him home."

Ruth and Kimberly get up to remove the soup bowls, and David goes to put on a record of Dvořák's "New World" Symphony. This is his mother's request. David says it's syrupy.

They are quiet, waiting for the music to start. Eva says, "How did you guys fall in love anyway? Was it a physical attraction?"

Ruth knocks her gently on the head with a soup bowl. "You ought to have your jaws wired shut," she says. "Don't forget I'm learning how to cope with disturbed children."

"Didn't it bother you, Mom being so much older?"

"You see what I mean about her?" Angela says.

"What do you know about love?" says George grandly. "Love suffereth long, and is kind. Similar to myself in that respect. Love is not puffed up . . . "

"I think that is a particular kind of love," says Kimberly, setting down the vegetables. "If you're quoting."

Under cover of a conversation about translation and the meanings of words (a subject of which George knows little but about which he is soon making sweeping, provocative statements, true to his classroom technique), Roberta says to Valerie, "The man's girlfriend said that the wonderful thing was that his wife had done the whole Mediterranean cruise with a front-end loader."

"A what?"

"Front-end loader. I looked blank, too, so she said, 'You know, his wife had one of those operations and she had to wear one of those bag things.' "

"Oh, God help us."

"She had big fat arms and a sprayed blonde hairdo. The wife did, in the pictures. The girlfriend was something the same, but trimmer. The wife had such a lewd, happy look. A good-times look."

"And a front-end loader."

So you see against what odds, and with what unpromising-looking persons, love takes root and flourishes, and I myself have no front-end loader, merely some wrinkles and slackness and sallowness and subtle withering. This is what Roberta is saying to herself. It's not my fault, she says to herself, as she has said so often before. Usually when she says it it's a whine, a plea, a whimper. Now it says itself matter-of-factly in her head; the tone in which it is stated is bored and tired. It seems as if this could be the truth.

By dessert the conversation has shifted to architecture. The only light on the verandah is from the candles on the table. Ruth has taken the big candles away and set in front of each place a single small candle in a black metal holder with a handle, like the candle in the nursery rhyme. Valerie and Roberta say it together: " 'Here comes a candle to light you to bed. Here comes a chopper to chop off your head!'"

Neither of them taught that rhyme to her children, and their children have never heard it before.

"I've neard it," says Kimberly.

"The pointed arch, for instance — that was just a fad," George is saying. "It was an architectural fashion, very like fashions today."

"Well, it wasn't only that," says David, temporizing. "It was more than a fashion. The people who built the cathedrals were not entirely like us."

"They were very unlike us," Kimberly says.

"I'm sure I was always taught, if I was taught at all in those far-off days," says Valerie, "that the pointed arch was a development of the Romanesque arch. It suddenly occurred to them to carry it further. And it looked more religious."

"Bull," says George happily. "Beggin' your pardon. I know that's what they used to say, but in fact the pointed arch is the most primitive. It's the easiest arch; it's not a development from the round arch at all — how could it be? They had pointed arches in Egypt. The round arch, the keystone arch, is the most sophisticated arch you can build. The whole thing has been reported ass backwards to favor Christianity."

"Well, it may be sophisticated, but I think it's depressing," says Ruth. "I think they're very depressing, those round arches. They're monotonous; they just go along blah-blah-blah — they don't exactly make your spirits soar."

"It must have expressed something the people deeply wanted," Kimberly says. "You can hardly call that a fad. They built those cathedrals, the people did; the plan wasn't dictated by some architect."

"A misconception. They did have architects. In some cases we even know who they were."

"Nevertheless, I think Kimberly's right," says Valerie. "In those cathedrals you feel so much of the aspirations of those people; you feel the Christian emotion in the architecture — "

"Never mind what you feel. The fact is, the Crusaders

brought the pointed arch back from the Arab world. Just as they brought back a taste for spicy food. It wasn't dreamed up by the collective unconscious to honor Jesus any more than I was. It was the latest style. The earliest examples you can see are in Italy, and then it worked north."

Kimberly is very pink in the face but is benignly, tightly smiling. Valerie, just because she so much dislikes Kimberly, is feeling a need to say anything at all to come to her rescue. Valerie never minds if she sounds silly; she will throw herself headlong into any conversation to turn it off its contentious course, to make people laugh and calm down. Ruth also has a knack for lightening things, though in her case it seems to be done not so deliberately but serenely and almost inadvertently, as a result of her faithful following of her own line of thought. What about David? At this moment David is caught up by Angela and not paying as much attention as he might be. Angela is trying out her powers; she will try them out even on a cousin she has known since she was child. Kimberly is endangered on two sides, Roberta thinks. But she will manage. She is strong enough to hold on to David through any number of Angelas, and strong enough to hold her smile in the face of George's attack on her faith. Does her smile foresee how he will burn? Not likely. She foresees, instead, how all of them will stumble and wander around and tie themselves in knots; what does it matter who wins the argument? For Kimberly all the arguments have already been won.

Thinking this, pinning them all down this way, Roberta feels competent, relieved. Indifference has rescued her. The main thing is to be indifferent to George—that's the great boon. But her indifference flows past him; it's generous, it touches everybody. She is drunk enough to feel like reporting some findings. "Sexual abdication is not enough," she might say to Valerie. She is sober enough to keep quiet.

Valerie has got George talking about Italy. Ruth and David and Kimberly and Angela have started talking about something else. Roberta hears Angela's voice speaking with impatience and authority, and with an eagerness, a shyness, only she can detect.

"Acid rain . . ." Angela is saying.

Eva flicks her fingers against Roberta's arm. "What are you thinking?" she says.

"I don't know."

"You can't not know. What are you thinking?"

"About life."

"What about life?"

"About people."

"What about people?"

"About the dessert."

Eva flicks harder, giggling. "What about the dessert?"

"I thought it was O.K."

Sometime later Valerie has occasion to say that she was not born in the nineteenth century, in spite of what David may think. David says that everybody born in this country before the Second World War was to all intents and purposes brought up in the nineteenth century, and that their thinking is archaic.

"We are more than products of our upbringing," Valerie says. "As you yourself must hope, David." She says that she has been listening to all this talk about overpopulation, ecological disaster, nuclear disaster, this and that disaster, destroying the ozone layer — it's been going on and on, on and on for years, talk of disaster — but here they sit, all healthy, relatively sane, with a lovely dinner and lovely wine inside them, in the beautiful, undestroyed countryside.

"The Incas eating off gold plates while Pizarro was landing on the coast," says David.

"Don't talk as if there's no solution," says Kimberly.

"I think maybe we're destroyed already," Ruth says dreamily. "I think maybe we're anachronisms. No, that's not what I mean. I mean relics. In some way we are already. Relics."

Eva raises her head from her folded arms on the table. Her curtain veil is pulled down over one eye; her makeup has leaked beyond its boundaries, so that her whole face is a patchy flower. She says in a loud, stern voice, "I am not a relic," and they all laugh.

"Certainly not!" says Valerie, and then begins the yawning, the pushing back of chairs, the rather sheepish and formal smiles, the blowing out of candles: time to go home.

"Smell the river now!" Valerie tells them. Her voice sounds forlorn and tender, in the dark.

"A gibbous moon."

It was Roberta who told George what a gibbous moon was, and so his saying this is always an offering. It is an offering now, as they drive between the black cornfields.

"So there is."

Roberta doesn't reject the offering with silence, but she doesn't welcome it, either. She is polite. She yawns, and there is a private sound to her yawn. This isn't tactics, though she knows indifference is attractive. The real thing is. He can spot an imitation; he can always withstand tactics. She has to go all the way, to where she doesn't care. Then he feels how light and distant she is and his love revives. She has power. But the minute she begins to value it it will begin to leave her. So she is thinking, as she yawns and wavers on the edge of caring and not caring. She'd stay on this edge if she could.

The half-ton truck bearing George and Roberta, with Eva and Angela in the back, is driving down the third concession road of Weymouth Township, known locally as the Telephone Road. It is a gravel road, fairly wide and well travelled. They turned on to it from the River Road, a much narrower road, which runs past Valerie's place. From the corner of the River Road to George's gate is a distance of about two and a quarter miles. Two side roads cut this stretch of the Telephone Road at right angles. Both these roads have stop signs; the Telephone Road is a through road. The first crossroad they have already passed. Along the second crossroad, from the west, a dark-green 1969 Dodge is travelling at between eighty and ninety miles an hour. Two young men are returning from a party to their home in Logan. One has passed out. The other is driving. He hasn't remembered to put the lights on. He sees the road by the light of the moon.

There isn't time to say a word. Roberta doesn't scream. George doesn't touch the brake. The big car flashes before them, a huge, dark flash, without lights, seemingly without sound. It comes out of the dark corn and fills the air right in front of them the way a big flat fish will glide into view suddenly in an aquarium tank. It seems to be no more than a yard in front of their headlights. Then it's gone — it has disappeared into the corn on the other side of the road. They drive on. They drive on down the Telephone Road and turn into the lane and come to a stop and are sitting in the truck in the yard in front of the dark shape of the half-improved house. What they feel is not terror or thanksgiving — not yet. What they feel is strangeness. They feel as strange, as flattened out and borne aloft, as unconnected with previous and future events as the ghost car was, the black fish. The shaggy branches of the pine trees are moving overhead, and under those branches the moonlight comes clear on the hesitant grass of their new lawn.

"Are you guys dead?" Eva says, rousing them. "Aren't we home?"

Mrs. Cross and Mrs. Kidd

Mrs. Cross and Mrs. Kidd have known each other eighty years, ever since Kindergarten, which was not called that then, but Primary. Mrs. Cross's first picture of Mrs. Kidd is of her standing at the front of the class reciting some poem, her hands behind her back and her small black-eyed face lifted to let out her self-confident voice. Over the next ten years, if you went to any concert, any meeting that featured entertainment, you would find Mrs. Kidd (who was not called Mrs. Kidd then but Marian Botherton), with her dark, thick bangs cut straight across her forehead, and her pinafore sticking up in starched wings, reciting a poem with the greatest competence and no hitch of memory. Even today with hardly any excuse, sitting in her wheelchair, Mrs. Kidd will launch forth.

> "*Today we French stormed Ratisbon,*"

she will say, or:

> "*Where are the ships I used to know*
> *That came to port on the Fundy tide?*"

She stops not because she doesn't remember how to go on but in order to let somebody say, "What's that one?" or, "Wasn't that in the Third Reader?" which she takes as a request to steam ahead.

> *"Half a century ago*
> *In beauty and stately pride."*

Mrs. Kidd's first memory of Mrs. Cross (Dolly Grainger) is of a broad red face and a dress with a droopy hem, and thick fair braids, and a bellowing voice, in the playground on a rainy day when they were all crowded under the overhang. The girls played a game that was really a dance, that Mrs. Kidd did not know how to do. It was a Virginia reel and the words they sang were:

> *"Jolting up and down in the old Brass Wagon*
> *Jolting up and down in the old Brass Wagon*
> *Jolting up and down in the old Brass Wagon*
> *You're the One my Darling!"*

Nobody whirled and stomped and sang more enthusiastically than Mrs. Cross, who was the youngest and smallest allowed to play. She knew it from her older sisters. Mrs. Kidd was an only child.

Younger people, learning that these two women have known each other for more than three-quarters of a century, seem to imagine this gives them everything in common. They themselves are the only ones who can recall what separated them, and to a certain extent does yet: the apartment over the Post Office and Customs house, where Mrs. Kidd lived with her mother and her father who was the Postmaster; the row-house on Newgate Street where Mrs. Cross lived with her mother and father and two sisters and four brothers; the fact that Mrs. Kidd went to the Anglican Church and Mrs. Cross to the Free Methodist; that Mrs. Kidd married, at the age of twenty-three, a high-school teacher of science, and Mrs. Cross married, at the age of seventeen, a man who worked on the lake boats and never got to be a captain. Mrs. Cross had six children, Mrs. Kidd had three. Mrs. Cross's husband died suddenly at forty-two with no life insurance; Mrs. Kidd's husband retired to Goderich with a pension after years of being principal of the high school in a nearby town. Only recently has the gap closed. The children equalled things out; Mrs. Cross's children, on the average, make as much money as Mrs. Kidd's children, though they do not have as much education. Mrs. Cross's grandchildren make more money.

Mrs. Cross has been in Hilltop Home three years and two months, Mrs. Kidd three years less a month. They both have bad hearts and ride around in wheelchairs to save their energy. During their first conversation, Mrs. Kidd said, "I don't notice any hilltop."

"You can see the highway," said Mrs. Cross. "I guess that's what they mean. Where did they put you?" she asked.

"I hardly know if I can find my way back. It's a nice room, though. It's a single."

"Mine is too, I have a single. Is it the other side of the dining-room or this?"

"Oh. The other side."

"That's good. That's the best part. Everybody's in fairly good shape down there. It costs more, though. The better you are, the more it costs. The other side of the dining-room is out of their head."

"Senile?"

"Senile. This side is the younger ones that have something like that the matter with them. For instance." She nodded at a Mongoloid man of about fifty, who was trying to play the mouth organ. "Down in our part there's also younger ones, but nothing the matter up here," she tapped her head. "Just some disease. When it gets to the point they can't look after themselves — upstairs. That's where you get the far-gone ones. Then the crazies is another story. Locked up in the back wing. That's the real crazies. Also, I think there is some place they have the ones that walk around but soil all the time."

"Well, we are the top drawer," said Mrs. Kidd with a tight smile. "I knew there would be plenty of senile ones, but I wasn't prepared for the others. Such as." She nodded discreetly at the Mongoloid who was doing a step-dance in front of the window.

Unlike most Mongoloids, he was thin and agile, though very pale and brittle-looking.

"Happier than most," said Mrs. Cross, observing him. "This is the only place in the county, everything gets dumped here. After a while it doesn't bother you."

"It doesn't *bother* me."

Mrs. Kidd's room is full of rocks and shells, in boxes and in bottles. She has a case of brittle butterflies and a case of stuffed songbirds. Her bookshelves contain *Ferns and Mosses of North America*, *Peterson's Guide to the Birds of Eastern North America*, *How to Know the Rocks and Minerals*, and a book of Star Maps. The case of butterflies and the songbirds once hung in the classroom of her husband, the science teacher. He bought the songbirds, but he and Mrs. Kidd collected the butterflies themselves. Mrs. Kidd was a good student of botany and zoology. If she had not had what was perceived at the time as delicate health, she would have gone on and studied botany at a university, though few girls did such a thing then. Her children, who all live at a distance, send her beautiful books on subjects they are sure will interest her, but for the most part these books are large and heavy and she can't find a way to look at them comfortably, so she soon relegates them to her bottom shelf. She would not admit it to her children, but her interest has waned, it has waned considerably. They say in their letters that they remember how she taught them about mushrooms; do you remember when we saw the destroying angel in Petrie's Bush when we were living in Logan? Their letters are full of remembering. They want her fixed where she was forty or fifty years ago, these children who are aging themselves. They have a notion of her that is as fond and necessary as any notion a parent ever had of a child. They celebrate what would in a child be called precocity: her brightness, her fund of knowledge, her atheism (a secret all those years her husband was in charge of the minds of young), all the ways in which she differs from the average, or expected, old lady. She feels it a duty to hide from them the many indications that she is not so different as they think.

Mrs. Cross also gets presents from her children, but not books. Their thoughts run to ornaments, pictures, cushions. Mrs.

Cross has a bouquet of artificial roses in which are set tubes of light, always shooting and bubbling up like a fountain. She has a Southern Belle whose satin skirts are supposed to form an enormous pincushion. She has a picture of the Lord's Supper, in which a light comes on to form a halo around Jesus's head. (Mrs. Kidd, after her first visit, wrote a letter to one of her children in which she described this picture and said she had tried to figure out what the Lord and his Disciples were eating and it appeared to be hamburgers. This is the sort of thing her children love to hear from her.) There is also, near the door, a life-size plaster statue of a collie dog which resembles a dog the Cross family had when the children were small: old Bonnie. Mrs. Cross finds out from her children what these things cost and tells people. She says she is shocked.

Shortly after Mrs. Kidd's arrival, Mrs. Cross took her along on a visit to the Second Floor. Mrs. Cross has been going up there every couple of weeks to visit a cousin of hers, old Lily Barbour.

"Lily is not running on all cylinders," she warned Mrs. Kidd, as they wheeled themselves into the elevator. "Another thing, it doesn't smell like Sweet Violets, in spite of them always spraying. They do the best they can."

The first thing Mrs. Kidd saw as they got off the elevator was a little wrinkled-up woman with wild white hair, and a dress rucked up high on her bare legs (Mrs. Kidd snatched her eyes away from that) and a tongue she couldn't seem to stuff back inside her mouth. The smell was of heated urine — you would think they had had it on the stove — as well as of floral sprays. But here was a smooth-faced sensible-looking person with a topknot, wearing an apron over a clean pink dress.

"Well, did you get the papers?" this woman said in a familiar way to Mrs. Cross and Mrs. Kidd.

"Oh, they don't come in till about five o'clock," said Mrs. Kidd politely, thinking she meant the newspaper.

"Never mind her," said Mrs. Cross.

"I have to sign them today," the woman said. "Otherwise it'll be a catastrophe. They can put me out. You see I never knew it was illegal." She spoke so well, so plausibly and confidentially, that Mrs. Kidd was convinced she had to make sense, but Mrs. Cross was wheeling vigorously away. Mrs. Kidd went after her.

"Don't get tied up in that rigamarole," said Mrs. Cross when Mrs. Kidd caught up to her. A woman with a terrible goitre, such as Mrs. Kidd had not seen for years, was smiling winningly at them. Up here nobody had teeth.

"I thought there was no such thing as a goitre any more," Mrs. Kidd said. "With the iodine."

They were going in the direction of a hollering voice.

"George!" the voice said. "George! Jessie! I'm here! Come and pull me up! George!"

Another voice was weaving cheerfully in and out of these yells. "Bad-bad-bad," it said. "Bad. Bad-bad. Bad-bad-bad. Bad-bad."

The owners of both these voices were sitting around a long table by a row of windows halfway down the hall. Nine or ten women were sitting there. Some were mumbling or singing softly to themselves. One was tearing apart a little embroidered cushion somebody had made. Another was eating a chocolate-covered ice-cream bar. Bits of chocolate had caught on her whiskers, dribbles of ice cream ran down her chin. None of them looked out the windows, or at each other. None of them paid any attention to George-and-Jessie, or to Bad-bad-bad, who were carrying on without a break.

Mrs. Kidd halted.

"Where is this Lily?"

"She's down at the end. They don't get her out of bed."

"Well, you go on and see her," said Mrs. Kidd. "I'm going back."

"There's nothing to get upset about," said Mrs. Cross. "They're all off in their own little world. They're happy as clams."

"They may be, but I'm not," said Mrs. Kidd. "I'll see you in the Recreation Room." She wheeled herself around and down the hall to the elevator where the pink lady was still inquiring urgently for her papers. She never came back.

Mrs. Cross and Mrs. Kidd used to play cards in the Recreation Room every afternoon. They put on earrings, stockings, afternoon dresses. They took turns treating for tea. On the whole, these afternoons were pleasant. They were well matched at cards.

Sometimes they played Scrabble, but Mrs. Cross did not take Scrabble seriously, as she did cards. She became frivolous and quarrelsome, defending words that were her own invention. So they went back to cards; they played rummy, most of the time. It was like school here. People paired off, they had best friends. The same people always sat together in the dining-room. Some people had nobody.

The first time Mrs. Cross took notice of Jack, he was in the Recreation Room, when she and Mrs. Kidd were playing cards. He had just come in a week or so before. Mrs. Kidd knew about him.

"Do you see that red-haired fellow by the window?" said Mrs. Kidd. "He's in from a stroke. He's only fifty-nine years old. I heard it in the dining-room before you got down."

"Poor chap. That young."

"He's lucky to be alive at all. His parents are still alive, both of them, they're still on a farm. He was back visiting them and he took the stroke and was lying face down in the barnyard when they found him. He wasn't living around here, he's from out west."

"Poor chap," said Mrs. Cross. "What did he work at?"

"He worked on a newspaper."

"Was he married?"

"That I didn't hear. He's supposed to have been an alcoholic, then he joined A.A. and got over it. You can't trust all you hear in this place."

(That was true. There was usually a swirl of stories around any newcomer; stories about the money people had, or the places they had been, or the number of operations they have had and the plastic repairs or contrivances they carry around in or on their bodies. A few days later Mrs. Cross was saying that Jack had been the editor of a newspaper. First she heard it was in Sudbury, then she heard Winnipeg. She was saying he had had a nervous break-down due to overwork; that was the truth, he had never been an alcoholic. She was saying he came from a good family. His name was Jack MacNeil.)

At present Mrs. Cross noticed how clean and tended he

looked in his gray pants and light shirt. It was unnatural, at least for him; he looked like something that had gone soft from being too long in the water. He was a big man, but he could not hold himself straight, even in the wheelchair. The whole left side of his body was loose, emptied, powerless. His hair and moustache were not even gray yet, but fawn-colored. He was white as if just out of bandages.

A distraction occurred. The Gospel preacher who came every week to conduct a prayer service, with hymns (the more established preachers came, in turn, on Sundays), was walking through the Recreation Room with his wife close behind, the pair of them showering smiles and greetings wherever they could catch an eye. Mrs. Kidd looked up when they had passed and said softly but distinctly, "Joy to the World."

At this, Jack, who was wheeling himself across the room in a clumsy way—he tended to go in circles—smiled. The smile was intelligent, ironic, and did not go with his helpless look. Mrs. Cross waved him over and wheeled part of the way to meet him. She introduced herself, and introduced Mrs. Kidd. He opened his mouth and said, "Anh-anh-anh,"

"Yes," said Mrs. Cross encouragingly. "Yes?"

"Anh-anh-*anh* ," said Jack. He flapped his right hand. Tears came into his eyes.

"Are we playing cards?" said Mrs. Kidd.

"I have to get on with this game," said Mrs. Cross. "You're welcome to sit and watch. Were you a card player?"

His right hand came out and grabbed her chair, and he bent his head weeping. He tried to get the left hand up to wipe his face. He could lift it a few inches, then it fell back in his lap.

"Oh, well," said Mrs. Cross softly. Then she remembered what you do when children cry; how to josh them out of it. "How can I tell what you're saying if you're going to cry? You just be patient. I have known people that have had strokes and got their speech back. Yes I have. You mustn't cry, that won't accomplish anything. You just take it slow. Boo-hoo-hoo," she said, bending towards him. "Boo-hoo-hoo. You'll have Mrs. Kidd and me crying next."

That was the beginning of Mrs. Cross's takeover of Jack. She got him to sit and watch the card game and to dry up, more or less, and make a noise which was a substitute for conversation (an-anh) rather than a desperate attempt at it (anh-anh-*anh*). Mrs. Cross felt something stretching in her. It was her old managing, watching power, her capacity for strategy, which if properly exercised could never be detected by those it was used on.

Mrs. Kidd could detect it, however.

"This isn't what I call a card game," she said.

Mrs. Cross soon found out that Jack could not stay interested in cards and there was no use trying to get him to play; it was conversation he was after. But trying to talk brought on the weeping.

"Crying doesn't bother me," she said to him. "I've seen tears and tears. But it doesn't do you any good with a lot of people, to get a reputation for being a cry-baby."

She started to ask him questions to which he could give yes-and-no answers. That brightened him up and let her test out her information.

Yes, he had worked on a newspaper. No, he was not married. No, the newspaper was not in Sudbury. Mrs. Cross began to reel off the name of every city she could think of but was unable to hit on the right one. He became agitated, tried to speak, and this time the syllables got close to a word, but she couldn't catch it. She blamed herself, for not knowing enough places. Then, inspired, she ordered him to stay right where he was, not to move, she would be back, and she wheeled herself down the hall to the Library. There she looked for a book with maps in it. To her disgust there was not such a thing, there was nothing but love stories and religion. But she did not give up. She took off down the hall to Mrs. Kidd's room. Since their card games had lapsed (they still played some days, but not every day), Mrs. Kidd spent many afternoons in her room. She was there now, lying on top of her bed, wearing an elegant purple dressing-gown with a high embroidered neck. She had a headache.

"Have you got one of those, like a geography book?" Mrs.

Cross said. "A book with maps in it." She explained that she wanted it for Jack.

"An atlas, you mean," said Mrs. Kidd. "I think there may be. I can't remember. You can look on the bottom shelf. I can't remember what's there."

Mrs. Cross parked by the bookcase and began to lift the heavy books onto her lap one by one, reading the titles at close range. She was out of breath from the speed of her trip.

"You're wearing yourself out," said Mrs. Kidd. "You'll get yourself upset and you'll get him upset, and what is the point of it?"

"I'm not upset. It just seems a crime to me."

"What does?"

"Such an intelligent man, what's he doing in here? They should have put him in one of those places they teach you things, teach you how to talk again. What's the name of them? You know. Why did they just stick him in here? I want to help him and I don't know what to do. Well, I just have to try. If it was one of my boys like that and in a place where nobody knew him, I just hope some woman would take the same interest in him."

"Rehabilitation," said Mrs. Kidd. "The reason they put him in here is more than likely that the stroke was too bad for them to do anything for him."

"Everything under the sun but a map-book," said Mrs. Cross, not choosing to answer this. "He'll think I'm not coming back." She wheeled out of Mrs. Kidd's room without a thank-you or good-bye. She was afraid Jack would think she hadn't meant to come back, all she intended to do was to get rid of him. Sure enough, when she got to the Recreation Room he was gone. She did not know what to do. She was near tears herself. She didn't know where his room was. She thought she would go to the office and ask; then she saw that it was five past four and the office would be closed. Lazy, those girls were. Four o'clock, get their coats on and go home, nothing matters to them. She went wheeling slowly along the corridor, wondering what to do. Then in one of the dead-end side corridors she saw Jack.

"There you are, what a relief! I didn't know where to look for you. Did you think I wasn't ever coming back? I'll tell you what I went for. I was going to surprise you. I went to look for one of those books with maps in, what do you call them, so you could show me where you used to live. Atlases!"

He was sitting looking at the pink wall as if it was a window. Against the wall was a whatnot with a vase of plastic daffodils on it, and some figurines, dwarfs and dogs; on the wall were three paint-by-number pictures that had been done in the Craft Room.

"My friend Mrs. Kidd has more books than the Library. She has a book on nothing but bugs. Another nothing but the moon, when they went there, close up. But not such a simple thing as a map."

Jack was pointing at one of the pictures.

"Which one are you pointing at?" said Mrs. Cross. "The one with the church with the cross? No? The one above that? The pine trees? Yes? What about it? The pine trees and the red deer?" He was smiling, waving his hand. She hoped he wouldn't get too excited and disappointed this time. "What about it? This is like one of those things on television. Trees? Green? Pine trees? Is it the deer? Three deer? No? Yes. Three red deer?" He flapped his arm up and down and she said, "I don't know, really. Three — red — deer. Wait a minute. That's a place. I've heard it on the news. Red Deer. Red Deer! That's the place! That's the place you lived in! That's the place where you worked on the newspaper! *Red Deer.*"

They were both jubilant. He waved his arm around in celebration, as if he was conducting an orchestra, and she leaned forward, laughing, clapping her hands on her knees.

"Oh, if everything was in pictures like that, we could have a lot of fun! You and me could have a lot of fun, couldn't we?"

Mrs. Cross made an appointment to see the doctor.

"I've heard of people that had a very bad stroke and their speech came back, isn't that so?"

"It can happen. It depends. Are you worrying a lot about this man?"

"It must be a terrible feeling. No wonder he cries."

"How many chidren did you have?"

"Six."

"I'd say you'd done your share of worrying."

She could see he didn't mean to tell her anything. Either he didn't remember much about Jack's case or he was pretending he didn't.

"I'm here to take care of people," the doctor said. "That's what I'm here for, that's what the nurses are here for. So you can leave all the worrying to us. That's what we get paid for. Right?"

And how much worrying do you do? she wanted to ask.

She would have liked to talk to Mrs. Kidd about this visit because she knew Mrs. Kidd thought the doctor was a fool, but once Mrs. Kidd knew Jack was the reason for the visit she would make some impatient remark. Mrs. Cross never talked to her any more about Jack. She talked to other people, but she could see them getting bored. Nobody cares about anybody else's misfortunes in here, she thought. Even when somebody dies they don't care, it's just *me, I'm still alive, what's for dinner?* The selfishness. They're all just as bad as the ones on the Second Floor, only they don't show it yet.

She hadn't been up to the Second Floor, hadn't visited Lily Barbour, since she took up with Jack.

They liked sitting in the corner with the Red Deer picture, the scene of their first success. That was established as their place, where they could be by themselves. Mrs. Cross brought a pencil and paper, fixed the tray across his chair, tried to see how Jack made out with writing. It was about the same as talking. He would scrawl a bit, push the pencil till he broke it, start to cry. They didn't make progress, either in writing or talking, it was useless. But she was learning to talk to him by the yes-and-no method, and it seemed sometimes she could pick up what was in his mind.

"If I was smarter I would be more of a help to you," she said. "Isn't it the limit? I can get it all out that's in my head, but there never was so much in it, and you've got your head crammed full but you can't get it out. Never mind. We'll have a cup of coffee, won't we? Cup of coffee, that's what you like. My friend Mrs. Kidd and I used to drink tea all the time, but now I drink coffee. I prefer it too."

"So you never got married? Never?"

Never.

"Did you have a sweetheart?"

Yes.

"Did you? Did you? Was it long ago? Long ago or recently?"

Yes.

"Long ago or recently? Both. Long ago and recently. Different sweethearts. The same? The same. The same woman. You were in love with the same woman years and years but you didn't get married to her. Oh, Jack. Why didn't you? Couldn't she marry you? She couldn't. Why not? Was she married already? Was she? Yes. Yes. Oh, my."

She searched his face to see if this was too painful a subject or if he wanted to go on. She thought he did want to. She was eager to ask where this woman was now, but something warned her not to. Instead she took a light tone.

"I wonder if I can guess her name? Remember Red Deer? Wasn't that funny? I wonder. I could start with A and work through the alphabet. Anne? Audrey? Annabelle? No. I think I'll just follow my intuition. Jane? Mary? Louise?"

The name was Pat, Patricia, which she hit on maybe her thirtieth try.

"Now, in my mind a Pat is always fair. Not dark. You know how you have a picture in your mind for a name? Was she fair? Yes? And tall, in my mind a Pat is always tall. Was she? Well! I got it right. Tall and fair. A good-looking woman. A lovely woman."

Yes.

She felt ashamed of herself, because she had wished for a moment that she had somebody to tell this to.

"That is a secret then. It's between you and me. Now. If you ever want to write Pat a letter you come to me. Come to me and I'll make out what you want to say to her and I'll write it."

No. No letter. Never.

"Well. I have a secret too. I had a boy I liked, he was killed in the First World War. He walked me home from a skating-party, it was our school skating-party. I was in the Senior Fourth. I was fourteen. That was before the war. I did like him, and I used to think about him, you know, and when I heard he was killed, that was after I was married, I was married at seventeen, well, when I heard he was killed I thought, now I've got something to look forward to, I could look forward to meeting him in Heaven. That's true. That's how childish I was.

"Marian was at that skating-party too. You know who I mean by Marian. Mrs. Kidd. She was there and she had the most beautiful outfit. It was sky-blue trimmed with white fur and a hood on it. Also she had a muff. She had a white fur muff. I never saw anything I would've like to have for myself as much as that muff."

Lying in the dark at night, before she went to sleep, Mrs. Cross would go over everything that had happened with Jack that day: how he had looked; how his color was; whether he had cried and how long and how often; whether he had been in a bad temper in the dining-room, annoyed with so many people around him or perhaps not liking the food; whether he had said good-night to her sullenly or gratefully.

Meanwhile Mrs. Kidd had taken on a new friend of her own. This was Charlotte, who used to live down near the dining-room but had recently moved in across the hall. Charlotte was a tall, thin, deferential woman in her mid-forties. She had multiple sclerosis. Sometimes her disease was in remission, as it was now; she could have gone home, if she had wanted to, and there had been a place for her. But she was happy where she was. Years of institutional life had made her childlike, affectionate, good-humored. She helped in the hairdressing shop, she loved doing that, she loved brushing and pinning up Mrs. Kidd's hair, marvelling at how much black there still was in it. She put an ash-blond rinse on her own hair and wore it in a bouffant, stiff with spray. Mrs. Kidd could smell the hairspray from her room and she would call out, "Charlotte! Did they move you down here for the purpose of asphyxiating us?"

Charlotte giggled. She brought Mrs. Kidd a present. It was a red felt purse, with an appliquéd design of green leaves and blue and yellow flowers; she had made it in the Craft Room. Mrs. Kidd thought how much it resembled those recipe-holders her children used to bring home from school; a whole cardboard pie-plate and a half pie-plate, stitched together with bright yarn. They didn't hold enough to be really useful. They were painstakingly created frivolities, like the crocheted potholders through which you could burn yourself; the cut-out wooden horse's head with a hook not quite big enough to hold a hat.

Charlotte made purses for her daughters, who were married, and for her small granddaughter, and for the woman who lived with her husband and used his name. The husband and this woman came regularly to see Charlotte; they were all good friends. It had been a good arrangement for the husband, for the children, and perhaps for Charlotte herself. Nothing was being put over on Charlotte. Most likely she had given in without a whimper. Glad of the chance.

"What do you expect?" said Mrs. Cross. "Charlotte's easy-going."

Mrs. Cross and Mrs. Kidd had not had any falling-out or any real coolness. They still had some talks and card games. But it was difficult. They no longer sat at the same table in the dining-room because Mrs. Cross had to watch to see if Jack needed help cutting up his meat. He wouldn't let anyone else cut it; he would just pretend he didn't want any and miss out on his protein. Then Charlotte moved into the place Mrs. Cross had vacated. Charlotte had no problems cutting her meat. In fact she cut her meat, toast, egg, vegetables, cake, whatever she was eating that would cut, into tiny regular pieces before she started on it. Mrs. Kidd told her that was not good manners. Charlotte was crestfallen but stubborn and continued to do it.

"Neither you nor I would have given up so quickly," said Mrs. Kidd, still speaking about Charlotte to Mrs. Cross. "We wouldn't've had the choice."

"That's true. There weren't places like this. Not pleasant places. They couldn't have kept us alive the way they do her. The drugs and so on. Also it may be the drugs makes her silly."

Mrs. Kidd remained silent, frowning at hearing Charlotte called silly, though that was just the blunt way of putting what she had been trying to say herself. After a moment she spoke lamely.

"I think she has more brains than she shows."

Mrs. Cross said evenly, "I wouldn't know."

Mrs. Kidd sat with her head bent forward, thoughtfully. She could sit that way for half an hour, easily, letting Charlotte brush and tend her hair. Was she turning into one of those old ladies that love to be waited on? Those old ladies also needed somebody to boss. They were the sort who went around the world on cruise ships, she had read about them in novels. They went around the world, and stayed at hotels, or they lived in grand decaying houses, with their companions. It was so easy to boss Charlotte, to make her play Scrabble and tell her when her manners were bad. Charlotte was itching to be somebody's slave. So why did Mrs. Kidd hope to restrain herself? She did not wish to be such a recognizable sort of old lady. Also, slaves cost more than they were worth. In the end, people's devotion hung like rocks around your neck. Expectations. She wanted to float herself clear. Sometimes she could do it by lying on her bed and saying in her head all the poems she knew, or the facts, which got harder and harder to hold in place. Other times she imagined a house on the edge of some dark woods or bog, bright fields in front of it running down to the sea. She imagined she lived there alone, like an old woman in a story.

Mrs. Cross wanted to take Jack on visits. She thought it was time for him to learn to associate with people. He didn't cry so often now, when they were alone. But sometimes at meals she was ashamed of him and had to tell him so. He would take offense at something, often she didn't know what, and sometimes his sulk would proceed to the point where he would knock over the sugar-bowl, or sweep all his cutlery on to the floor. She thought that if only he could get used to a few more people as he was to her, he would calm down and behave decently.

The first time she took him to Mrs. Kidd's room, Mrs. Kidd said she and Charlotte were just going out, they were going to the Crafts Room. She didn't ask them to come along. The next time they came, Mrs. Kidd and Charlotte were sitting there playing Scrabble, so they were caught.

"You don't mind if we watch you for a little while," Mrs. Cross said.

"Oh no. But don't blame me if you get bored. Charlotte takes a week from Wednesday to make up her mind."

"We're not in any hurry. We're not expected anywhere. Are we, Jack?"

She was wondering if she could get Jack playing Scrabble. She didn't know the extent of his problem when he tried to write. Was it that he couldn't form the letters, was that all? Or couldn't he see how they made the words? This might be the very thing for him.

At any rate he was taking an interest. He edged his chair up beside Charlotte, who picked up some letters, put them back, picked them up, looked at them in her hand, and finally made *wind*, working down from the *w* in Mrs. Kidd's word *elbow*. Jack seemed to understand. He was so pleased that he patted Charlotte's knee in congratulation. Mrs. Cross hoped Charlotte would realize that was just friendliness and not take offense.

She needn't have worried. Charlotte did not know how to take offense.

"Well good for you," said Mrs. Kidd, frowning, and right away she made *demon* across from the *d*. "Triple word!" she said, and was writing down the score. "Pick up your letters, Charlotte."

Charlotte showed her new letters to Jack, one by one, and he made a noise of appreciation. Mrs. Cross kept an eye on him, hoping nothing would happen to turn him bad-tempered and spoil this show of friendliness. Nothing did. But he was not having a good effect on Charlotte's concentration.

"You want to help?" Charlotte said, and moved the little stand with the letters on it so that it was in front of both of them. He bent over so that he almost had his head on her shoulder.

"Anh-anh-anh," said Jack, but he sounded cheerful.

"Anh-anh-anh?" said Charlotte, teasing him. "What kind of a word is that, *anh-anh-anh*?"

Mrs. Cross waited for the skies to fall, but the only thing Jack did was giggle, and Charlotte giggled, so that there was a sort of giggling-match set up between the two of them.

"Aren't you the great friends," said Mrs. Kidd.

Mrs. Cross thought it would be just as well not to exasperate Mrs. Kidd if they wanted to make a habit of visiting.

"Now Jack, don't distract Charlotte," she said affably. "You let her play."

Even as she finished saying this, she saw Jack's hand descend clumsily on the Scrabble board. The letters went flying. He turned and showed her his ugly look, worse than she had ever seen it. She was amazed and even frightened, but she did not mean to let him see.

"Now what have you done?" she said. "Fine behavior!"

He made a sound of disgust and pushed the Scrabble board and all the letters to the floor, all the time looking at Mrs. Cross so that there could be no doubt that this disgust and fury had been aroused by her. She knew that it was important at this moment to speak coldly and firmly. That was what you must do with a child or an animal; you must show them that your control has not budged and that you are not hurt or alarmed by such displays. But she was not able to say a word, such a feeling of grief, and shock, and helplessness rose in her heart. Her eyes filled with tears, and at the sight of her tears his expression grew even more hateful and menacing as if the feelings he had against her were boiling higher every moment.

Charlotte was smiling, either because she could not switch out of her giggling mood of a moment before or because she did not know how to do anything but smile, no matter what happened. She was pink-faced, apologetic, excited.

Jack managed to turn his chair around, with a violent, awkward motion. Charlotte stood up. Mrs. Cross made herself speak.

"Yes, you better push him home now. He better go home and cool off and repent of his bad manners. He better."

Jack made a taunting sound, which seemed to point out that Mrs. Cross was just telling Charlotte to do what Charlotte was going to do anyway; Mrs. Cross was just pretending to have control of things. Charlotte had hold of the wheelchair and was pushing it towards the door, her smiling lips pressed together in concentration as she avoided the bookshelves and the butterfly case leaning against the wall. Perhaps it was hard for her to steer, perhaps the ordinary reflexes and balances of her body were not there for her to rely on. But she looked pleased; she raised her hand to them and released her smile, and set off down the corridor. She was just like one of those old-fashioned dolls, not the kind Mrs. Cross and Mrs. Kidd used to have but the kind their mothers had, with the long, limp bodies and pink-and-white faces and crimped china hair and ladylike smiles. Jack kept his face turned away; the bit of it Mrs. Cross could see was flushed red.

"It would be easy for any man to get the better of Charlotte," said Mrs. Kidd when they were gone.

"I don't think he's so much of a danger," said Mrs. Cross. She spoke in a dry tone but her voice was shaking.

Mrs. Kidd looked at the Scrabble board and the letters scattered all over the floor.

"We can't do much about picking them up," she said. "If either one of us bends over we black out." That was true.

"Useless old crocks, aren't we?" said Mrs. Cross. Her voice was under better control now.

"We won't try. When the girl comes in with the juice I'll ask her to do it. We don't need to say how it happened. That's what we'll do. We won't bend over and end up smashing our noses."

Mrs. Cross felt her heart give a big flop. Her heart was like an old crippled crow, flopping around in her chest. She crossed her hands there, to hold it.

"Well, I never told you, I don't think I did," said Mrs. Kidd, with her eyes on Mrs. Cross's face. "I never told you what happened that time I got out of bed too fast in my apartment, and I fell over on my face. I blacked out. Fortunately the woman was home, in the apartment underneath me, and she heard the crash and got the whatyamacallit, the man with the keys, the superintendent. They came and found me out cold and took me in the ambulance. I don't remember a thing about it. I can't remember anything that happened throughout the next three weeks. I wasn't unconscious. I wish I had been. I was conscious and saying a lot of foolish things.

Do you know the first thing I remember? The psychiatrist coming to see me! They had got a psychiatrist in to determine whether I was loony. But nobody told me he was a psychiatrist. That's part of it, they don't tell you. He had a thing like an army jacket on. He was quite young. So I thought he was just some fellow who had walked in off the street.

" 'What is the name of the Prime Minister?' he said to me.

"Well! I thought *he* was loony. So I said, 'Who cares?' And I turned my back on him as if I was going to sleep, and from that time on I remember everything."

"*Who cares!*"

As a matter of fact, Mrs. Cross had heard Mrs. Kidd tell this story before, but it was a long time ago and she laughed now not just to be obliging; she laughed with relief. Mrs. Kidd's firm voice had spread a numbing ointment over her misery.

Out of their combined laughter, Mrs. Kidd shot a quick serious question.

"Are you all right?"

Mrs. Cross lifted her hands from her chest, waited.

"I think so. Yes. But I think I'll go and lie down."

In this exchange it was understood that Mrs. Kidd also said, "Your heart is weak, you shouldn't put it at the mercy of these emotions," and Mrs. Cross replied, "I will do as I do, though there may be something in what you say."

"You haven't got your chair," Mrs. Kidd said. Mrs. Cross was sitting on an ordinary chair. She had come here walking slowly behind Jack's chair, to help him steer.

"I can walk," she said. "I can walk if I take my time."

"No. You ride. You get in my chair and I'll push you."

"You can't do that."

"Yes I can. If I don't use my energy I'll get mad about my Scrabble game."

Mrs. Cross heaved herself up and into Mrs. Kidd's wheel-chair. As she did so she felt such weakness in her legs that she knew Mrs. Kidd was right. She couldn't have walked ten feet.

"Now then," said Mrs. Kidd, and she negotiated their way out of the room into the corridor.

"Don't strain yourself. Don't try to go too fast."

"No."

They proceeded down the corridor, turned left, made their way successfully up a very gentle ramp. Mrs. Cross could hear Mrs. Kidd's breathing.

"Maybe I can manage the rest by myself."

"No you can't."

They made another left turn at the top of the ramp. Now Mrs. Cross's room was in sight. It was three doors ahead of them.

"What I am going to do now," said Mrs. Kidd, with emphasis and pauses to hide her breathlessness, "is give you a push. I can give you a push that will take you exactly to your own door."

"Can you?" said Mrs. Cross doubtfully.

"Certainly. Then you can turn yourself in and get on the bed and take your time to get yourself settled, then ring for the girl and get her to deliver the chair back to me."

"You won't bash me into anything?"

"You watch."

With that Mrs. Kidd gave the wheelchair a calculated, delicately balanced push. It rolled forward smoothly and came to a stop just where she had said it would, in exactly the right place in front of Mrs. Cross's door. Mrs. Cross had hastily raised her feet and hands for this last bit of the ride. Now she dropped them. She gave a single, satisfied, conceding nod and turned and glided safely into her own room.

Mrs. Kidd, as soon as Mrs. Cross was out of sight, sank down and sat with her back against the wall, her legs stuck straight out in front of her on the cool linoleum. She prayed no nosy person would come along until she could recover her strength and get started on the trip back.

Hard-Luck Stories

Julie is wearing a pink-and-white-striped shirtwaist dress, and a hat of lacy beige straw, with a pink rose under the brim. I noticed the hat first, when she came striding along the street. For a moment I didn't realize it was Julie. Over the last couple of years I have experienced moments of disbelief when I meet my friends in public. They look older than I think they should. Julie didn't look older, but she did catch my attention in a way she had never done before. It was the hat. I thought there was something gallant and absurd about it, on that tall, tomboyish woman. Then I saw that it was Julie and hurried to greet her, and we got a table under an umbrella at this sidewalk restaurant where we are having lunch.

We have not seen each other for two months, not since the conference in May. I am down in Toronto for the day. Julie lives here.

She soon tells me what is going on. Sitting down, she looks pretty, with the angles of her face softened and shaded by the hat, and her dark eyes shining.

"It makes me think of a story," Julie says. "Isn't it like one of those ironical-twist-at-the-end sort of stories that used to be so popular? I really did think that I was asked along to protect you. No, not exactly protect, that's too vulgar, but I thought you felt something and you were being prudent, and that was why me. Wouldn't it make a good story? Why did those stories go out of style?"

"They got to seem too predictable," I said. "Or people thought, that isn't the way things happen. Or they thought, who cares the way things happen?"

"Not to me! Not to me was anything predictable!" says Julie. One or two people look our way. The tables are too close together here.

She makes a face, and pulls the hat down on both cheeks, scrunching the rose against her temple.

"I must be crowing," she says. "I have a tendency now to get light-headed. It just seems to me so remarkable. Is this hat silly? No, seriously, do you remember when we were driving down and you told about the visit you went on, the visit that man took you on, to see the rich people? The rich woman? The awful one? Do you remember you said then about there being the two kinds of love, and the one kind nobody wants to think they've missed out on? Well, I was thinking then, have I missed out on every kind? I haven't even got to tell the different kinds apart."

I am about to say "Leslie," which is the name of Julie's husband.

"Don't say 'Leslie,'" Julie says. "You know that doesn't count. I can't help it. It doesn't count. So I was thinking, I was ready to make a joke about it but I was thinking, how I'd like to get some crumbs, even!"

"Douglas is better than crumbs," I say.

"Yes he is."

When the conference last May had ended and the buses were standing at the door of the summer hotel, waiting to take people back to Toronto or to the airport, I went into Julie's room and found her doing up her backpack.

"I've got us a ride to Toronto," I said. "If you'd rather that than the bus. Remember the man I introduced you to last night? Douglas Reider?"

"All right," said Julie. "I'm mildly sick of all these people. Do we have to talk?"

"Not much. He will."

I helped her hoist her backpack. She probably doesn't own an overnight case. She was wearing her hiking boots and a denim jacket. She wasn't faking. She could have walked to Toronto. Every summer she and her husband and some of their children walk the Bruce Trail. Other things fit the picture. She makes her own yogurt, and whole-grain bread, and granola. You'd think I would have worried about introducing her to Douglas, who is driven by any display of virtue into the most extraordinary provocations. I've heard him tell people that yogurt causes cancer, and smoking is good for your heart, and whales are an abomination. He does this lightheartedly but with absolute assurance, and adds a shocking, contemptuous embroidery of false statistics and invented detail. The people he takes on are furious or confused or wounded—sometimes all of those things at once. I don't remember thinking about how Julie would have handled him, but I suppose, if I did think about it, I must have decided that she would be all right. Julie isn't simple. She knows her own stratagems, her efforts, her doubts. You couldn't get at her through her causes.

Julie and I have been friends for years. She is a children's librarian, in Toronto. She helped me get the job I have now, or at least, she told me about it. I drive a bookmobile in the Ottawa Valley. I have been divorced for a long time, and so it is natural that Julie should talk to me about a problem she says she cannot discuss with many people. It is a question, more than a problem. The question is: should Julie herself try living alone? She says her husband Leslie is cold-hearted, superficial, stubborn, emotionally stingy, loyal, honest, high-minded, and vulnerable. She says she never really wants him. She says she thinks she might miss him more than she could stand, or perhaps just being alone would be more than she could stand. She says she has no illusions about being able to attract another man. But sometimes she feels her emotions, her life, her something-or-other—all that is being wasted.

I listen, and think this sounds like the complaints many women make, and in fact it sounds a lot like the complaints I used to make, when I was married. How much is this meant, how deep does it go? How much is it an exercise that balances the marriage and keeps it afloat? I've asked her, has she ever been in love, in love with somebody else? She says she once thought she was, with a boy she met on the beach, but it was all nonsense, it all evaporated. And once in recent years a man thought he was in love with her, but that was nonsense too, nothing came of it. I tell her that being alone has its grim side, certainly; I tell her to think twice. I think that I am in some ways a braver person than Julie, because I have taken the risk. I have taken more than one risk.

Julie and Douglas Reider and I had lunch at a restaurant in an old white wooden building overlooking a small lake. The lake is one of a chain of lakes, and there was a dock where the lake boats used to come in before the road was built; boats brought the holidayers then, and the supplies. The trees came down to the shore, on both sides of the building. Most of them were birch and poplar. The leaves were not quite out here, even though it was May. You could see all the branches with just an impression of green, as if that was the color of the air. Under the trees there were hundreds of white trilliums. The day was cloudy, though the sun had been trying to break through. The water looked bright and cold.

We sat on old, unmatched, brightly painted kitchen chairs, on a long glassed-in verandah. We were the only people there. It was a bit late for lunch. We ate roast chicken.

"It's Sunday dinner, really," I said. "It's Sunday dinner after church."

"It's a lovely place," said Julie. She asked Douglas how he knew it existed.

Douglas said he got to know where everything was, he spent so much time travelling around the province. He is in charge of collecting, buying up for the Provincial Archives, all sorts of old diaries, letters, records, that would otherwise perish, or be sold to collectors outside the province or the country. He pursues various clues and hunches, and when he finds a treasure it is not always his immediately. He often has to persuade reticent or suspicious or greedy owners, and to outwit private dealers.

"He's a sort of pirate, really," I said to Julie.

He was talking about the private dealers, telling stories about his rivals. Sometimes they would get hold of valuable material, and then impudently try to sell it back to him. Or they would try to sell it out of the country to the highest bidders, a disaster he has sworn to prevent.

Douglas is tall, and most people would think of him as lean, disregarding the little bulge over his belt which can be seen as a recent, unsuitable, perhaps temporary, development. His hair is gray, and cut short, perhaps to reassure elderly and conservative diary-owners. To me he is a boyish-looking man. I don't mean to suggest by that a man who is open-faced and ruddy and shy. I am thinking of the hard youthfulness, the jaunty grim looks you often see in photographs of servicemen in the Second World War. Douglas was one of those, and is preserved, not ripened. Oh, the modesty and satisfaction of those faces, clamped down on their secrets! With such men the descent into love is swift and private and amazing — so is their recovery. I watched him as he told Julie about the people who deal in old books and papers, how they are not fusty and shadowy, as in popular imagination, not mysterious old magpies, but bold rogues with the instincts of gamblers and confidence men. In this, as in any other enterprise where there is the promise of money, intrigues and lies and hoodwinking and bullying abound.

"People have that idea about anything to do with books," Julie said. "They have it about librarians. Think of the times you hear people say that somebody is not a typical librarian. Haven't you wanted to say it about yourself?"

Julie was excited, drinking her wine. I thought it was because she had flourished, at the conference. She has a talent for conferences, and no objection to making herself useful. She can speak up in general meetings without her mouth going dry and her knees shaking. She knows what a point of order is. She says she has to admit to rather liking meetings, and committees, and newsletters. She has worked for the P.T.A. and the N.D.P. and the Unitarian Church, and for Tenants' Associations, and Great Books Clubs; she has given a lot of her life to organizations. Maybe it's an addiction, she says, but she looks around her at meetings and she can't help thinking that meetings are good for people. They make people feel everything isn't such a muddle.

Now, at this conference, Julie said, who, who, were the typical librarians? Where could you find them? Indeed, she said, you might think there had been a too-strenuous effort to knock that image on the head.

"But it isn't a calculated knocking-on-the-head," she said. "It really is one of those refuge-professions." Which didn't mean, she said, that all the people in it were scared and spiritless. Far from it. It was full of genuine oddities and many flamboyant and expansive personalities.

"Old kooks," Douglas said.

"Still, the image prevails somewhere," Julie said. "The Director of the Conference Centre came and talked to the Chairman this morning and asked if she wanted a list of the people who were out of their rooms during the night. Can you imagine them thinking we'd want to know that?"

"Wouldn't we?" I said.

"I mean, officially. How do they get that kind of information on people, anyway?"

"Spies," said Douglas. "A.G.P.M. Amateur Guardians of the Public Morality. I'm a member myself. It's like being a fire warden."

Julie didn't pick this up. Instead she said morosely, "It's the younger ones, I guess."

"Envious of the Sexual Revolution," said Douglas, shaking his head. "Anyway I thought it was all over. Isn't it all over?" he said, looking at me.

"So I understand," I said.

"Well that's not fair," said Julie. "For me it never happened. No, really. I wish I'd been born younger. I mean, later. Why not be honest about it?" Sometimes she set herself up to be preposterously frank. There was something willed and coquettish — childishly coquettish — about this; yet it seemed not playful. It seemed, at the moment, necessary. It made me nervous for her. We were working down into our second bottle of wine and she had drunk more than either Douglas or I had.

"Well all right," she said. "I know it's funny. Twice in my life there have been possibilities and both turned out very funny. I mean very strange. So I think it is not meant. No. Not God's will."

"Oh, Julie," I said.

"You don't know the whole story," she said.

I thought that she really was getting drunk, and I ought to do what I could to keep the tone light, so I said, "Yes, I know. You met a psychology student while you were throwing a cake into the sea."

I was glad that Douglas laughed.

"Really?" he said. "Did you always throw your cakes into the sea? Were they that bad?"

"Very good," said Julie, speaking in an artificial, severely joking style. "Very good and very elaborate. Gateau St. Honoré. A monstrosity. It's got cream and custard and butterscotch. No. The reason I was throwing it into the sea — and I've told you this," she said to me, "was that I had a secret problem at the time. I had a problem about food. I was just newly married and we were living in Vancouver, near Kitsilano Beach. I was one of those people who gorge, then purge. I used to make cream puffs and eat them all one after the other, or make fudge and eat a whole panful, then take mustard and water to vomit or else massive doses of epsom salts to wash it through. Terrible. The guilt. I was compelled. It must have had something to do with sex. They say now it does, don't they?

"Well, I made this horrific cake and I pretended I was making it for Leslie, but by the time I got it finished I knew I was making it for myself, I was going to end up eating it all myself, and I went to put it in the garbage but I knew I might fish it out again. Isn't that disgusting? So I put the whole mess in a brown paper bag and I went down to the rocky end of the beach and I heaved it into the sea. But — this boy saw me. He gave me a look, so I knew what he thought. What's naturally the first thought, when you see a girl throw a brown paper bag into the sea? I had to tell him it was a cake. I said I'd goofed on the ingredients and I was ashamed it was such a failure. Then within fifteen minutes' conversation I was telling him the truth, which I never dreamed of telling anybody. He told me he was a psychology student at U.B.C. but he had dropped out because they were all behaviorists there. I didn't know—I didn't know what a behaviorist *was*.

"So," said Julie, resigned now, and marveling. "So, he became my boyfriend. For about six weeks. He wanted me to read Jung. He had very tight curly hair the color of mouse-skin. We'd lie behind the rocks and neck up a storm. It was February or March, still pretty cold. He could only meet me one day a week, always the same day. We didn't progress very far. The upshot was—well, the upshot was, really, that I discovered he was in a mental hospital. That was his day out. I don't know if I discovered that first or the scars on his neck. Did I say he had a beard? Beards were very unusual then. Leslie abhorred them. He's got one himself now. He'd tried to cut his throat. Not Leslie."

"Oh, Julie," I said, though I had heard this before. Mention of suicide is like innards pushing through an incision; you have to push it back and clap some pads on, quickly.

"It wasn't that bad. He was recovering. I'm sure he did recover. He was just a very intense kid who'd had a crisis. But I was so scared. I was scared because I felt I wasn't too far from being loony myself. With the gorging and vomiting and so on. And at the same time he confessed that he was really only seventeen years old. He'd lied to me about his age. That really did it. To think I'd been fooling around with a boy three years younger than I was. That shamed me. I told him a pack of lies about how I understood and it didn't matter and I'd meet him next week and I went home and told Leslie I couldn't stand living in a basement apartment any more, we had to move. I cried. I found us a place on the North Shore within a week. I never would go to Kits Beach. When the kids were little and we took them to the beach I would always insist on Spanish Banks or Ambleside. I wonder what became of him."

"Probably he's okay," I said. "He is probably a celebrated Jungian."

"Or a celebrated behaviorist," said Douglas. "Or a sportscaster. You don't look as if you ate too many cream puffs now."

"I got over it. I think when I got pregnant. Life is so weird."

Douglas ceremonially poured out the rest of the wine.

"You said two occasions," he said to Julie. "Are you going to leave us hanging?"

It's all right, I thought, he isn't bored or put off, he likes her. While she talked I had been watching him, wondering. Why is there always this twitchiness, when you introduce a man to a woman friend, about whether the man will be bored or put off?

"The other was weirder," said Julie. "At least I understand it less. I shouldn't bother telling such stupid stuff but now I'm on the brink I suppose I will. Well. This puzzles me. It bewilders me totally. This was in Vancouver too, but years later. I joined what was called an Encounter Group. It was just a sort of group-therapy thing for ordinary functioning miserable mixed-up people. That sort of thing was very in at the time and it was the West Coast. There was a lot of talk about getting rid of masks and feeling close to one another, which it's easy to laugh at but I think it did more good than harm. And it was all sort of new. I must sound as if I'm trying to justify myself. Like saying, I was doing macramé fifteen years ago before it was the fad. When it's probably better never to have done macramé, ever."

Douglas said, "I don't even know what macramé is."

"That's best of all," I said.

"A man from California, named Stanley, was running several of these groups. He wouldn't have said he was running them. He was very low-key. But he got paid. We did pay him. He was a psychologist. He had lovely long curly dark hair and of course he had a beard too, but beards were nothing by then. He sort of barged around in an awkward innocent way. He'd say, 'Well, this is going to sound kind of crazy but I wonder—' He had a technique of making everybody feel they were smarter than he was. He was very sincere. He'd say, 'You—don't—realize—how *lovable* you are.' No. I'm making him sound such a phony. It's got to be more complicated than that. Anyway, before long he wrote me a letter. Stanley did. It was an appreciation of my mental and physical and spiritual qualities and he said he had fallen in love with me.

"I was very mature about it. I wrote back and said he hardly knew me. He wrote oh, yes, he did. He phoned to apologize for being such a nuisance. He said he couldn't help himself. He asked if we could have coffee. No harm. We had coffee various times. I'd be doing the cheery conversation and he'd break in and say I had beautiful eyebrows. He'd say he wondered what my nipples were like. I have very ordinary eyebrows. I stopped having coffee and he took to lurking around my house in his old van. He did. I'd be shopping in the supermarket and there he'd be beside me peering into the dairy goods, with his woebegone expression. I'd get sometimes three letters a day from him, rhapsodies about myself and how much I meant to him and confessions of self-doubt and how he didn't want to turn into a guru and how good I was for him because I was so aloof and wise. What rot. I knew it was all ludicrous but I won't deny I got to depend on it, in a way. I knew the exact time of day the postman came. I decided I wasn't too old to wear my hair long.

"And about half a year after this started, another woman in our group phoned me up one day. She told me all hell had broken loose. Some woman in one of the groups had confessed to her husband she was sleeping with Stanley. The husband got very mad, he wasn't a group person, and the story got out and then another woman, and another and another, revealed the same thing, they confessed they were sleeping with Stanley, and pretty soon there was no blame attached, it was like being a victim of witchcraft. It turned out he'd been quite systematic, he'd picked one from each group, and he already had one in the group I was in so presumably it wasn't to be me. Always a married woman, not a single one who could get bothersome. Nine of them. Really. Nine women."

Douglas said, "Busy."

"All the men took that attitude," Julie said. "They all chortled. Except of course the husbands. There was a big sort of official meeting of group people at one of the women's houses. She had a lovely kitchen with a big chopping block in the middle and I remember thinking, did they do it on that? Everybody was too cool to say they were shocked about adultery or anything like that so we had to say we were mad at Stanley's betrayal of trust. Actually I think some women were mad about being left out. I said that, as a kind of joke. I never told a word about how he'd been acting with me. If there'd been anybody else getting the same treatment I was, she didn't tell either. Some of the chosen women cried. Then they'd comfort each other and compare notes. What a scene, now when I think of it! And I was so bewildered. I couldn't put it together. How can you put it together? I thought of Stanley's wife. She was a nice-looking rather nervous girl with lovely long legs. I used to meet her sometimes and to think: little do you know what your husband's been saying to me. And there were all those other women meeting her and thinking, little do you know, etcetera. Maybe she knew about them all, us all, maybe she was thinking: little do you know how many others there are. Is it possible? I'd said to him once, you know this is really just a farce, and he said, don't say that, don't say that to me! I thought he might cry. So what can you make of it? The energy. I don't mean just the physical part of it. In a way that's the least of it."

"Did the husbands get him?" Douglas said.

"A delegation went to see him. He didn't deny anything. He said he acted in good faith and from good motives and their possessiveness and jealousy was the problem. But he had to leave town, his groups had collapsed, he and his wife and their little kids left town in the van. But he sent back bills. Everybody got their bills. The women he'd been sleeping with got theirs with the rest. I got mine. No more letters, just the bill. I paid. I think most people paid. You had to think of the wife and kids.

"So there you are. I only attract the bizarre. And a good thing, because I'm married all along and virtuous at heart in spite of whatever I may have said. We should have coffee."

We drove on the back roads, in the sandy country, poor country, south of Lake Simcoe. Grass blows on the dunes. We hardly saw another car. We got out the road map to see where we were, and Douglas sidetracked to drive us through a village where he had once almost got his hands on a valuable diary. He showed us the very house. An old woman had burned it, finally—or that was what she told him—because parts of it were scandalous.

"They dread exposure," Douglas said. "Unto the third and fourth generation."

"Not like me," said Julie. "Laying bare my ridiculous almost-affairs. I don't care."

"Back and side lay bare, lay bare," sang Douglas. "Both foot and hand go cold—"

"I can lay bare," I said. "It may not be very entertaining."

"Will we risk it?" Douglas said.

"But it is interesting," I said. "I was thinking back at the restaurant about a visit I went on with a man I was in love with. This was before you came down to Toronto, Julie. We were going to visit some friends of his who had a place up in the hills on the Quebec side of the Ottawa River. I've never seen such a house. It was like a series of glass cubes with ramps and decks joining them together. The friends were Keith and Caroline. They were married, they had children, but the children weren't there. The man I was with wasn't married, he hadn't been married for a long time. I asked him on the way up what Keith and Caroline were like, and he said they were rich. I said that wasn't much of a description. He said it was Caroline's money, her daddy owned a brewery. He told me which one. There was something about the way he said 'her daddy' that made me see the money on her, the way he saw it, like long lashes or a bosom — like a luxuriant physical thing. Inherited money can make a woman seem like a treasure. It's not the same with money she's made herself, that's just brassy and ordinary. But then he said, she's very neurotic, she's really a bitch, and Keith's just a poor honest sod who works for the government. He's an A.D.M., he said. I didn't know what that was."

"Assistant Deputy Minister," Julie said.

"Even cats and children know that," said Douglas.

"Thank you," said Julie.

I was sitting in the middle. I turned mostly towards Julie as I talked.

"He said they liked to have some friends who weren't rich people or government people, people they could think of as eccentric or independent or artistic, sometimes a starveling artist Caroline could get her hooks into, to torment and show off and be bountiful with."

"Sounds as if he didn't like his friends much," Julie said.

"I don't know if he'd think of it that way. Liking or disliking. I expected them to be physically intimidating, at least I expected her to be, but they were little people. Keith was very fussy and hospitable. He had little freckled hands. I think of his hands because he was always handing you a drink or something to eat or a cushion for your back. Caroline was a wisp. She had long limp hair and a high white forehead and she wore a gray cotton dress with a hood. No makeup. I felt big and gaudy. She stood with her head bent and her hands up the sleeves of the dress while the men talked about the house. It was new. Then she said in her wispy voice how much she loved the way it was in the winter with the snow deep outside and the white rugs and the white furniture. Keith seemed rather embarrassed by her and said it was like a squash court, no depth perception. I felt sympathetic because she seemed just on the verge of making some sort of fool of herself. She seemed to be pleading with you to reassure her, and yet reassuring her seemed to involve you in a kind of fakery. She was like that. There was such a strain around her. Every subject seemed to get caught up in such emotional extravagance and fakery. The man I was with got very brusque with her, and I thought that was mean. I thought, even if she's faking, it shows she wants to feel something, doesn't it, oughtn't decent people to help her? She just didn't seem to know how.

"We sat out on a deck having drinks. Their house guest appeared. His name was Martin and he was in his early twenties. Maybe a bit older. He had a pretty superior style. Caroline asked him in a very submissive way if he would get some blankets—it was chilly on the deck—and when he went off she said he was a playwright. She said he was just a marvelous, marvelous play-wright but his plays were too European to be successful here, they were too spare and rigorous. Too spare and rigorous. Then she said, oh, the state of the theater, the state of literature in this country, it is an embarrassment, isn't it? It is the triumph of the second-rate. I thought, she mustn't know that I am a contributor to this sorry situation. Because at that time I was the assistant editor of a little magazine, you know, it was *Thousand Islands*, and I had published a poem or two. But right then she asked if I could put Martin in touch with some of the people I knew through the magazine. Straight from insult to asking favors, in that suffering sensitive little voice. I began to think she was a bitch, all right. When Martin came back with the blankets she went into a fit of shivering that was practically a ballet act and thanked him as if she was going to weep. He just dumped a blanket on her, and that way I knew they were lovers. The man I was with had told me she had lovers. What he said was, Caroline's a sexual monster. I asked if he had ever slept with her, and he said oh, yes, long ago. I wanted to ask something about his not liking her, hadn't that been any sort of impediment, but I knew that would be a very stupid question.

"Martin asked me to go for a walk. We walked down a great flight of steps and sat on a bench by the water, and he turned out to be sinister. He was vicious about some people he said he knew, in the theater in Montreal. He said that Caroline used to be fat and after she lost weight she had to have tucks taken in her belly, because the skin was so loose. He had a stuffy smell. He smoked those little cigars. I began to feel sorry for Caroline all over again. This is what you have to put up with, for the sake of your fantasies. If you have to have a literary-genius lover, this is what you're liable to end up with. If you're a fake, worse fakes will get you. That was what I was thinking.

"Well. Dinner. There was lots of wine, and brandy afterwards, and Keith kept fussing, but nobody was easy. Martin was poisonous in an obvious sneering way, trying to get one up on everybody, but Caroline was poisonous in an exquisitely moral way, she'd take every topic and twist it, so that somebody seemed crass. Martin and the man I was with finally got into a filthy argument, it was filthy mean, and Caroline cooed and whimpered. The man I was with got up and said he was going to bed, and Martin wrapped himself up in a big sulk and Caroline all of a sudden started being sweet to Keith, drinking brandy with him, ignoring Martin.

"I went to my room and the man I was with was there, in bed, though we'd been given separate rooms. Caroline was very decorous in spite of all. He stayed the night. He was furious. Before, during, and after making love, he kept on the subject of Martin, what a slimy fraud he was, and I agreed. But he's their problem, I said. So he said, they're welcome to him, the posturing shit, and at last he went to sleep and I did too, but in the middle of the night I woke up. I wakened with a revelation. Occasionally you do. I rearranged myself and listened to his breathing, and I thought — he's in love with Caroline. I knew it. I knew it. I was trying not to know it, not just because it wasn't encouraging but also because it didn't seem decent, for me to know it. But once you know something like that you never can really stop. Everything seemed clear to me. For instance Martin. That was an arrangement. She'd arranged to have the old lover and the new lover there together, just to stir things up. There was something so crude about it, but that didn't mean it wouldn't work. There was something crude about *her.* All that poetic stuff, the sensibility stuff, it was crudely done; she wasn't a talented fake, but that didn't mattter. What matters is to want to do it enough. To have the will to disturb. To be a femme fatale you don't have to be slinky and sensuous and disastrously beautiful, you just have to have the will to disturb.

"And I thought, why should I be surprised? Isn't this just what you always hear? How love isn't rational, or in one's best interests, it doesn't have anything to do with normal preferences?"

"Where do you always hear that?" Douglas said.

"It's standard. There's the intelligent sort of love that makes an intelligent choice. That's the kind you're supposed to get married on. Then there's the kind that's anything but intelligent, that's like a possession. And that's the one, that's the one, everybody really values. That's the one nobody wants to have missed out on."

"Standard," said Douglas.

"You know what I mean. You know it's true. All sorts of hackneyed notions are true."

"Hackneyed," he said. "That's a word you don't often hear."

"That's a sad story," Julie said.

"Yours were sad too," I said.

"Mine were really sort of ridiculous. Did you ask him if he was in love with her?"

"Asking wouldn't have got me anywhere," I said. "He'd brought me there to counter her with. I was his sensible choice. I was the woman he liked. I couldn't stand that. I couldn't stand it. It was so humiliating. I got very touchy and depressed. I told him he didn't really love me. That was enough. He wouldn't stand for anybody telling him things about himself."

We stopped at a country church within sight of the highway.
"Something to soothe the spirit, after all these hard-luck stories, and before the Sunday traffic," Douglas said.
We walked around the graveyard first, looking at the oldest tombstones, reading names and dates aloud.
I read out a verse I found.

"Afflictions sore long time she bore,
Physicians were in vain,
Till God did please to give her ease,
And waft her from her Pain."

"Waft," I said. "That sounds nice."
Then I felt something go over me — a shadow, a chastening. I heard the silly sound of my own voice against the truth of the lives laid down here. Lives pressed down, like layers of rotting fabric, disintegrating dark leaves. The old pain and privation. How strange, indulged, and culpable they would find us — three middle-aged people still stirred up about love, or sex.
The church was unlocked. Julie said that was very trusting of them, even Anglican churches which were supposed to be open all the time were usually locked up nowadays, because of vandals. She said she was surprised the diocese let them keep it open.
"How do you know about dioceses?" said Douglas.
"My father was a parson. Couldn't you guess?"
It was colder inside the church than outside. Julie went ahead, looking at the Roll of Honour, and memorial plaques on the walls. I looked over the back of the last pew at a row of footstools, where people could kneel to pray. Each stool was covered with needle-work, in a different design.
Douglas put his hand on my shoulder blade, not around my shoulders. If Julie turned she wouldn't notice. He brushed his hand down my back and settled at my waist, applying a slight pressure to

the ribs before he passed behind me and walked up the outer aisle, ready to explain something to Julie. She was trying to read the Latin on a stained-glass window.

On one footstool was the Cross of St. George, on another the Cross of St. Andrew.

I hadn't expected there would be any announcement from him, either while I was telling the story, or after it was over. I did not think that he would tell me that I was right, or that I was wrong. I heard him translating, Julie laughing, but I couldn't attend. I felt that I had been overtaken—stumped by a truth about myself, or at least a fact, that I couldn't do anything about. A pressure of the hand, with no promise about it, could admonish and comfort me. Something unresolved could become permanent. I could be always bent on knowing, and always in the dark, about what was important to him, and what was not.

On another footstool there was a dove on a blue ground, with the olive branch in its mouth; on another a lamp, with lines of straight golden stitching to show its munificent rays; on another a white lily. No—it was a trillium. When I made this discovery, I called out for Douglas and Julie to come and see it. I was pleased with this homely emblem, among the more ancient and exotic. I think I became rather boisterous, from then on. In fact all three of us did, as if we had each one, secretly, come upon an unacknowledged spring of hopefulness. When we stopped for gas, Julie and I exclaimed at the sight of Douglas's credit cards, and declared that we didn't want to go back to Toronto. We talked of how we would all run away to Nova Scotia, and live off the credit cards. Then when the crackdown came we would go into hiding, change our names, take up humble occupations. Julie and I would work as barmaids. Douglas could set traps for lobsters. Then we could all be happy.

Visitors

Mildred had just come into the kitchen and was looking at the clock, which said five to two. She had thought it might be at least half past. Wilfred came in from the back, through the utility room, and said, "Hadn't you ought to be out there keeping them company?"

His brother Albert's wife, Grace, and her sister, Vera, were sitting out in the shade of the carport making lace tablecloths. Albert was out at the back of the house, sitting beside the patch of garden where Wilfred grew beans, tomatoes, and cucumbers. Every half-hour Wilfred checked to see which tomatoes were ripe enough to pick. He picked them half-ripe and spread them out on the kitchen windowsill, so the bugs wouldn't get them.

"I was," said Mildred. She ran a glass of water. "I maybe might take them for a drive," she said when she had finished drinking it.

"That's a good idea."

"How is Albert?"

Albert had spent most of the day before, the first full day of the visit, lying down.

"I can't figure out."

"Well surely if he felt sick he'd say so."

"That's just it," said Wilfred. "That's just what he wouldn't."

This was the first time Wilfred had seen his brother in more than thirty years.

Wilfred and Mildred were retired. Their house was small and they weren't, but they got along fine in the space. They had a kitchen not much wider than a hallway, a bathroom about the usual size, two bedrooms that were pretty well filled up when you got a double bed and a dresser into them, a living room where a large sofa sat five feet in front of a large television set, with a low table about the size of a coffin in between, and a small glassed-in porch.

Mildred had set up a table on the porch to serve meals on. Ordinarily, she and Wilfred ate at the table under the kitchen window. If one of them was up and moving around, the other always stayed sitting down. There was no way five people could have managed there, even when three of them were as skinny as these visitors were.

Fortunately there was a daybed on the porch, and Vera, the sister-in-law, slept on that. The sister-in-law had been a surprise to Mildred and Wilfred. Wilfred had done the talking on the phone (nobody in his family, he said, had ever written a letter); according to him, no sister-in-law had been mentioned, just Albert and his wife. Mildred thought Wilfred might not have heard, because he was so excited. Talking to Albert on the phone, from Logan, Ontario, to Elder, Saskatchewan, taking in the news that his brother proposed to visit him, Wilfred had been in a dither of hospitality, reassurances, amazement.

"You come right ahead," he yelled over the phone to Saskatchewan. "We can put you up as long as you want to stay. We got plenty of room. We'll be glad to. Never mind your return tickets. You get on down here and enjoy the summer." It might have been while he was going on like this that Albert was explaining about the sister-in-law.

"How do you tell them apart?" said Wilfred on first meeting Grace and Vera. "Or do you always bother?" He meant it for a joke.

"They're not twins," said Albert, without a glance at either of them. Albert was a short, thin man in dark clothes, who looked as if he might weigh heavy, like dense wood. He wore a string tie and a westerner's hat, but these did not give him a jaunty appearance. His pale cheeks hung down on either side of his chin.

"You look like sisters, though," said Mildred genially to the two dried-out, brown-spotted, gray-haired women. Look what the prairie did to a woman's skin, she was thinking. Mildred was vain of her own skin; it was her compensation for being fat. Also, she put an ash-gold rinse on her hair and wore coordinated pastel pants and tops. Grace and Vera wore dresses with loose pleats over their flat chests, and cardigans in summer. "You look a lot more like sisters than those two look like brothers."

It was true. Wilfred had a big head as well as a big stomach, and an anxious, eager, changeable face. He looked like a man who put a high value on joking and chatting, and so he did.

"It's lucky there's none of you too fleshy," Wilfred said. "You can all fit into the one bed. Naturally Albert gets the middle."

"Don't pay attention to him," said Mildred. "There's a good daybed if you don't mind sleeping on the porch," she said to Vera. "It's got blinds on the windows and it gets the best breeze of anywhere."

God knows if the women even caught on to what Wilfred was joking about.

"That'll be fine," said Albert.

With Albert and Grace sleeping in the spare room, which was where Mildred usually slept, Mildred and Wilfred had to share a double bed. They weren't used to it. In the night, Wilfred had one of his wild dreams, which were the reason Mildred had moved to the spare room in the first place.

"Grab ahold!" yelled Wilfred, in terror. Was he on a lake boat, trying to pull somebody out of the water?

"Wilfred, wake up! Stop hollering and scaring everybody to death."

"I am awake," said Wilfred. "I wasn't hollering."

"Then I'm Her Majesty the Queen."

They were lying on their backs. They both heaved, and turned to face the outside. Each kept a courteous but firm hold on the top sheet.

"Is it whales that can't turn over when they get up on the beach?" Mildred said.

"I can still turn over," said Wilfred. They aligned backsides. "Maybe you think that's the only thing I can do."

"Keep still, now, you've got them all listening."

In the morning she said, "Did Wilfred wake you up? He's a terrible hollerer in his sleep."

"I hadn't got to sleep anyway," Albert said.

She went out and got the two ladies into the car. "We'll take a little drive and raise a breeze to cool us off," she said. They sat in the back, because there wasn't really room left over in the front, even for two such skinnies.

"I'm the chauffeur!" said Mildred merrily. "Where to, your ladyships?"

"Just anyplace you'd like," said one of them. When she wasn't looking at them Mildred couldn't be sure which was talking.

She drove them around Winter Court and Chelsea Drive to look at the new houses with their landscaping and swimming pools. Then she took them to the Fish and Game Club, where they saw the ornamental fowl, the family of deer, the raccoons, and the caged bobcat. She felt as tired as if she had driven to Toronto, and in need of refreshment, so she headed out to the place on the highway to buy ice-cream cones. They both asked for a small vanilla. Mildred had a mixed double: rum-raisin and praline cream. They sat at a picnic table licking their ice-cream cones and looking at a field of corn.

"They grow a lot of corn around here," Mildred said. Albert had been the manager of a grain elevator before he retired, so she supposed they might be interested in crops. "Do they grow a lot of corn out west?"

They thought about it. Grace said, "Well. Some."

Vera said, "I was wondering."

"Wondering what?" said Mildred cheerfully.

"You wouldn't have a Pentecostal Church here in Logan?"

They set out in the car again, and after some blundering, Mildred found the Pentecostal Church. It was not one of the handsomer churches in town. It was a plain building, of cement blocks, with the doors and the window-trim painted orange. A sign told the minister's name and the times of service. There was no shade tree near it and no bushes or flowers, just a dry yard. Maybe that would remind them of Saskatchewan.

"Pentecostal Church," said Mildred, reading the sign. "Is that the church you people go to?"

"Yes."

"Wilfred and I are not regular churchgoers. If we went, I guess we would go to the United. Do you want to get out and see if it's unlocked?"

"Oh, no."

"If it was locked, we could try and locate the minister. I don't know him, but there's a lot of Logan people I don't know yet. I know the ones that bowl and the ones that play euchre at the Legion. Otherwise, I don't know many. Would you like to call on him?"

They said no. Mildred was thinking about the Pentecostal Church, and it seemed to her that it was the one where people spoke in tongues. She thought she might as well get something out of the afternoon, so she went ahead and asked them: was that true?

"Yes, it's true."

"But what are tongues?"

A pause. One said, with difficulty, "It's the voice of God."

"Heavens," said Mildred. She wanted to ask more — did they speak in tongues themselves? — but they made her nervous. It was clear that she made them nervous, too. She let them look a few minutes more, then asked if they had seen enough. They said they had, and thanked her.

If she had married Wilfred when they were young, Mildred thought, she would have known something about his family and what to expect of them. Mildred and Wilfred had married in late middle age, after a courtship of only six weeks. Neither of them had been married before. Wilfred had moved around too much, or so he said. He had worked on the lake boats and in lumber camps, he had helped build houses and had pumped gas and had pruned trees; he had worked from California to the Yukon and from the east coast to the west. Mildred had spent most of her life in the town of McGaw, twenty miles from Logan, where she now lived. She had been an only child, and had been given tap-dancing lessons and then sent to business school. From business school she went into the office of the Toll Shoe Factory, in McGaw, and shortly became the sweetheart of Mr. Toll, who owned it. There she stayed.

It was during the last days of Mr. Toll's life that she met Wilfred. Mr. Toll was in the psychiatric hospital overlooking Lake Huron. Wilfred was working there as a groundsman and guard. Mr. Toll was eighty-two years old and didn't know who Mildred was, but she visited him anyway. He called her Sadie, that being the name of his wife. His wife was dead now but she had been alive all the time Mr. Toll and Mildred were taking their little trips together, staying at hotels together, staying in the cottage Mr. Toll had bought for Mildred at Amberley Beach. In all the time she had known him, Mildred had never heard him speak of his wife except in a dry, impatient way. Now she had to listen to him tell Sadie he loved her, ask Sadie's forgiveness. Pretending she was Sadie, Mildred said she forgave him. She dreaded some confession regarding a brassy-headed floozy named Mildred. Nevertheless, she kept on visiting. She hadn't the heart to deprive him. That had been her trouble all along. But when the sons or daughters or Sadie's sisters showed up, she had to make herself scarce. Once, taken by surprise, she had to get Wilfred to let her out a back way. She sat down on a cement wall by the back door and had a cigarette, and Wilfred asked her if anything was the matter. Being upset, and having nobody in McGaw to talk to, she told him what was going on, even about the letter she had received from a lawyer telling her she had to get out of the Amberley cottage. She had thought all along it was in her name, but it wasn't.

Wilfred took her side. He went in and spied on the visiting family, and reported that they were sitting staring at the poor old man like crows on a fence. He didn't point out to Mildred what she already knew: that she should have seen the writing on the wall. She herself said it.

"I should've gotten out while I still had something going for me."

"You must've been fond of him," said Wilfred reasonably.

"It was never love," said Mildred sadly. Wilfred scowled with deep embarrassment. Mildred had the sense not to go on, and couldn't have explained, anyway, how she had been transfixed by Mr. Toll in his more vigorous days, when his need for her was so desperate she thought he would turn himself inside out.

Mr. Toll died in the middle of the night. Wilfred phoned Mildred at seven in the morning.

"I didn't want to wake you up," he said. "But I wanted to make sure you knew before you heard it out in public."

Then he asked her to have supper with him in a restaurant. Being used to Mr. Toll, she was surprised at Wilfred's table manners. He was nervous, she decided. He got upset because the waitress hadn't brought their glasses of water. Mildred told him she was going to quit her job, she wanted to get clear of McGaw, she might end up out west.

"Why not end up in Logan?" Wilfred said. "I've got a house there. It's not so big a house, but it'll take two."

So it dawned on her. His nervousness, his bad temper with the waitress, his sloppiness, must all relate to her. She asked if he had ever been married before, and if not, why not?

He said he had always been on the go, and besides, it wasn't often you met a good-hearted woman. She was about to make sure he had things straight, by pointing out that she expected nothing from Mr. Toll's will (nothing was what she got), but she saw in the nick of time that Wilfred was the kind of man who would be insulted.

Instead, she said, "You know I'm secondhand goods?"

"None of that," he said. "We won't have any of that kind of talk around the house. Is it settled?"

Mildred said yes. She was glad to see an immediate improvement in his behavior to the waitress. In fact, he went overboard, apologizing for his impatience earlier, telling her he had worked in a restaurant himself. He told her where the restaurant was, up on the Alaska Highway. The girl had trouble getting away to serve coffee at the other tables.

No such improvement took place in Wilfred's table manners. She guessed that this was one of his bachelor ways she would just have to learn to live with.

"You better tell me a bit about where you were born, and so on," Mildred said.

He told her he had been born on a farm in Hullett Township, but left there when he was three days old.

"Itchy feet," he said, and laughed. Then he sobered, and told her that his mother had died within a few hours of his birth, and his aunt had taken him. His aunt was married to a man who worked on the railway. They moved around, and when he was twelve his aunt died. Then the man she was married to looked at Wilfred and said, "You're a big boy. What size shoe do you wear?"

"Number nine," said Wilfred.

"Then you're big enough to earn your own living."

"Him and my aunt had eight kids of their own," said Wilfred. "So I don't blame him."

"Did you have any brothers and sisters in your real family?" Mildred thought cozily of her own life long ago: her mother fixing her curls in the morning, the kitten, named Pansy, that she used to dress up in doll's clothes and wheel round the block in the doll buggy.

"I had two older sisters, married. Both dead now. And one brother. He went out to Saskatchewan. He has a job managing a grain elevator. I don't know what he gets paid but I imagine it's pretty good. He went to business college, like yourself. He's a different person than me, way different."

The day that Albert had stayed in bed, he wanted the curtains shut. He didn't want a doctor. Wilfred couldn't get out of him what was wrong. Albert said he was just tired.

"Then maybe he is tired," said Mildred. "Let him rest."

But Wilfred was in and out of the spare room all day. He was talking, smoking, asking Albert how he felt. He told Albert he had cured himself of migraine headaches by eating fresh leeks from the bush in the spring. Albert said he didn't have a migraine headache, even if he did want the curtains closed. He said he had never had a bad headache in his life. Wilfred explained that you could have migraine headaches without knowing it — that is, without having the actual ache — so that could be what Albert had. Albert said he didn't see how that was possible.

Early that afternoon Mildred heard Wilfred crashing around in the clothes closet. He emerged calling her name.

"Mildred! Mildred! Where is the Texas mickey?"

"In the buffet," said Mildred, and she got it out for him so he wouldn't be rummaging around in there in her mother's china. It was in a tall box, gold-embossed, with the Legion crest on it. Wilfred bore it into the bedroom and set it on the dresser for Albert to see.

"What do you think that is and how do you think I come by it?"

It was a bottle of whiskey, a gallon bottle of whiskey, 140-proof, that Wilfred had won playing darts at the tournament in Owen Sound. The tournament had taken place in February three years before. Wilfred described the terrible drive from Logan to Owen Sound, himself driving, the other members of the dart team urging him to stop in every town they reached, and not to try to get farther. A blizzard blew off Lake Huron, they were enveloped in whiteouts, trucks and buses loomed up in front of their eyes out of the wall of snow, there was no room to maneuver because the road was walled with drifts ten feet high. Wilfred kept driving; driving blind, driving through skids and drifts across the road. At last, on Highway No. 6, a blue light appeared ahead of him, a twirling blue light, a beacon, a rescue-light. It was the snowplow, travelling ahead of them. The road was filling in almost as fast as the snowplow cleared it, but by keeping close behind the plow they were guided safe into Owen Sound. There they played in the tournament, and were victorious.

"Do you ever play darts yourself?" Mildred heard Wilfred ask his brother.

"As a rule they play darts in places that serve liquor," Albert said. "As a rule I don't go into those places."

"Well, this here is liquor I would never consider drinking. I keep it for the honor of it."

Their sitting took on a regular pattern. In the afternoon Grace and Vera sat in the driveway crocheting their tablecloths. Mildred sat with them off and on. Albert and Wilfred sat at the back of the house, by the vegetables. After supper they all sat together, moving their chairs to the lawn in front of the flower beds, which was then in the shade. Grace and Vera went on crocheting as long as they could see.

Wilfred admired the crocheting.

"How much would you get for one of those things?"

"Hundreds of dollars," Albert said.

"It's sold for the church," said Grace.

"Blanche Black," said Wilfred, "was the greatest crocheter, knitter, sewer, what-all, and cook of any girl I ever knew."

"What a name," said Mildred.

"She lived in the state of Michigan. It was when I got fed up with working on the boats and I had a job over there working on a farm. She could make quilts or anything. And bake bread, fancy cake, anything. But not very good-looking. In fact, she was about as good-looking as a turnip, and about the shape."

Now came a story that Mildred had heard before. It was told when the subject of pretty girls and homely girls came up, or baking, or box socials, or pride. Wilfred told how he and a friend went to a box social, where at an intermission in the dancing you bid on a box, and the box contained a lunch, and you ate lunch with the girl whose box you had bought. Blanche Black brought a box lunch and so did a pretty girl, a Miss Buchanan, and Wilfred and his friend got into the back room and switched all the wrappings around on these two boxes. So when it came time to bid, a fellow named Jack Fleck, who had a very good opinion of himself and a case on Miss Buchanan, bid for the box he thought was hers, and Wilfred and his friend bid for the box that everybody thought was Blanche Black's. The boxes were given out, and to his consternation Jack Fleck was compelled to sit down with Blanche Black. Wilfred and his friend were set up with Miss Buchanan. Then Wilfred looked in the box and saw there was nothing but sandwiches with a kind of pink paste on them.

"So over I go to Jack Fleck and I say, 'Trade you the lunch and the girl.' I didn't do it entirely on account of the food but because I saw how he was going to treat that poor creature. He agreed like a shot and we sat down. We ate fried chicken. Home-cured ham and biscuits. Date pie. Never fed better in my life. And tucked down at the bottom of the box she had a mickey of whiskey. So I sat eating and drinking and looking at him over there with his paste sandwiches."

Wilfred must have started that story as a tribute to ladies whose crocheting or baking or whatever put them away ahead of ladies who had better looks to offer, but Mildred didn't think even Grace and Vera would be pleased to be put in the category of Blanche Black, who looked like a turnip. And mentioning the mickey of whiskey was a mistake. It was a mistake as far as she was concerned, too. She thought of how much she would like a drink at this moment. She thought of Old Fashioneds, Brown Cows, Pink Ladies, every fancy drink you could imagine.

"I better go and see if I can fix that air-conditioner," Wilfred said. "We'll roast tonight if I don't."

Mildred sat on. Over in the next block there was a blue light that sizzled loudly, catching bugs.

"I guess those things make a difference with the flies," she said.

"Fries them," said Albert.

"I don't like the noise, though."

She thought he wasn't going to answer but he finally said, "If it doesn't make a noise it can't destroy the bugs."

When she went into the house to put on some coffee (a good thing Pentecostals had no ban on that), Mildred could hear the air-conditioner humming away. She looked into the bedroom and saw Wilfred stretched out asleep. Worn out.

"Wilfred?"

He jumped. "I wasn't asleep."

"They're still sitting out front. I thought I'd make us some coffee." Then she couldn't resist adding, "I'm glad it isn't anything too serious the matter with the air-conditioner."

On the next-to-last day of the visit, they decided to drive forty-five miles over to Hullett Township to see the place where Wilfred and Albert were born. This was Mildred's idea. She had thought Albert might suggest it, and she was waiting for that, because she didn't want to push Albert into doing anything he was too tired to do. But at last she mentioned it. She said she had been trying for a long time to get Wilfred to take her, but he said he wouldn't know where to go, since he had never been back after being taken away as a baby. The buildings were all gone, the farms were gone; that whole part of the township had become a conservation area.

Grace and Vera brought along their tablecloths. Mildred wondered why they didn't get sick, working with their heads down in a moving car. She sat between them in the back seat, feeling squashed, although she knew she was the one doing the squashing. Wilfred drove and Albert sat beside him.

Wilfred always got into an argumentative mood when driving.

"Now what is so wrong with taking a bet?" he said. "I don't mean gambling. I don't mean you go down to Las Vegas and you throw all your money away on those games and machines. With betting you can sometimes be lucky. I had a free winter in the Soo on a bet."

"Sault Ste. Marie," Albert said.

"We always said The Soo. I was off the *Kamloops*, I was in for the winter. The old *Kamloops*, that was a terrible boat. One night in the bar they were listening to the hockey game on the radio. Before television. Playing Sudbury. Sudbury four, the Soo nothing."

"We're getting to where we turn off the highway," Albert said.

Mildred said, "Watch for the turn, Wilfred."

"I am watching."

Albert said, "Not this one but the next one."

"I was helping them out in there, I was slinging beer for tips because I didn't have a union card, and this grouchy fellow was cursing at the Soo. They might come out of it yet, I said, the Soo might beat them yet."

"Right here," said Albert.

Wilfred made a sharp turn. "Put your money where your mouth is! Put your money where your mouth is! That's what he said to me. Ten to one. I didn't have the money, but the fellow that owned the hotel was a good fellow, and I was helping him out, so he says, take the bet, Wilfred! He says, you go ahead and take the bet!"

"The Hullett Conservation Area," Mildred read from a sign. They drove along the edge of a dark swamp.

"Heavens, it's gloomy in there!" she said. "And water standing, at this time of the year."

"The Hullett Swamp," said Albert. "It goes for miles."

They came out of the swamp and on either side was wasteland, churned-up black earth, ditches, uprooted trees. The road was very rough.

"I'll back you, he says. So I went ahead and took the bet."

Mildred read the crossroad signs: "Dead end. No winter maintenance beyond this point."

Albert said, "Now we'll want to turn south."

"South?" said Wilfred. "South. I took it and you know what happened? The Soo came through and beat Sudbury seven to four!"

There was a large pond and a lookout stand, and a sign saying "Wildfowl Observation Point."

"Wildfowl," said Mildred. "I wonder what there is to see?"

Wilfred was not in the mood to stop. "You wouldn't know a crow from a hawk, Mildred! The Soo beat Sudbury seven to four and I had my bet. That fellow sneaked out when I was busy but the manager knew where he lived and next day I had a hundred dollars. When I got called to go back on the *Kamloops* I had exactly to the penny the amount of money I had when I got off before Christmas. I had the winter free in the Soo."

"This looks like it," Albert said.

"Where?" asked Wilfred.

"Here."

"Here? I had the winter free, all from one little bet."

They turned off the road into a rough sort of lane, where there were wooden arrows on a post. "Hawthorn Trail. Sugar Bush Trail. Tamarack Trail. No motor vehicles beyond this point." Wilfred stopped the car and he and Albert got out. Grace got out to let Mildred out and then got back in. The arrows were all pointing in the same direction. Mildred thought some children had probably tampered with them. She didn't see any trails at all. They had climbed out of the low swampland and were among rough little hills.

"This where your farm was?" she asked Albert.

"The house was up there," said Albert, pointing uphill. "The lane ran up there. The barn was behind."

There was a brown wooden box on the post under the arrows. She opened it up and took out a handful of brightly colored pamphlets. She looked through them.

"These tell about the different trails."

"Maybe they'd like something to read if they aren't going to get out," said Wilfred, nodding toward the women in the car. "Maybe you should go and ask them."

"They're busy," Mildred said. She thought she should go and tell Grace and Vera to roll down the windows so they wouldn't suffocate, but she decided to let them figure that out for themselves. Albert was setting off up the hill and she and Wilfred followed him, plowing through goldenrod, which, to her surprise, was easier than grass to walk in. It didn't tangle you so, and felt silky. Goldenrod she knew, and wild carrot, but what were these little white flowers on a low bush, and this blue one with coarse petals, and this feathery purple? You always heard about the spring flowers, the buttercups and the trilliums and marsh marigolds, but here were just as many, names unknown, at the end of summer. There were also little frogs leaping from underfoot, and small white butterflies, and hundreds of bugs she couldn't see that nibbled at and stung her bare arms.

Albert walked up and down in the grass. He made a turn, he stopped and looked around and started again. He was trying to get the outline of the house. Wilfred frowned at the grass, and said, "They don't leave you much."

"Who?" said Mildred faintly. She fanned herself with goldenrod.

"Conservation people. They don't leave one stone of the foundation, or the cellar hole, or one brick or beam. They dig it all out and fill it all in and haul it all away."

"Well, they couldn't leave a pile of rubble, I guess, for people to fall over."

"You sure this is where it would have been?" Wilfred said.

"Right about here," said Albert, "facing south. Here would've been the front door."

"You could be standing on the step, Albert," said Mildred, with as much interest as she had energy for.

But Albert said, "We never had a step at the front door. We only opened it once that I can remember, and that for Mother's coffin. We put some chunks of wood down then, to make a temporary step."

"That's a lilac," said Mildred, noticing a bush near where he was standing. "Was that there then? It must have been there then."

"I think it was."

"Is it a white one or a purple?"

"I can't say."

That was the difference between him and Wilfred, she thought. Wilfred would have said. Whether he remembered or not, he would have said, and then believed himself. Brothers and sisters were a mystery to her. There were Grace and Vera, speaking like two mouths out of the same head, and Wilfred and Albert without a thread of connection between them.

They ate lunch in a café down the road. It wasn't licensed, or Mildred would have ordered beer, never mind how she shocked Grace and Vera or how Wilfred glared at her. She was hot enough. Albert's face was a bright pink and his eyes had a fierce, concentrating look. Wilfred looked cantankerous.

"It used to be a lot bigger swamp," Albert said. "They've drained it."

"That's so people can get in and walk and see different things," said Mildred. She still had the red and green and yellow pamphlets in her hand, and she smoothed them out and looked at them.

"Squawks, calls, screeches, and cries echo throughout this bush," she read. "Do you recognize any of them? Most are made by birds." What else would they be made by? she wondered.

"A man went into the Hullett Swamp and remained there," Albert said.

Wilfred made a mess of his ketchup and gravy, then dipped his french fries into it with his fingers.

"For how long?" he said.

"Forever."

"You going to eat them?" said Wilfred, indicating Mildred's french fries.

"Forever?" said Mildred, dividing them and sliding half onto Wilfred's plate. "Did you know him, Albert?"

"No. It was too long ago."

"Did you know his name?"

"Lloyd Sallows."

"Who?" said Wilfred.

"Lloyd Sallows," said Albert. "He worked on a farm."

"I never heard of him," Wilfred said.

"How do you mean, he went into the swamp?" said Mildred.

"They found his clothes on the railway tracks and that's what they said, he went into the swamp."

"Why would he go in there without his clothes on?"

Albert thought for a few minutes and said, "He could have wanted to go wild."

"Did he leave his shoes, too?"

"I would think so."

"He might have committed suicide," Mildred said briskly. "Did they look for a body?"

"They did look."

"Or might have been murdered. Did he have any enemies? Was he in trouble? Maybe he was in debt or in trouble about a girl."

"No," said Albert.

"So they never found a trace of him?"

"No."

"Was there any suspicious sort of person around at the time?"

"No."

"Well, there must be some explanation," said Mildred. "A person, if they're not dead, they go on living somewhere."

Albert forked the hamburger patty out of his bun onto his plate, where he proceeded to cut it up into little pieces. He had not yet eaten anything.

"He was thought to be living in the swamp."

"They should've looked in the swamp, then," Wilfred said.

"They went in at both ends and said they'd meet in the middle but they didn't."

"Why not?" said Mildred.

"You can't just walk your way through that swamp. You couldn't then."

"So they thought he was in there?" Wilfred persisted. "Is that what they thought?"

"Most did," said Albert, rather grudgingly. Wilfred snorted.

"What was he living on?"

Albert put down his knife and fork and said somberly, "Flesh."

All of a sudden, after being so hot, Mildred's arms came out in goose bumps.

"Did anybody ever see him?" she asked, in a more subdued and thoughtful voice than before.

"Two said so."

"Who were they?"

"One was a lady that when I knew her, she was in her fifties. She had been a little girl at the time. She saw him when she was sent back to get the cows. She saw a long white person running behind the trees."

"Near enough that she could tell if it was a boy or a girl?" said Wilfred.

Albert took the question seriously.

"I don't know how near."

"That was one person," Mildred said. "Who was the other?"

"It was a boy fishing. This was years later. He looked up and saw a white fellow watching him from the other bank. He thought he'd seen a ghost."

"Is that all?" said Wilfred. "They never found out what happened?"

"No."

"I guess he'd be dead by now anyway," Mildred said.

"Dead long ago," said Albert.

If Wilfred had been telling that story, Mildred thought, it would have gone someplace, there would have been some kind of ending to it. Lloyd Sallows might reappear stark naked to collect on a bet, or he would come back dressed as a millionaire, maybe having tricked some gangsters who had robbed him. In Wilfred's stories you could always be sure that the gloomy parts would give way to something better, and if somebody behaved in a peculiar way there was an explanation for it. If Wilfred figured in his own stories, as he usually did, there was always a stroke of luck for him somewhere, a good meal or a bottle of whiskey or some money. Neither luck nor money played a part in this story. She wondered why Albert had told it, what it meant to him.

"How did you happen to remember that story, Albert?"

As soon as she said that, she knew she shouldn't have spoken. It was none of her business.

"I see they have apple or raisin pie," she said.

"No apple or raisin pie in the Hullett Swamp!" said Wilfred raucously. "I'm having apple."

Albert picked up a cold piece of hamburger and put it down and said, "It's not a story. It's something that happened."

Mildred had stripped the bed the visitors had slept in, and hadn't got it made up again, so she lay down beside Wilfred, on their first night by themselves.

Before she went to sleep she said to Wilfred, "Nobody in their right mind would go and live in a swamp."

"If you did want to live someplace like that," said Wilfred, "the place to live would be the bush, where you wouldn't have so much trouble making a fire if you wanted one."

He seemed restored to good humor. But in the night she was wakened by his crying. She was not badly startled, because she had known him to cry before, usually at night. It was hard to tell how she knew. He wasn't making any noise and he wasn't moving. Maybe that in itself was the unusual thing. She knew that he was lying beside her on his back with tears welling up in his eyes and wetting his face.

"Wilfred?"

Any time before, when he had consented to tell her why he was crying, the reason had seemed to her very queer, something thought up on the spur of the moment, or only distantly connected with the real reason. But maybe it was as close as he could get.

"Wilfred."

"Albert and I will probably never see each other again," said Wilfred in a loud voice with no trace of tears, or any clear indication of either satisfaction or regret.

"Unless we did go to Saskatchewan," said Mildred. An invitation had been extended, and she had thought at the time she would be as likely to visit Siberia.

"Eventually," she added.

"Eventually, maybe," Wilfred said. He gave a prolonged, noisy sniff that seemed to signal content. "Not next week."

The Moons of Jupiter

I found my father in the heart wing, on the eighth floor of Toronto
General Hospital. He was in a semi-private room. The other bed
was empty. He said that his hospital insurance covered only a bed
in the ward, and he was worried that he might be charged extra.

"I never asked for a semi-private," he said.

I said the wards were probably full.

"No. I saw some empty beds when they were wheeling me
by."

"Then it was because you had to be hooked up to that thing,"
I said. "Don't worry. If they're going to charge you extra, they tell
you about it."

"That's likely it," he said. "They wouldn't want those
doohickeys set up in the wards. I guess I'm covered for that kind of
thing."

I said I was sure he was.

He had wires taped to his chest. A small screen hung over his
head. On the screen a bright jagged line was continually being
written. The writing was accompanied by a nervous electronic
beeping. The behavior of his heart was on display. I tried to ignore
it. It seemed to me that paying such close attention—in fact,
dramatizing what ought to be a most secret activity—was asking

for trouble. Anything exposed that way was apt to flare up and go crazy.

My father did not seem to mind. He said they had him on tranquillizers. You know, he said, the happy pills. He did seem calm and optimistic.

It had been a different story the night before. When I brought him into the hospital, to the emergency room, he had been pale and closemouthed. He had opened the car door and stood up and said quietly, "Maybe you better get me one of those wheelchairs." He used the voice he always used in a crisis. Once, our chimney caught on fire; it was on a Sunday afternoon and I was in the dining room pinning together a dress I was making. He came in and said in that same matter-of-fact, warning voice, "Janet. Do you know where there's some baking powder?" He wanted it to throw on the fire. Afterwards he said, "I guess it was your fault — sewing on Sunday."

I had to wait for over an hour in the emergency waiting room. They summoned a heart specialist who was in the hospital, a young man. He called me out into the hall and explained to me that one of the valves of my father's heart had deteriorated so badly that there ought to be an immediate operation.

I asked him what would happen otherwise.

"He'd have to stay in bed," the doctor said.

"How long?"

"Maybe three months."

"I meant, how long would he live?"

"That's what I meant, too," the doctor said.

I went to see my father. He was sitting up in bed in a curtained-off corner. "It's bad, isn't it?" he said. "Did he tell you above the valve?"

"It's not as bad as it could be," I said. Then I repeated, even exaggerated, anything hopeful the doctor had said. "You're not in any immediate danger. Your physical condition is good, otherwise."

"Otherwise," said my father, gloomily.

I was tired from the drive — all the way up to Dalgleish, to get him, and back to Toronto since noon — and worried about getting the rented car back on time, and irritated by an article I had been reading in a magazine in the waiting room. It was about another writer, a woman younger, better-looking, probably more talented than I am. I had been in England for two months and so I had not seen this article before, but it crossed my mind while I was reading that my father would have. I could hear him saying, Well, I didn't see anything about you in *Maclean's*. And if he had read something about me he would say, Well, I didn't think too much of that writeup. His tone would be humorous and indulgent but would produce in me a familiar dreariness of spirit. The message I got from him was simple: Fame must be striven for, then apologized for. Getting or not getting it, you will be to blame.

I was not surprised by the doctor's news. I was prepared to hear something of the sort and was pleased with myself for taking it calmly, just as I would be pleased with myself for dressing a wound or looking down from the frail balcony of a high building. I thought, Yes, it's time; there has to be something, here it is. I did not feel any of the protest I would have felt twenty, even ten, years before. When I saw from my father's face that he felt it — that refusal leapt up in him as readily as if he had been thirty or forty years younger — my heart hardened, and I spoke with a kind of badgering cheerfulness. "Otherwise is plenty," I said.

The next day he was himself again.

That was how I would have put it. He said it appeared to him now that the young fellow, the doctor, might have been a bit too eager to operate. "A bit knife-happy," he said. He was both mocking and showing off the hospital slang. He said that another doctor had examined him, an older man, and had given it as his opinion that rest and medication might do the trick.

I didn't ask what trick.

"He says I've got a defective valve, all right. There's certainly some damage. They wanted to know if I had rheumatic fever when I was a kid. I said I didn't think so. But half the time then you weren't diagnosed what you had. My father was not one for getting the doctor."

The thought of my father's childhood, which I always pictured as bleak and dangerous — the poor farm, the scared sisters, the harsh father — made me less resigned to his dying. I thought of him running away to work on the lake boats, running along the railway tracks, toward Goderich, in the evening light. He used to tell about that trip. Somewhere along the track he found a quince tree. Quince trees are rare in our part of the country; in fact, I have never seen one. Not even the one my father found, though he once took us on an expedition to look for it. He thought he knew the crossroad it was near, but we could not find it. He had not been able to eat the fruit, of course, but he had been impressed by its existence. It made him think he had got into a new part of the world.

The escaped child, the survivor, an old man trapped here by his leaky heart. I didn't pursue these thoughts. I didn't care to think of his younger selves. Even his bare torso, thick and white—he had the body of a workingman of his generation, seldom exposed to the sun—was a danger to me; it looked so strong and young. The wrinkled neck, the age-freckled hands and arms, the narrow, courteous head, with its thin gray hair and mustache, were more what I was used to.

"Now, why would I want to get myself operated on?" said my father reasonably. "Think of the risk at my age, and what for? A few years at the outside. I think the best thing for me to do is go home and take it easy. Give in gracefully. That's all you can do, at my age. Your attitude changes, you know. You go through some mental changes. It seems more natural."

"What does?" I said.

"Well, death does. You can't get more natural than that. No, what I mean, specifically, is not having the operation."

"That seems more natural?"

"Yes."

"It's up to you," I said, but I did approve. This was what I would have expected of him. Whenever I told people about my father I stressed his independence, his self-sufficiency, his forbearance. He worked in a factory, he worked in his garden, he read history books. He could tell you about the Roman emperors or the Balkan wars. He never made a fuss.

Judith, my younger daughter, had come to meet me at Toronto Airport two days before. She had brought the boy she was living with, whose name was Don. They were driving to Mexico in the morning, and while I was in Toronto I was to stay in their apartment. For the time being, I live in Vancouver. I sometimes say I have my headquarters in Vancouver.

"Where's Nichola?" I said, thinking at once of an accident or an overdose. Nichola is my older daughter. She used to be a student at the Conservatory, then she became a cocktail waitress, then she was out of work. If she had been at the airport, I would probably have said something wrong. I would have asked her what her plans were, and she would have gracefully brushed back her hair and said, "Plans?"—as if that was a word I had invented.

"I knew the first thing you'd say would be about Nichola," Judith said.

"It wasn't. I said hello and I—"

"We'll get your bag," Don said neutrally.

"Is she all right?"

"I'm sure she is," said Judith, with a fabricated air of amusement. "You wouldn't look like that if I was the one who wasn't here."

"Of course I would."

"You wouldn't. Nichola is the baby of the family. You know, she's four years older than I am."

"I ought to know."

Judith said she did not know where Nichola was exactly. She said Nichola had moved out of her apartment (that dump!) and had actually telephoned (which is quite a deal, you might say, Nichola phoning) to say she wanted to be incommunicado for a while but she was fine.

"I told her you would worry," said Judith more kindly on the way to their van. Don walked ahead carrying my suitcase. "But don't. She's all right, believe me."

Don's presence made me uncomfortable. I did not like him to hear these things. I thought of the conversations they must have had, Don and Judith. Or Don and Judith and Nichola, for Nichola and Judith were sometimes on good terms. Or Don and Judith and

Nichola and others whose names I did not even know. They would have talked about me. Judith and Nichola comparing notes, relating anecdotes; analyzing, regretting, blaming, forgiving. I wished I'd had a boy and a girl. Or two boys. They wouldn't have done that. Boys couldn't possibly know so much about you.

I did the same thing at that age. When I was the age Judith is now I talked with my friends in the college cafeteria or, late at night, over coffee in our cheap rooms. When I was the age Nichola is now I had Nichola herself in a carry-cot or squirming in my lap, and I was drinking coffee again all the rainy Vancouver afternoons with my one neighborhood friend, Ruth Boudreau, who read a lot and was bewildered by her situation, as I was. We talked about our parents, our childhoods, though for some time we kept clear of our marriages. How thoroughly we dealt with our fathers and mothers, deplored their marriages, their mistaken ambitions or fear of ambition, how competently we filed them away, defined them beyond any possibility of change. What presumption.

I looked at Don walking ahead. A tall ascetic-looking boy, with a St. Francis cap of black hair, a precise fringe of beard. What right did he have to hear about me, to know things I myself had probably forgotten? I decided that his beard and hairstyle were affected.

Once, when my children were little, my father said to me, "You know those years you were growing up—well, that's all just a kind of a blur to me. I can't sort out one year from another." I was offended. I remembered each separate year with pain and clarity. I could have told how old I was when I went to look at the evening dresses in the window of Benbow's Ladies' Wear. Every week through the winter a new dress, spotlit—the sequins and tulle, the rose and lilac, sapphire, daffodil—and me a cold worshipper on the slushy sidewalk. I could have told how old I was when I forged my mother's signature on a bad report card, when I had measles, when we papered the front room. But the years when Judith and Nichola were little, when I lived with their father—yes, blur is the word for it. I remember hanging out diapers, bringing in and folding diapers; I can recall the kitchen counters of two houses and where the clothesbasket sat. I remember the television programs— *Popeye the Sailor*, *The Three Stooges*, *Funorama*. When

Funorama came on it was time to turn on the lights and cook supper. But I couldn't tell the years apart. We lived outside Vancouver in a dormitory suburb: Dormir, Dormer, Dormouse — something like that. I was sleepy all the time then; pregnancy made me sleepy, and the night feedings, and the West Coast rain falling. Dark dripping cedars, shiny dripping laurel; wives yawning, napping, visiting, drinking coffee, and folding diapers; husbands coming home at night from the city across the water. Every night I kissed my homecoming husband in his wet Burberry and hoped he might wake me up; I served up meat and potatoes and one of the four vegetables he permitted. He ate with a violent appetite, then fell asleep on the living-room sofa. We had become a cartoon couple, more middle-aged in our twenties than we would be in middle age.

Those bumbling years are the years our children will remember all their lives. Corners of the yards I never visited will stay in their heads.

"Did Nichola not want to see me?" I said to Judith.

"She doesn't want to see anybody, half the time," she said. Judith moved ahead and touched Don's arm. I knew that touch — an apology, an anxious reassurance. You touch a man that way to remind him that you are grateful, that you realize he is doing for your sake something that bores him or slightly endangers his dignity. It made me feel older than grandchildren would to see my daughter touch a man — a boy — this way. I felt her sad jitters, could predict her supple attentions. My blunt and stocky, blonde and candid child. Why should I think she wouldn't be susceptible, that she would always be straightforward, heavy-footed, self-reliant? Just as I go around saying that Nichola is sly and solitary, cold, seductive. Many people must know things that would contradict what I say.

In the morning Don and Judith left for Mexico. I decided I wanted to see somebody who wasn't related to me, and who didn't expect anything in particular from me. I called an old lover of mine, but his phone was answered by a machine: "This is Tom Shepherd speaking. I will be out of town for the month of September. Please record your message, name, and phone number."

Tom's voice sounded so pleasant and familiar that I opened

my mouth to ask him the meaning of this foolishness. Then I hung up. I felt as if he had deliberately let me down, as if we had planned to meet in a public place and then he hadn't shown up. Once, he had done that, I remembered.

I got myself a glass of vermouth, though it was not yet noon, and I phoned my father.

"Well, of all things," he said. "Fifteen more minutes and you would have missed me."

"Were you going downtown?"

"Downtown Toronto."

He explained that he was going to the hospital. His doctor in Dalgleish wanted the doctors in Toronto to take a look at him, and had given him a letter to show them in the emergency room.

"Emergency room?" I said.

"It's not an emergency. He just seems to think this is the best way to handle it. He knows the name of a fellow there. If he was to make me an appointment, it might take weeks."

"Does your doctor know you're driving to Toronto?" I said.

"Well, he didn't say I couldn't."

The upshot of this was that I rented a car, drove to Dalgleish, brought my father back to Toronto, and had him in the emergency room by seven o'clock that evening.

Before Judith left I said to her, "You're sure Nichola knows I'm staying here?"

"Well, I told her," she said.

Sometimes the phone rang, but it was always a friend of Judith's.

"Well, it looks like I'm going to have it," my father said. This was on the fourth day. He had done a complete turnaround overnight. "It looks like I might as well."

I didn't know what he wanted me to say. I thought perhaps he looked to me for a protest, an attempt to dissuade him.

"When will they do it?" I said.

"Day after tomorrow."

I said I was going to the washroom. I went to the nurses' station and found a woman there who I thought was the head nurse. At any rate, she was gray-haired, kind, and serious-looking.

"My father's having an operation the day after tomorrow?" I said.

"Oh, yes."

"I just wanted to talk to somebody about it. I thought there'd been a sort of decision reached that he'd be better not to. I thought because of his age."

"Well, it's his decision and the doctor's." She smiled at me without condescension. "It's hard to make these decisions."

"How were his tests?"

"Well, I haven't seen them all."

I was sure she had. After a moment she said, "We have to be realistic. But the doctors here are very good."

When I went back into the room my father said, in a surprised voice, "*Shore*-less seas."

"What?" I said. I wondered if he had found out how much, or how little, time he could hope for. I wondered if the pills had brought on an untrustworthy euphoria. Or if he had wanted to gamble. Once, when he was talking to me about his life, he said, "The trouble was I was always afraid to take chances."

I used to tell people that he never spoke regretfully about his life, but that was not true. It was just that I didn't listen to it. He said that he should have gone into the Army as a tradesman — he would have been better off. He said he should have gone on his own, as a carpenter, after the war. He should have got out of Dalgleish. Once, he said, "A wasted life, eh?" But he was making fun of himself, saying that, because it was such a dramatic thing to say. When he quoted poetry, too, he always had a scoffing note in his voice, to excuse the showing-off and the pleasure.

"Shoreless seas," he said again. " 'Behind him lay the gray Azores,/ Behind the Gates of Hercules;/ Before him not the ghost of shores,/ Before him only shoreless seas.' That's what was going through my head last night. But do you think I could remember what kind of seas? I could not. Lonely seas? Empty seas? I was on the right track but I couldn't get it. But there now when you came into the room and I wasn't thinking about it at all, the word popped into my head. That's always the way, isn't it? It's not all that surprising. I ask my mind a question. The answer's there, but I can't see all the connections my mind's making to get it. Like a computer. Nothing out of the way. You know, in my situation the thing is, if there's anything you can't explain right away, there's a great temptation to—well, to make a mystery out of it. There's a great temptation to believe in—You know."

"The soul?" I said, speaking lightly, feeling an appalling rush of love and recognition.

"Oh, I guess you could call it that. You know, when I first came into this room there was a pile of papers here by the bed. Somebody had left them here—one of those tabloid sort of things I never looked at. I started reading them. I'll read anything handy. There was a series running in them on personal experiences of people who had died, medically speaking—heart arrest, mostly—and had been brought back to life. It was what they remembered of the time when they were dead. Their experiences."

"Pleasant or un-?" I said.

"Oh, pleasant. Oh yes. They'd float up to the ceiling and look down on themselves and see the doctors working on them, on their bodies. Then float on further and recognize some people they knew who had died before them. Not see them exactly but sort of sense them. Sometimes there would be a humming and sometimes a sort of—what's that light that there is or color around a person?"

"Aura?"

"Yes. But without the person. That's about all they'd get time for; then they found themselves back in the body and feeling all the mortal pain and so on—brought back to life."

"Did it seem—convincing?"

"Oh, I don't know. It's all in whether you want to believe that kind of thing or not. And if you are going to believe it, take it seriously, I figure you've got to take everything else seriously that they print in those papers."

"What else do they?"

"Rubbish—cancer cures, baldness cures, bellyaching about the younger generation and the welfare bums. Tripe about movie stars."

"Oh, yes. I know."

"In my situation you have to keep a watch," he said, "or you'll start playing tricks on yourself." Then he said, "There's a few practical details we ought to get straight on," and he told me about his will, the house, the cemetery plot. Everything was simple.

"Do you want me to phone Peggy?" I said. Peggy is my sister. She is married to an astronomer and lives in Victoria.

He thought about it. "I guess we ought to tell them," he said finally. "But tell them not to get alarmed."

"All right."

"No, wait a minute. Sam is supposed to be going to a conference the end of this week, and Peggy was planning to go along with him. I don't want them wondering about changing their plans."

"Where is the conference?"

"Amsterdam," he said proudly. He did take pride in Sam, and kept track of his books and articles. He would pick one up and say, "Look at that, will you? And I can't understand a word of it!" in a marvelling voice that managed nevertheless to have a trace of ridicule.

"Professor Sam," he would say. "And the three little Sams." This is what he called his grandsons, who did resemble their father in braininess and in an almost endearing pushiness — an innocent energetic showing-off. They went to a private school that favored old-fashioned discipline and started calculus in Grade Five. "And the dogs," he might enumerate further, "who have been to obedience school. And Peggy . . ."

But if I said, "Do you suppose she has been to obedience school, too?" he would play the game no further. I imagine that when he was with Sam and Peggy he spoke of me in the same way — hinted at my flightiness just as he hinted at their stodginess, made mild jokes at my expense, did not quite conceal his amazement (or pretended not to conceal his amazement) that people paid money for things I had written. He had to do this so that he might never seem to brag, but he would put up the gates when the joking got too rough. And of course I found later, in the house, things of mine he had kept — a few magazines, clippings, things I had never bothered about.

Now his thoughts travelled from Peggy's family to mine. "Have you heard from Judith?" he said.

"Not yet."

"Well, it's pretty soon. Were they going to sleep in the van?"

"Yes."

"I guess it's safe enough, if they stop in the right places."

I knew he would have to say something more and I knew it would come as a joke.

"I guess they put a board down the middle, like the pioneers?"

I smiled but did not answer.

"I take it you have no objections?"

"No," I said.

"Well, I always believed that, too. Keep out of your children's business. I tried not to say anything. I never said anything when you left Richard."

"What do you mean, 'said anything'? Criticize?"

"It wasn't any of my business."

"No."

"But that doesn't mean I was pleased."

I was surprised — not just at what he said but at his feeling that he had any right, even now, to say it. I had to look out the window and down at the traffic to control myself.

"I just wanted you to know," he added.

A long time ago, he said to me in his mild way, "It's funny. Richard when I first saw him reminded me of what my father used to say. He'd say if that fellow was half as smart as he thinks he is, he'd be twice as smart as he really is."

I turned to remind him of this, but found myself looking at the line his heart was writing. Not that there seemed to be anything wrong, any difference in the beeps and points. But it was there.

He saw where I was looking. "Unfair advantage," he said.

"It is," I said. "I'm going to have to get hooked up, too."

We laughed, we kissed formally; I left. At least he hadn't asked me about Nichola, I thought.

The next afternoon I didn't go to the hospital, because my father was having some more tests done, to prepare for the operation. I was to see him in the evening instead. I found myself wandering through the Bloor Street dress shops, trying on clothes. A preoccupation with fashion and my own appearance had descended on me like a raging headache. I looked at the women in the street, at the clothes in the shops, trying to discover how a transformation might be made, what I would have to buy. I recognized this obsession for what it was but had trouble shaking it. I've had people tell me that waiting for life-or-death news they've stood in front of an open refrigerator eating anything in sight — cold boiled potatoes, chili sauce, bowls of whipped cream. Or have been unable to stop doing crossword puzzles. Attention narrows in on something — some distraction — grabs on, becomes fanatically serious. I shuffled clothes on the racks, pulled them on in hot little changing rooms in front of cruel mirrors. I was sweating; once or twice I thought I might faint. Out on the street again, I thought I must remove myself from Bloor Street, and decided to go to the museum.

I remembered another time, in Vancouver. It was when Nichola was going to Kindergarten and Judith was a baby. Nichola had been to the doctor about a cold, or maybe for a routine examination, and the blood test revealed something about her white blood cells — either that there were too many of them or that they were enlarged. The doctor ordered further tests, and I took Nichola to the hospital for them. Nobody mentioned leukemia but I knew, of course, what they were looking for. When I took Nichola home I asked the babysitter who had been with Judith to stay for the afternoon and I went shopping. I bought the most daring dress I ever owned, a black silk sheath with some laced-up arrangement in front. I remembered that bright spring afternoon, the spike-heeled shoes in the department store, the underwear printed with leopard spots.

I also remembered going home from St. Paul's Hospital over the Lions Gate Bridge on the crowded bus and holding Nichola on my knee. She suddenly recalled her baby name for bridge and whispered to me, "Whee — over the whee." I did not avoid touching my child — Nichola was slender and graceful even then, with a pretty back and fine dark hair — but realized I was touching her with a difference, though I did not think it could ever be detected. There was a care — not a withdrawal exactly but a care —

not to feel anything much. I saw how the forms of love might be maintained with a condemned person but with the love in fact measured and disciplined, because you have to survive. It could be done so discreetly that the object of such care would not suspect, any more than she would suspect the sentence of death itself. Nichola did not know, would not know. Toys and kisses and jokes would come tumbling over her; she would never know, though I worried that she would feel the wind between the cracks of the manufactured holidays, the manufactured normal days. But all was well. Nichola did not have leukemia. She grew up — was still alive, and possibly happy. Incommunicado.

I could not think of anything in the museum I really wanted to see, so I walked past it to the planetarium. I had never been to a planetarium. The show was due to start in ten minutes. I went inside, bought a ticket, got in line. There was a whole class of schoolchildren, maybe a couple of classes, with teachers and volunteer mothers riding herd on them. I looked around to see if there were any other unattached adults. Only one — a man with a red face and puffy eyes, who looked as if he might be here to keep himself from going to a bar.

Inside, we sat on wonderfully comfortable seats that were tilted back so that you lay in a sort of hammock, attention directed to the bowl of the ceiling, which soon turned dark blue, with a faint rim of light all around the edge. There was some splendid, commanding music. The adults all around were shushing the children, trying to make them stop crackling their potato-chip bags. Then a man's voice, an eloquent professional voice, began to speak slowly, out of the walls. The voice reminded me a little of the way radio announcers used to introduce a piece of classical music or describe the progress of the Royal Family to Westminster Abbey on one of their royal occasions. There was a faint echo-chamber effect.

The dark ceiling was filling with stars. They came out not all at once but one after another, the way the stars really do come out at night, though more quickly. The Milky Way appeared, was moving closer; stars swam into brilliance and kept on going, disappearing beyond the edges of the sky-screen or behind my head. While the flow of light continued, the voice presented the stunning facts. A few light-years away, it announced, the sun appears as a bright star, and the planets are not visible. A few dozen light-years away, the sun is not visible, either, to the naked eye. And that distance — a few dozen light-years — is only about a thousandth part of the distance from the sun to the center of our galaxy, one galaxy, which itself contains about two hundred billion suns. And is, in turn, one of millions, perhaps billions, of galaxies. Innumerable repetitions, innumerable variations. All this rolled past my head, too, like balls of lightning.

Now realism was abandoned, for familiar artifice. A model of the solar system was spinning away in its elegant style. A bright bug took off from the earth, heading for Jupiter. I set my dodging and shrinking mind sternly to recording facts. The mass of Jupiter two and a half times that of all the other planets put together. The Great Red Spot. The thirteen moons. Past Jupiter, a glance at the eccentric orbit of Pluto, the icy rings of Saturn. Back to Earth and moving in to hot and dazzling Venus. Atmospheric pressure ninety times ours. Moonless Mercury rotating three times while circling the sun twice; an odd arrangement, not as satisfying as what they used to tell us — that it rotated once as it circled the sun. No perpetual darkness after all. Why did they give out such confident information, only to announce later that it was quite wrong? Finally, the picture already familiar from magazines: the red soil of Mars, the blooming pink sky.

When the show was over I sat in my seat while the children clambered across me, making no comments on anything they had just seen or heard. They were pestering their keepers for eatables and further entertainments. An effort had been made to get their attention, to take it away from canned pop and potato chips and fix it on various knowns and unknowns and horrible immensities, and it seemed to have failed. A good thing, too, I thought. Children have a natural immunity, most of them, and it shouldn't be tampered with. As for the adults who would deplore it, the ones who promoted this show, weren't they immune themselves to the extent that they could put in the echo-chamber effects, the music, the churchlike solemnity, simulating the awe that they supposed they ought to feel? Awe — what was that supposed to be? A fit of the shivers when you looked out the window? Once you knew what it was, you wouldn't be courting it.

Two men came with brooms to sweep up the debris the audience had left behind. They told me that the next show would start in forty minutes. In the meantime, I had to get out.

"I went to the show at the planetarium," I said to my father. "It was very exciting — about the solar system." I thought what a silly word I had used: "exciting." "It's like a slightly phony temple," I added.

He was already talking. "I remember when they found Pluto. Right where they thought it had to be. Mercury, Venus, Earth, Mars," he recited. "Jupiter, Saturn, Nept — no, Uranus, Neptune, Pluto. Is that right?"

"Yes," I said. I was just as glad he hadn't heard what I said about the phony temple. I had meant that to be truthful, but it sounded slick and superior. "Tell me the moons of Jupiter."

"Well, I don't know the new ones. There's a bunch of new ones, isn't there?"

"Two. But they're not new."

"New to us," said my father. "You've turned pretty cheeky now I'm going under the knife."

" 'Under the knife.' What an expression."

He was not in bed tonight, his last night. He had been detached from his apparatus, and was sitting in a chair by the window. He was bare-legged, wearing a hospital dressing gown, but he did not look self-conscious or out of place. He looked thoughtful but good-humored, an affable host.

"You haven't even named the old ones," I said.

"Give me time. Galileo named them. Io."

"That's a start."

"The moons of Jupiter were the first heavenly bodies discovered with the telescope." He said this gravely, as if he could see the sentence in an old book. "It wasn't Galileo named them, either; it was some German. Io, Europa, Ganymede, Callisto. There you are."

"Yes."

"Io and Europa, they were girlfriends of Jupiter's, weren't they? Ganymede was a boy. A shepherd? I don't know who Callisto was."

"I think she was a girlfriend, too," I said. "Jupiter's wife — Jove's wife — changed her into a bear and stuck her up in the sky. Great Bear and Little Bear. Little Bear was her baby."

The loudspeaker said that it was time for visitors to go.

"I'll see you when you come out of the anesthetic," I said.

"Yes."

When I was at the door, he called to me, "Ganymede wasn't any shepherd. He was Jove's cupbearer."

When I left the planetarium that afternoon, I had walked through the museum to the Chinese garden. I saw the stone camels again, the warriors, the tomb. I sat on a bench looking toward Bloor Street. Through the evergreen bushes and the high grilled iron fence I watched people going by in the late-afternoon sunlight. The planetarium show had done what I wanted it to after all — calmed me down, drained me. I saw a girl who reminded me of Nichola. She wore a trenchcoat and carried a bag of groceries. She was shorter than Nichola — not really much like her at all — but I thought that I might see Nichola. She would be walking along some street maybe not far from here — burdened, preoccupied, alone. She was one of the grownup people in the world now, one of the shoppers going home.

If I did see her, I might just sit and watch, I decided. I felt like one of those people who have floated up to the ceiling, enjoying a brief death. A relief, while it lasts. My father had chosen and Nichola had chosen. Someday, probably soon, I would hear from her, but it came to the same thing.

I meant to get up and go over to the tomb, to look at the relief carvings, the stone pictures, that go all the way around it. I always mean to look at them and I never do. Not this time, either. It was getting cold out, so I went inside to have coffee and something to eat before I went back to the hospital.

About the Author

Alice Munro grew up in Wingham, Ontario, and attended the University of Western Ontario. She has published more than ten collections of stories as well as a novel, *Lives of Girls and Women*. During her distinguished career she has been the recipient of many awards and prizes, including three of Canada's Governor General's Literary Awards and its Giller Prize, the Rea Award for the Short Story, the Lannan Literary Award, the W. H. Smith Literary Award, and the National Book Critics Circle Award. Her stories have appeared in *The New Yorker*, *The Atlantic Monthly*, *The Paris Review*, and other publications, and her collections have been translated into thirteen languages. She was awarded the Nobel Prize in Literature in 2013.

INTERNATIONAL

OPEN SECRETS

In *Open Secrets*, Munro uncovers the devastating power of old love suddenly recollected. She tells of vanished young schoolgirls, indentured frontier brides, an eccentric recluse who finds love at a dinner party, and a Canadian woman fleeing a husband and a lover. These stories resonate with sorrow, humor, and wisdom, confirming Munro as one of the most gifted writers of our time.

Fiction/Literature/Short Stories/978-0-679-75562-3

THE PROGRESS OF LOVE

A divorced woman returns to her childhood home and confronts the memory of her parents' confounding yet deep bond. The accidental near-drowning of a child exposes the fragility of the trust between children and parents. A man brings his lover on a visit to his ex-wife, only to feel unexpectedly closer to his estranged partner. Drawing us into the most intimate corners of ordinary lives, Munro reveals much about ourselves, our choices, and our experiences of love.

Fiction/Literature/Short Stories/978-0-375-72470-1

SOMETHING I'VE BEEN MEANING TO TELL YOU

In these thirteen stories, Munro demonstrates the precise observation, straightforward prose style, and masterful technique that led no less a critic than John Updike to compare her to Chekhov. The sisters, mothers and daughters, aunts, grandmothers, and friends in these stories shimmer with hope and love, anger and reconciliation, as they contend with their histories and their present, and what they can see of the future.

Fiction/Literature/Short Stories/978-0-375-70748-3

ALSO AVAILABLE

The Beggar Maid, 978-0-679-73271-6
Friend of My Youth, 978-0-679-72957-0
Lives of Girls and Women, 978-0-375-70749-0
Runaway, 978-1-4000-7791-5
Vintage Munro, 978-1-4000-3395-9
Selected Stories, 978-0-679-76674-2

VINTAGE INTERNATIONAL
Available at your local bookstore, or visit www.randomhouse.com